P9-CBJ-768

MATCHMAKING STRATEGY ACCORDING TO A FOUR-YEAR-OLD VAMP:

√ Invite Michael, the nice man who just moved in next door, to a backyard tea party

√ Make him tell me daddy stories

√ See if he can come for dinner since Mommy is too chicken to ask him

√ Hope Mommy doesn't ground me!

Dear Reader,

You're about to rejoin the Holiday cousins—Peter, Michael, Raymond and Jared. They're four sexy guys with two things in common: the Holiday name and humbug in the heart! But this year, Cupid's working overtime, and by Christmas he's aiming to have the Holiday men singing love songs!

Linda Cajio brings you the second book in THE HOLIDAY HEART miniseries. Here, cousin Michael's about to have a close encounter of the Mother's Day kind—can he escape it before he becomes a father? In the months ahead, follow the other cousins' stories set around Labor Day and Christmas.

Readers of romance know Linda Cajio, the author of over twenty bestselling contemporary and historical romances. She's a past president of Romance Writers of America and has won several writing awards. Linda lives in New Jersey with her family.

Be sure you don't miss any of the Holiday men in THE HOLIDAY HEART miniseries!

Regards,

Debra Matteucci
Senior Editor & Editorial Coordinator
Harlequin
300 East 42nd Street
New York, New York 10017

BACHELOR DADDY
Linda Cajio

Harlequin Books

TORONTO • NEW YORK • LONDON
AMSTERDAM • PARIS • SYDNEY • HAMBURG
STOCKHOLM • ATHENS • TOKYO • MILAN
MADRID • WARSAW • BUDAPEST • AUCKLAND

ISBN 0-373-16678-8

BACHELOR DADDY

Copyright © 1997 by Linda Cajio.

This edition published by arrangement with Harlequin Books S.A.

® and TM are trademarks of the publisher. Trademarks indicated with
® are registered in the United States Patent and Trademark Office, the
Canadian Trade Marks Office and in other countries.

Printed in U.S.A.

Prologue

Never think with the brain below your waist. It will get you into trouble every time.

—Michael Holiday
Man Can Definitely Live by Bread Alone

"As you can see, the master bedroom has a three-window alcove, perfect for a small group seating...or a chaise for your wife."

Michael Holiday walked over to the alcove with its three windows set in a bay. He glanced at the Realtor. "No wife."

The Realtor's polite smile turned more intimate. She was in her late thirties and her invitation was clear. She'd like to get to know him better. Michael considered the options.

From her age and figure he guessed she was encumbered with children—probably grown ones—maybe even a husband, although she wore no wedding ring. He decided to pass. He *never* involved himself with a mother. Even one date meant complications well out of a man's control. That was not for him.

But it did remind him tomorrow was Mother's Day. He had ordered flowers for his mother, but he needed to call her, too. She was the one woman he never passed on. There would be hell to pay if he did.

"What's the closet space like for this room?" he asked. "My girlfriend needs a big closet."

"Oh." The Realtor turned businesslike again. The girlfriend ploy always worked. "It's a walk-in, over here...."

Michael followed the woman into the closet, which was spacious enough for several wardrobes. He wondered what the hell he was doing, looking at a four-bedroom suburban colonial in Marshfield, New Jersey, rather than staying at his two-bedroom town house in center-city Philadelphia—or even moving to a singles community. He didn't need the space. Despite what he'd said to the Realtor, he had no girlfriend and preferred it that way. The whole problem between men and women were two deceptively innocuous words: *love* and *commitment*. He had seen the pain they caused. He had been subjected to it more than once. Never again.

No, he needed a general life change, new blood for his syndicated newspaper columns on suburban life through the eyes of a single yuppie. And he needed a good tax write-off against his half-million-dollar advance from his publisher. Gotham Publishing already had huge orders for his first book, *Man Can Definitely Live by Bread Alone: Advice for the Single Male*. Gotham even expected the book to hit the *New York Times* bestseller list, which meant more money and higher taxes. A large, expensive house would help the cause greatly. Michael was happy to pay the government its due, but not a penny more.

He had had this urge lately to put down deeper roots, too. The notion disturbed him on some level, yet he couldn't ignore it no matter how he tried. Just because his cousin Peter, another long-time bachelor, had recently married didn't mean Michael had the least urge to do the same.

He needed the house for a lot more important reasons, hence the hunting in suburban New Jersey.

"Doing this on Mother's Day weekend is *not* prophetic," he muttered under his breath. He could add his golf swing to the nondomestic list. There was a great course just down the road from Marshfield.

"Pardon me?" the Realtor asked.

"Nothing." He walked out of the closet and over to the alcove again, wondering what he'd do with it. A wife probably would put a chaise or group seating here. Maybe he would set up his skiing exerciser, to catch the morning light....

Gazing down on the backyard, he smiled at the jumble of shrubs and trees crying out in neglect. The house had been empty for nearly a year. It needed work inside and out, challenging his old gardening skills, garnered working at a nursery during college summers.

A splotch of pink in the yard behind the house caught his attention. A woman lay on a mat, the sunlight making her slender body glow. *What a body,* Michael thought, looking at the pink leotard that clung like a second skin to full breasts, flat stomach and taut thighs. She had pulled her dark brown hair back into a ponytail or braid—he couldn't really tell which and didn't care; it just looked damn good. So did her profile, with its snub nose and determined chin. She couldn't be more than twenty-five, he decided.

And then she did the most extraordinary thing.

She bent her knees, leaving a good space between her legs. Michael's breath hung in his throat. Slowly, very slowly, she raised her hips until she had created a perfect incline of her body from shoulders to raised knees. As she held the position for a long count, he could see the outline of her stomach muscles, the beautifully tight derriere.

Slowly, as slowly as before, the woman lowered her body to the ground.

She did the languorous movement again. And again. Michael wondered what it would be like to lie on top of the woman when she raised herself like that…to be inside her when she did.

His mouth went dry as his brain conjured the imagined sensation. Sweat broke on his forehead. A certain part of his anatomy rose up in perfect timing with her next repetition—and stayed up.

Michael swallowed and wiped the perspiration away with a shaky hand. God, perfection in the next backyard. And he would see it every day if he lived here. Southern New Jersey had many, many very fine days, too, weatherwise. He bet she worked out outside on every damn one of them.

After a few more incredible hip lifts, the goddess finally stood. The body was everything it promised—lithe and strong. She turned her back to him, bent over and grabbed her ankles, the stretch giving him a view that rivaled any in the civilized world. Michael heard a faint moan and realized it came from his throat. He cleared it, embarrassed to have had such an adolescent reaction at the age of thirty-six.

Her hair hung over her face. Ponytail confirmed. The goddess continued her eye-popping stretch. Thoughts raced through Michael's head. This woman was younger than he, a fact he usually liked. She exercised outside, clearly making her a sun worshipper. All in the next backyard. Had he missed anything?

His lower body pulsed urgently, confirming his deductions.

"I'll take the house," he said hoarsely.

To his surprise, he found the Realtor already at his side. "I thought you might."

Chapter One

*If you should meet a woman with children, run, run, run!
In the other direction as fast as you can.*
—Michael Holiday
Man Can Definitely Live by Bread Alone

"A ghost is moving into the haunted house! A ghost is moving into the haunted house!"

Janice Parker firmed her lips as she watched her nine-year-old triplets race through the kitchen while screaming at the top of their lungs.

"Stop!" she shouted at the top of hers.

Chris and C.J. crashed into the usual leader, their sister Cat, who immediately obeyed the order.

"Catherine, Christopher and Cameron James Parker," Janice began sternly. "I will not have running and screaming in the house."

"But, Mom! The ghost!" the three whined in scary unison. Their eyes shone with excitement only kids could have. They fed off each other all the time, although Cat, the eldest of the three, led while the boys followed.

"Is there a ghost, Mommy?" Amy asked, wide-eyed.

"No, honey, we do not have a ghost moving into the house behind us today," she said to her four-year-old.

"Ghosts do not *move* into houses. They especially don't move in with moving vans, okay? And do you three understand?"

The three nodded.

"You stay away from the house," she added for good measure. "Or you'll probably scare the poor people half to death. I know you do me."

Her triplets grinned.

"Now, before I begin inspection rounds...have you cleaned your rooms?"

"Yes."

"And your bathroom?"

"Oh, yes."

"And your toys from the television room?"

"Yes, Mom."

Janice smiled, pleased. "Good job, guys. As your reward, you can pick up all the papers, twigs and other trash from the yard before David mows the grass. Then you can sort today's laundry for me."

"Mom...!"

"What a lovely whine," Janice said in appreciation. "A 97 out of 100, I believe, with just a hint of petulance."

"What's petulance?" Cat asked.

"Chore number three—look it up in the dictionary: *P-E-T-U-L-A-N-C-E.* I dare you to use it properly in a sentence three times today. I love you all. Now move!"

The triplets shambled grumpily out of the room. Janice sighed and turned back to stacking the breakfast dishes in the dishwasher. Little Amy helped her. Keeping those three out of trouble was like keeping the sun from rising, Janice thought. It would be a grand effort ultimately doomed to failure.

"At least it's not tax season," she muttered, grateful her accounting business was in its annual postseason lull.

"I hate tax season," Amy said solemnly.

"Me, too. But it pays the mortgage."

"For our house," Amy said, having heard the mantra many times before.

"Mom, can you give Jen and me a ride to the mall?"

Janice turned and eyed her eldest. Fifteen-year-old Heather's makeup was sedate, her hair hung in lovely brown waves around her thin shoulders and her clothes, while stylishly baggy, would have elicited only a tiny "harrumph" from Janice's own mother. Janice knew it could be far worse. Even though her time was already tight, how could she say no to a good kid?

"I suppose…but what are you doing for money? I don't have any—"

Shrieks erupted from somewhere in the backyard. Janice muttered a sailor's curse and ran out the kitchen door. No triplets were in sight, although the shrieks reached a piercing pitch. Despite the mystery of the missing triplets, she had no doubt about what was happening.

She went to the fence between her property and the neighbor's behind, Amy running to keep up. Janice squeezed through a small break in the slats, popping open two shirt buttons in the process. She broke her way through the undergrowth of the neglected back garden. Shrubs grabbed at her, but finally she found the grassy knoll behind the house. Amy screamed. Janice grabbed her up in her arms, pulling her out of a clinging, overgrown wisteria.

Sure enough, the terrible trio, instead of policing their own yard, had instantly turned into little criminals and entered forbidden territory. They were now running in circles around a man, all three screaming that he was a ghost.

Janice knew a simple command to stop wouldn't work this time. She took out her secret weapon, put the trusty whistle to her lips and blasted the air with it.

The man staggered back in shock. But the triplets, knowing they had been caught red-handed and were in deep trouble, immediately sat on the ground in one graceful movement.

"Impressive angelic act, kids," she said. "But you're in it up to your necks."

"But, Mom!" the three sang in unison.

"No buts. Not five minutes after you were told not to come here, you're scaring our new neighbor to death. Now apologize to Mr...." She turned and looked fully at the man, to get his name.

Instead, something invisible slammed into her chest, taking her breath from her body. Her neighbor was tall, with slightly wavy, thick brown hair and features so sharply defined they could have been chiseled in stone. His eyes were a lovely shade of green and he had lashes a woman would kill for. Men would kill for his broad shoulders, flat stomach and narrow hips. Yet he had something elusive about him that triggered all her feminine instincts to capture and tame him for her own.

He was staring at her, as if as captured as she. She didn't understand the sensations running through her, but they urged her toward him. She managed to stay put, but she couldn't get her mouth to work.

"Mommy? Is he the ghost?" Amy asked, into the dead silence.

Janice cleared her throat. Belatedly, she realized she'd neglected her open shirt. Quickly buttoning the two buttons under the man's watchful eye, she said, "No, Amy. He's just a man." She looked directly at him, tried to hold on to her soaring heart and said, "I apologize for my children. They are usually better behaved than this—"

"You're their *mother?*" he asked, pointing to the triplets and Amy.

"Yes." She grinned wryly and pulled a twig from her hair, just becoming aware of how disheveled she must look. "You might as well have the bad news now. There's two more at home—"

"Two more!" He gaped. "You have *six* kids!"

She nodded. "But the other two won't bother you or your family—"

"Mrs. Baranowski complained about Heather's stereo being too loud," C.J. interjected.

"Mrs. Baranowski was right, even though she complains about everything," Janice said, by way of explanation about the lonely old lady next door to them.

The kids giggled.

"You have six kids," the man repeated.

Janice frowned. "Yes."

"You *can't* have six kids," he said.

"I can't?"

"No."

Janice stared at him, dumbfounded. "Well, if they're not my kids, someone forgot to tell me."

"No...I mean..." Something passed over the man's face, like a reality check, for he added, "I'm sorry. I'm not being sensible." He held out his hand for her to shake. "I'm Michael Holiday."

The name seemed vaguely familiar. Janice pushed the thought aside. "I'm Janice Parker. Welcome to the neighborhood."

She took his hand and immediately felt a jangle of awareness sweep up her arm. It ran through her veins at his touch. What the heck was this?

Worse, he didn't shake her hand up and down in a friendly way. He only held it, his palm warm against hers. Janice didn't want him to let go. Finally, he did.

Covering the awkward moment, she said, "These three

are Chris, Cat, short for Catherine, and Cameron James, also known as C.J. And yes, they are triplets, and yes, I hang myself regularly from the rafters."

Michael Holiday smiled.

"And this one—" she patted her youngest's shoulder "—this is little Amy."

"I'm four," Amy said proudly.

"I see." He looked less shell-shocked, dealing with one child. "Four's pretty good."

Amy grinned happily.

"Shake hands with Mr. Holiday, kids," Janice said, reminding her children of their manners.

The triplets shrank back, but Amy stepped forward and gravely shook Michael's hand.

"I don't care if you're a ghost," she said. "You're nice."

"Thank you. I'm glad somebody thinks so." He smiled at the little girl. "You're nice yourself."

Amy positively preened. Janice hid a smile.

When Amy returned to her side, the four-year-old turned to the triplets and stuck out her tongue. "I'm not scared and you are! I'm not scared and you are!"

"Shut up, you baby," the three groused. But they found some Dutch courage and each went over and shook Michael's hand.

"Ah, the sweet challenge of the youngest," Janice said. She looked sternly at the three. "Don't you guys owe Mr. Holiday something?"

"We're sorry," they said together.

"Now get back to your chores," she told them. "And take Amy with you."

The four took off at a run, Amy trailing behind.

Janice turned to the man. One look took her breath again, worse this time because she had no children to distract her. On an objective level, she recognized that he was nice looking, but not anything extraordinary. So why was she having a reaction that rivaled any Heather had to the latest teen heartthrob?

Janice pulled herself together. "I want to assure you my children won't be a problem again. Usually they're fairly good, but they get funny notions sometimes."

"Like I'm a ghost. Why would they think that?"

"The house has been empty for a year, since the last owner, Mr. Hobarth, died. Not in the house, but all the kids in the neighborhood decided the place was haunted. Mr. Hobarth wasn't particularly friendly with them." She waved a hand toward the jungle of a back garden. "The grounds look ominous since they've become so over-grown, adding to the atmosphere. I guess the kids decided you had to be a ghost because only ghosts would live in a haunted house. They also saw *Casper* one too many times. Please assure your wife—"

He interrupted her. "I'm not married."

Janice swallowed. Somehow that was news she didn't need to know. "Well...I'll make sure you're not disturbed again—"

"Mom...!" A new whine broke out, coming across the yard like a fire siren. "The mall! Jen's waiting! I've got to go *now!*"

"Ah, the dulcet voice of my eldest, Heather," Janice commented. She smiled. "I promised her I would drive her and her friend to the mall today. If my kids bother you again—although I doubt it after I'm through with them— let me know. And welcome to the neighborhood."

She didn't offer her hand a second time before she turned toward her house.

She wasn't that dumb.

MICHAEL DIRECTED the moving men to put the last boxes in the house, all the while keeping a wary eye on the gang of kids standing with their bikes just outside his property line. They looked like vultures waiting for their chance at the kill. It had to be after eight, even if it was a still-sunny May evening. Didn't their parents know where they were?

The Parker triplets led the flock.

How the hell could he have been so wrong about the love goddess? Because he hadn't investigated carefully, he thought, in answer to his question. He had been led by his gonads instead of his brain. He, of all people! That Realtor had known Janice's status and had been laughing up her real-estate jacket sleeve the entire time.

Six kids. Six kids!

He had seen or heard only five, but he didn't doubt the number. Janice had said six, and she would know. She was a drill sergeant in disguise.

She must be phenomenal in bed, he thought. Otherwise, how would she have gotten so many? And with that body... Up close, she had been as spectacular as he re-membered, with her full breasts, flat waist and flaring hips. Her heart-shaped face and clear brown eyes had imprinted themselves in his brain. She hadn't worn an ounce of makeup, and freckles lightly dusted her nose. Laugh lines proudly crinkled near her eyes when she smiled. Sexual maturity radiated out of her.

And her touch! When he'd taken her hand, good God, but he had thought he touched Heaven. Somehow, her skin had been like cool fire, waiting to be ignited. He couldn't explain all the things that had jumbled together inside him, but never in his life had he felt so drawn to a woman. He, who was also always in control of his emotions. *Always.*

Michael cursed himself for letting his thoughts stray yet again. One piece of advice he *always* adhered to was never to involve himself with a woman who had kids. One date in such a case was practically a major commitment on a man's part. Besides, she must be married, another taboo in his book. Literally. He had learned both lessons the hard way. His parents had had a bitter divorce, leaving him as the Ping-Pong ball in endless custody battles. His refuge had been his grandparents' house at the shore. Summers with the other grandsons—his cousins, Peter, Jared and Raymond—had been magical, a stable time in his unstable world.

Most magical of all, his grandmother had fussed over and pampered him. Probably she'd understood his hurt and confusion, and had known he needed pampering. He had thrived on it all. But when he was ten, his grandmother had had an affair with a man. She had never been the same after, and neither had the family. The magical summers had vanished. His grandmother withdrew from everyone.

Michael had learned the lesson very well: men and women weren't made to be together forever. Now he preferred the quiet life and controlled relationships.

"Hi, mister."

Michael turned to find little Amy behind him. She was a miniature version of her mother, with long, dark brown hair and gorgeous doe eyes. Something inside him melted at her sunny smile.

"Hi, Amy," he said.

"What's in the boxes?" she asked, coming alongside him. "Your toys?"

He laughed. "No. Well, yes. Adult toys, like my computer and my kitchen things."

"You mean your mommy's kitchen things."

"No. Mine. My mom lives somewhere else, so I like to cook."

Her gaze widened.

"Amy! You get away from there or I'm telling Mom!"

"Shut up, Cat," little Amy shouted back to her older sister.

Michael stifled a smile. This one was feisty. He couldn't help liking her.

The biker gang wheeled as one and took off down the street.

"Can I hire you?" Michael asked, watching the flight in awe. How the hell had Amy done it?

"You could lift me and then I'd be higher," Amy said.

Michael frowned, then chuckled when he realized she hadn't understood his comment. "I meant, will you come over and scare off your brothers and sister and their friends?"

"Sure. They're all babies anyway."

He decided that in ten years time, Amy would be a major breaker of hearts. She had his in the palm of her hand already.

"Do you have any kids, mister?"

"Nope. And you can call me Michael." Why not? He liked this child. But the thought of actually having one of his own made him shudder. He would never put a child of his at risk for a custody battle.

Amy smiled. She could melt chocolate. "Michael's a nice name. I'm going to kindergarten next year."

"Wow. Kindergarten."

"My mom says she can't wait 'cause she'll be real proud of me 'cause all us kids will be at school all day."

Michael hid another smile. "I'll bet she can't wait."

"Do you have a daddy?" Amy asked, then wandered over to look at a flower in the overgrown front garden.

"Yes."

"Tell me a daddy story, please."

Michael paused, confused. "A daddy story?"

Amy straightened and nodded. "Tell me a story about your daddy. My daddy died when I was a baby, so I don't have any daddy stories."

She didn't have a daddy. Michael stared at Amy, appalled to think of Janice raising six children *alone*.

"Amy Lynn Parker, what were you told?"

Michael turned to find his love goddess blazing with anger. She was magnificent with that fire in her eyes. A grim-faced teenager stood behind her. She looked enough like Janice to be a daughter, too. He realized it must be Heather, the eldest. Like her mother and her sister, she was a heartbreaker. God, but these Parker women were killing him.

Out of the corner of his eye, he saw that the biker gang was back. A chill went up his spine. *Kids.*

"I came to say hello to Michael," Amy said, looking steadily at her mother. "The triples were mean to him, so I wanted to be nice. I was real nice, Mommy. You should be very proud of me."

Janice's lips thinned. Michael had an urge to kiss them to lusciousness again. He knew she was hiding a smile. He didn't bother to hide his.

"Actually, she's been fine," he told Janice.

"That may be, but Amy knows she was supposed to stay in her own yard."

Amy looked at the ground. "Was I bad, Mommy?"

"Yes, you were bad. You will stay in the house all day tomorrow. You know Mommy has to know where you are at all times."

Amy sniffed dramatically.

Janice was unmoved. "I'm sorry you're crying, but that doesn't change anything. Now what will you do to make tomorrow better?"

"Be even nicer to Michael?" Amy suggested, taking her new friend's hand for protection.

Michael looked on, helpless. Damn, but she was cute.

"Wrong answer, my angel," Janice said sternly. "Heather, take Amy home. I'll be there in a minute, to discuss the merits of remembering what she's supposed to do every day."

"I 'member!"

"Good. I can't wait to hear it. Now get home with your sister."

Amy clung to Michael's hand. "Just don't punish Michael. He didn't do nothing."

Michael burst into laughter. He couldn't help it.

"Don't worry, young lady. I won't punish Michael," Janice said. "The punishment is all on your head."

Amy let go of Michael's hand. She patted him on the leg. "You can tell me about your daddy later."

She blithely skipped away, taking her older sister in tow. Amy had one last parting shot for the biker gang, clearly Janice's source of information, before she disappeared around the side of the house; "You big pigs!"

Janice waved off the gang. "Curfew time, kids. Everybody home."

They grumbled but dispersed.

She turned back to him. "I am really sorry. You must think you moved behind the Addams family."

"Maybe," he conceded.

She laughed. "No maybe about it. Positively. I would if I were you. I'm very sorry another one of mine bothered you again."

"Amy didn't bother me," he said quickly. "She's cute and very sweet."

"She milks it for all it's worth, believe me. I know the apology doesn't make up for the behavior, but I'll make sure you're not annoyed. They are good kids, really. They're just excitable.'' Janice grinned wryly. "I'll bet the Realtor didn't tell you about us. We're not exactly a selling point for the house."

"Well, no, she didn't." *Damn her,* Michael thought, meaning the realtor. He would hardly damn Janice. Up close, she mesmerized him. Her lithe body belied her bearing six kids. Six kids! He doubted he'd ever get over that.

He should have been warned just by wanting to buy a home on Mother's Day weekend. He should have known a woman—a mother—would ambush him like this.

She had to be around his own age of thirty-six, yet she looked ten years younger. A vision of her doing those sensual exercises danced through his head. That had happened more times than he cared to count since he had first seen her. Even the kids couldn't quite kill it. God, but she was delectable.

And all wrong for him. *All wrong.*

"Could you come inside for a moment?" he asked, remembering something he'd seen. "Maybe you can solve a mystery for me."

The oddest thing happened to him when she stepped over the threshold of his new home. It felt right. Usually women were an invasion he allowed because of other circumstances involved, but never had it felt right before.

He shook off the notion and led her to the back laundry room. A box sat in the corner. "I found this in a closet. I think the previous owner's family missed it when they cleaned out the house."

She looked inside, then gasped. "Oh! That's Chris's baseball glove. He thought he lost it last year. And the baseballs must be David's. We bought so many when he went out for Little League because he deliberately kept hitting them over the fences, wanting to duplicate out-of-the-park home runs. And Amy's bear!'' Janice lifted out a stuffed teddy, half-stiff with dirt. "I can't tell you the screaming nights we had when Boo-Boo here went missing."

"I don't think I want to know," Michael said honestly.

She chuckled. "I bet not. What an old bastard Mr. Hobarth was, to keep all this stuff and never say a word. For years!"

"At least he kept it," Michael replied. "He could have tossed it all and you'd never have these memories back."

"You're right." Her grateful look pierced his heart. "Thank you so much, Mr. Holiday."

"Michael. Please." His heart burst inside him. He wanted to kiss her, the urge almost overwhelming his common sense. But he hung on, blurting out the first thing that came into his head. "I can't believe all those kids are yours."

Her gratitude faded. "Oh, yes, they're mine. I even have the stretch marks to prove it."

Her face turned rosy, as if she wished she'd never said the words. He felt heat in his own face. Stretch marks were beyond his ken. They meant a lifetime of commitment. He wanted no part of commitment.

"Well," she said into the breach, "I better go."

"Right."

After picking up the box of her children's lost things, he walked her through the old house, around his own packing boxes and the other paraphernalia that littered the rooms. She murmured polite phrases about the house in general, although it needed modernizing. He paid little attention to her words, only wanting this woman, who disturbed his equilibrium so much, to leave.

She was almost to the door when something stopped her. "Omigod! You're *that* Michael Holiday!"

She pointed to the framed copy of his first syndicated column.

He set the heavy box on a larger one and smiled. "Yes, that's me."

She turned to him, her mouth gaping.

Not able to resist, he reached out and pushed her chin up, closing her mouth. But his hand didn't come away, intrigued as he was by the soft delicacy of her jawline. His fingers explored her flesh for a moment—an undeniable moment. He leaned forward. His lips just brushed hers before she stepped out of his reach.

"Excuse me," she said, picking up the box. "But I think you got enough column fodder from my kids today, Mr. Holiday, without including me."

"Janice..." he began, knowing he had to apologize to her.

"That's *Mrs.* Parker."

"You're a widow," he said.

"I see Amy's been talking. Sorry, not interested." She went out the door before he could stop her.

He closed the door afterward and leaned against it. He had nearly kissed a woman with children. What the hell was wrong with him? Stretch marks, teddy bears and baseball gloves made no dent against his idiocy.

Mr. Hobarth had the right idea. Collect the junk, hide it away for years and then croak.

Either that or sell the house.

Tomorrow.

JANICE SET THE BOX on her kitchen counter and fanned herself. She wasn't overheated from carrying a box. Nope, her trouble was a sensual man. What the hell had happened back there, anyway?

A man had kissed her, that's what happened. And she

had nearly allowed it. Worse, she had nearly kissed him back. She could still feel that moment when his lips settled warmly on her own. The entire room had spun....

"What's that?" Heather asked, coming into the kitchen.

Janice brought her reeling mind into focus—as much as she could for the moment. "Mr. Holiday found a bunch of our stuff that Mr. Hobarth kept."

Heather looked inside the box. "Hey! That's my Minnie Mouse sneaker. Remember I kept taking off my shoes when I was five and hiding them?"

Janice smiled. "I remember. And I remember all the trouble you got into when you came home with only one that time."

"Dad was mad, wasn't he?"

"Very. But you were positive a monster ate your shoe."

"It was the only thing I could think of to get out of trouble," Heather confessed.

Heather's mention of her father put the rest of Janice's brain into focus. Tom had died two months after Amy was born. Janice missed her husband terribly at times, especially when life overwhelmed her. People thought he had been a good husband and father. He had been, in his way. But Tom had had his secrets, secrets she'd never suspected.

Amy and the triplets wandered in. Janice handed out their things, Amy especially ecstatic about her bear, dirty or not.

"See?" she said. "Michael is a very nice man."

"Amy, you don't call Mr. Holiday by his first name," Janice corrected. She should have taken this in hand earlier, but she needed to now. "It's not respectful."

"But he told me to." Amy skipped out of the room, happy as a clam with her bear, while she added, "If he says so, then it's okay."

"She's gonna be tough," Janice muttered, thinking of the discussion yet to come over disappearing out of the yard.

Heather giggled, clearly liking her mother's predicament.

"David!" Janice shouted.

"What?"

Her eldest son was still alive at least. In typical thirteen-year-old fashion, he rarely emerged from his video games. Janice shouted again, "I've got a bunch of your baseballs from when you were the home-run king and they went over Mr. Hobarth's fence. Mr. Holiday gave them back. Do you want them?"

"I'll get them later!"

"His life's story," Janice said. For David everything was "later."

Heather laughed, then said, "You know, Mr. Holiday's pretty cute for an old man."

"He can't be any older than I am."

Heather just looked pointedly at her.

"Thanks a lot," Janice muttered.

"You're welcome," Heather said, laughing as she left the room.

Janice was losing the battle of the kids. Still, "old" or not, she didn't need reminding that Michael Holiday was "cute." She'd found that out up close and personal. At least Heather hadn't latched on to the real crux of the matter.

Michael Holiday was very sexy.

Janice swallowed, trying to dispel the tightness in her chest. The kids seemed emotionally healthy most of the time, her main concern. She had kept home and hearth together somehow, although exhaustion was her usual state of being. But she hadn't had a twinge of a sexual urge in more than three years.

Until today. Today, she'd had more than one.

Michael Holiday celebrated his single status in his columns, liking to place himself in the puzzlement of suburbia and comment wryly from his bachelor point of view. She'd found his pieces amusing generally, but some of his condescending comments annoyed her, too. Of all people to get a twinge for! A rip-roaring twinge at that.

Janice pushed the thought aside. It was bound to happen sooner or later. She was a still-functioning female, after all. Michael Holiday was only the conduit for her first spark.

She remembered how she had reacted to that spark, though—like a schoolgirl with all defenses up. Next time she would stay calm, like any normal adult woman facing a moment of mutual attraction. She'd just say "how nice, but no, thanks" and move on in platonic neighborly fashion.

As she went in search of Amy to "discuss" the child's behavior, Janice reminded herself to take care of the Wrens' Hardware monthly bank statement tonight. If she didn't do it now, she'd get bogged down with the rest of her accounting clients. Everything had to be kept in careful balance or she'd drown very, very fast.

Same as in her personal life.

She had no doubt her kids would probably get featured in Holiday's future columns—probably the entire family would be a wellspring of material for him.

Grinning, she bet he'd never been this close to a woman with six kids before.

She bet the For Sale sign went back up tomorrow.

Chapter Two

Tell a woman as little as possible about yourself. And don't ask questions of her, either. The less you both know about each other, the better your relationship will be.

—Michael Holiday
Man Can Definitely Live by Bread Alone

It was hard to turn down a community party in one's honor.

Michael wished he had, after shaking hands with yet another blustering upstanding citizen of Marshfield. He'd been inundated with invitations in the few weeks since his move; word had obviously got out about his columns. He'd thought the mayor's party would be the best for getting to know his neighbors in a one-shot deal, only the small salt-box Cape Cod was mobbed with people. He'd smiled so damn much his cheeks felt like they would burst any second. Worse, everyone had a story to tell that they were positive would be great for his column. The only good thing was that he had met a couple of potential golf partners.

"I think you're finding Marshfield quite a friendly place," the mayor said with satisfaction.

"Very friendly," Michael admitted ruefully.

The man's toupee was pitch black and an obvious fake. Michael resisted the urge to straighten the piece from its slightly tipped angle. The thing was disconcerting as hell, and the man clearly proud to wear it.

Michael vowed that should his own hair ever thin to the point of needing help, he wouldn't resort to a cheap toupee.

At least, he hoped he wouldn't.

He spotted a rescuer standing in the doorway, looking around the living room.

Janice Parker's hair hung free, the thick brown strands curling around her creamy shoulders. He hadn't seen her in more than a week, not since their kiss. He had been afraid to, and with good reason. Her rose sheath dress clung to her curves, a little satin bow under her breasts emphasizing their fullness. Her legs could have been in a hosiery commercial, her high heels enhancing their luscious length. If she had six kids, then he was a monkey's uncle.

He *was* a monkey's uncle.

"Excuse me," Michael said to the mayor. "I see someone I actually know and need to speak to."

He walked over to Janice and said, "I want to apologize for my behavior the last time we saw each other."

"No," she said. "I apologize. I was rude when a simple 'no thanks' would do."

Her tone was cool. So was her look. Somehow that aggravated him more than her original stiff-necked response. He pushed the notion aside, wanting her warmer. Wanting her help. "Do me a favor. Rescue me, please. If I have to meet another new person who has a story for my column, I'll go nuts."

She smiled reluctantly. "What did you expect? You're

the new kid on the block and you'll put Marshfield on the map, besides. This is suburbia as you write it.''

He shuddered. ''Don't remind me.''

''I just hope my kids haven't been bothering you again.''

''No. I haven't seen them.'' The lack of triplets had been a relief; they scared him. But he missed Amy a little. Usually he didn't take to kids, but she had been a charmer.

''I'm glad to hear they haven't. So how are you settling in?''

''Still trying to find things,'' he admitted. ''All the bathroom stuff was in a box marked Cellar.''

''What was in the bathroom box?'' she asked.

''Old brake pads and a pair of Jockey shorts.''

She laughed, although her cheeks flushed slightly. ''Only a man would pack those things together.''

He grinned. ''Moving is hell on wheels.''

She laughed harder. ''That's a column by itself.''

''Good point...if I could get some writing done.''

Michael wondered if she knew who played the mournful horn every evening around seven-thirty. The practice session hit right at his best writing time. While the horn didn't sound like a wounded moose or anything, he found himself distracted because he couldn't quite figure out the songs being played. The music sounded familiar. He knew he knew it...and yet he didn't. Either the horn or his writing time would have to go—and it wouldn't be his writing time.

''I'm sure you'll get into the swing of it again,'' Janice said. ''I'll send my kids back, if you like. You're bound to get a column in ten minutes. Or the bargain rate of three for fifteen.''

''*Et tu, Brute?*'' he asked.

She chuckled, recognizing Caesar's words to Brutus

when the latter had turned traitor and stabbed the Roman emperor to death. "Oh, I'm not offering stories for your column. I'm offering kids for inspiration. *You* figure out the stories, and I get a break for an afternoon. Fifteen minutes, anyway."

"I think I'll pass," Michael said.

"I don't blame you."

"Janice, help! Help!" A man rushed up to them. "I got a letter from the IRS!"

"What did it say, Rich?" Janice asked calmly.

Michael, however, felt the newcomer's words hit him in the solar plexus.

The man, Rich, paused. "I don't remember." He took her arm, stroking it a little. "Can you come over tonight and see it? I know you'll want to. I really need you to, Janice."

Michael recognized that the man was hitting on Janice. Probably he'd gotten a letter, but he was using it to entice her. An odd anger shot through Michael. He didn't like this guy.

Janice stepped away from Rich, very casually and very effectively removing her arm from his touch. "I'll be happy to see it in the morning, during my regular business hours," she advised. "It's not like the IRS is open tonight, Rich."

The mayor picked that moment to bring over several newcomers, and Michael became separated from Janice at that point. *So much for a rescue,* he thought, as he was introduced to more people. Too bad, since the rescuer was so very attractive....

Get a grip, man, he told himself. Wrong woman. Very wrong woman.

He found her again later, at the buffet table. He wanted to say something about the man who had hit on her, but knew he had no claim. Nor did he want to have, he told himself. Instead, he asked, "What do you do that people come to you with their tax problems?"

"I have an accounting business I run out of my home," she said, loading a plate with food. "I do a lot of taxes and bookkeeping in Marshfield."

"I bet you kick butt with the IRS."

"I *love* going into their offices on behalf of a client." She grinned wolfishly. "It's a challenge to refute their audit."

"I bet you kill them. Euphemistically, I mean."

"I try."

He would love to see her fight that institution. She probably treated the IRS staff as she treated her kids—no nonsense and no getting away with anything. The more he learned about her, the more intrigued he became.

Red flags went up in his brain. He promised himself he wouldn't ignore them, just talk to Janice a little more. It was the neighborly thing to do, after all.

"Oh, goody. Myra's Seven-Up salad. You have to try that."

"Okay." He plopped a spoonful of the coconut-studded Jell-O salad on his plate. "I can't believe you're an accountant. You look more like a model."

She laughed. "Not hardly. Why wouldn't you think I'm an accountant? A lot of women are."

"I don't know. You're more like a drill sergeant."

"I have six kids. Someone has to be."

People interrupted them, to say hello. Michael found most of the townsfolk were fond of Janice. At least most sounded concerned and affectionate. They even spoke kindly of her children.

An accountant. Six kids and now a deadly dull profession. Boy, had his instincts been all haywire about her.

And by the number of people who knew her, she did a good business, too.

He pointed out a couple of free chairs on the patio. When she agreed to join him, his heart beat faster. He didn't have any explanation for furthering his acquaintance with her. She symbolized trouble with a big *T*. Only he couldn't stop himself. She fascinated him. How many more outward signs didn't match the inner reality? He had to know.

"I don't understand you," he admitted, when they were relatively alone. "You hardly look like an accountant. You take care of your body. I saw you exercising in the yard the day I toured at the house. Yet you eat like a horse." He pointed to her plate. "You look like Snow White, but sound like—"

"The wicked witch?" she asked, grinning. The amusement didn't reach her eyes, however.

"No." He chuckled. "God, no. I keep thinking drill sergeant—my drill sergeant when I was in the service."

"What's not to understand?" She shrugged, her shoulders rising and dipping prettily. "I take care of my body because I'm all my kids have now, so I have to be strong and healthy for them. And because I have six kids, it's easier to have a job at home. Actually, it's a necessity, so I've utilized my math skills and worked hard to make it happen. The drill sergeant goes without saying when you have kids."

"So it all comes back to the children?"

"Everything I do is for the children. How could I not?"

She was his antithesis in women. Totally maternal. He had seen the ultimate mother on her ultimate holiday. He should get up and leave. He should. He didn't.

"I think you are an admirable woman," he said. He meant it.

She chuckled. "You sound like you hate admirable women. There's nothing particularly admirable about what I do. I'm just playing the hand I was dealt."

"I don't hate admirable women, believe me."

"But you don't like them, either. So tell me why you picked Marshfield to live. Suburban New Jersey hardly seems like the place for a sophisticated guy like you."

"I grew up not far from here, in Cherry Hill," he admitted. "Before my parents divorced. I'm coming back to my roots, I suppose. I've always been fascinated by suburbia and its undercurrents."

"Well, you'll get them here." She leaned over and whispered, "How do you like the mayor's toupee?"

"Not my color." Her perfume swirled through his senses. It was light, like sandalwood and jasmine.

"He wears it to impress the women. He thinks he's a real ladies' man."

Michael grinned. "Really? How did he get elected if he's a ladies' man?"

"Oh, he never acts on it. At least, I've never heard he has. He just likes to *think* he is." She straightened, leaving him feeling slightly disappointed. "It's interesting that you're moving back to your roots. Despite your single-guy columns, you must want to settle down and raise a family."

"Bite your tongue." Better still, he thought, let him bite it. "I have no familial urges. That would be bad for my columns, let alone my first book, which is on advice to the single guy."

She laughed. "Don't bet you don't have family urges. It hits everyone at one time or another. It packed a wallop with me." She waved a hand. "What else are you doing with a huge colonial on an acre of ground *except* putting down familial roots? I know! I'll help you find a really nice woman to marry—or are you as much a jerk as you sometimes seem in your columns?''

Her brown eyes sparkled with mirth. He realized she was needling him. He couldn't be a jerk in his columns, surely. He said, ''Let's hope I'm not. But I can't resist asking. Who do you have in mind for me?''

He deliberately didn't mention her. The kiss was best forgotten.

''Mmm.'' The way she pursed her lips hardly helped his cause. ''That's a toughie. I know. Barbara Neidermyer's sweet, and she has her own teeth, too.''

''That sounds promising.'' He had no clue who Barbara Neidermyer was, but he'd play along for fun. Or rather, to watch Janice have fun with him.

''Maybe Buffy Wilmont. She's very rich—''

''All Buffies are. But that's *very* promising.''

''I should warn you that she's gone European and thrown out her razors and depilatories.''

''Scratch that before she scratches me.''

''I don't blame you.''

He tried some of the dish she had recommended earlier. ''Hey! This Jell-O salad thing is really good. What about the lady who made it?''

''Myra?'' Janice grinned evilly. ''So you like older women?'' She pointed to a wizened, grandmotherly female. ''That's Myra.''

''I don't like older women that much,'' he admitted.

''You're really narrowing the field,'' she complained, eating the last bit on her plate.

''Do you have a wooden leg?'' he asked, enviously watching her.

''I work it off. That's the beauty of exercise...and running after six kids. Besides, I missed dinner. The triplets had a Little League game at five. I barely had time to change.''

"I thank you for coming then."

"It's good for business, frankly," she admitted. "My clients can see me in a social setting, and we chat. I also make new connections, which is important for future business. As long as I don't spill punch down my front, I'm okay. Besides, I thought I'd better be neighborly after, uh...where were we?"

Her reluctance to mention their last meeting wasn't lost on him. He decided to help her out. "Discussing wooden legs. It's good to see a woman eat."

"I take it you've been on the anorectic-model route."

"A time or two." They might look good in photos, but Michael had found the allure quickly waned in person.

"You definitely need help," she said. Her tone sounded more serious.

"So does your assistance in finding me a woman, at least so far," he replied, trying to keep the tone light. He didn't want her serious. He didn't want her disapproval about anything, including his choice of bachelorhood. Light and easy was his name.

"I can't say we have any model types here, although the women's club holds a fashion show every year where everyone models the clothes."

"I bet you're their top draw."

To his surprise, her face became shuttered. "You really are obsessed with the model type, aren't you?"

He sat up a little, surprised. "No. I was just commenting on you."

"On my *appearance*. Don't you ever look past that to a woman's heart?"

"Of course I look past appearances," he said defensively.

"You don't sound like it. You mentioned mine. You don't like Myra because she's old—"

"I love Myra!" he exclaimed, feeling backed into a corner and wondering how the hell he'd gotten there. "Her salad's great. And I was only trying to pay you a compliment."

"While you criticize my eating habits in the process," she continued. "You want women who shave regularly and have their own teeth."

"I did not criticize your eating habits. And *you* brought up Buffy's not using her razor and that Barbara Whoever having her own teeth!"

Janice glared. Michael realized dead silence surrounded them. Everyone on the patio stared their way, mouths gaping. Several others stood on the threshold of the French doors. Clearly his "discussion" with Janice had attracted attention. *Great first impression,* he thought.

Janice rose and set her empty plate on her seat. "I have to go. Welcome to Marshfield. I hope you like living here."

She walked out with grace and dignity—and a little sexy swivel to her hips.

Michael again cursed himself, this time for actually having her body movements even register, let alone receive approval. He looked up at everyone still staring expectantly at him and knew he should be cursing Mrs. Janice Parker. She had left him holding the bag.

Women.

JANICE GAZED at the broken fence slat, told herself not to be a wimp, girded her mental loins and slipped through the narrow opening.

The wood grabbed at her T-shirt but let her pass. She

pushed her way through the shrubbery of Michael's back garden until she stood in the grassy yard.

She hadn't been able to sleep, had seen his lights still on and knew what she had to do. Apologize for her atrocious behavior.

While walking to his back door, she wondered where her bitchiness had come from. Granted, she had been run off her feet today, but exhaustion was no excuse. She had snapped at him, with no provocation. Okay, so he had touched a nerve, sounding like he condemned women who ate more than a melba toast and a handful of strawberries. She should have held her temper better. But she'd felt an odd jealousy when they'd been trying to find him a woman. While she'd stifled it, the emotion had erupted suddenly when he'd been talking about her weight. His remarks had mirrored many she'd heard when she'd been a chubby child, and had irritated her all over again.

She shouldn't have left him abruptly like that. She hadn't been fair.

When she reached his back door, she wanted to turn tail and run. Having told the kids often enough that they had to accept the consequences of their actions, she couldn't ignore her own scoldings. Right now, she needed scolding more than the kids. Mostly, she needed to make it right. She wouldn't sleep until she did.

"Oh, God," she muttered, and knocked on his back door. It took several more knocks before he answered, but eventually Michael did.

He was wearing a pair of sleeping shorts. *Only* a pair of sleeping shorts.

"Oh, God!" Janice murmured again, then tore her gaze away from his defined chest, where a sprinkling of dark hair narrowed down to his waist and beyond. Unfortunately, she couldn't quite focus on his face. She cleared her throat. "I...am I here at a bad time, Michael?"

Now that was stupid, she thought.

"Not really," he replied, frowning. "Is something wrong at your house?"

"No...well, yes. Me." She screwed up her courage. "I behaved really badly earlier tonight, and I wanted to apologize."

"Now?"

"I know it seems bizarre," she admitted. "You're a new neighbor, and I've acted worse than my kids. I felt so badly afterward that I couldn't sleep. When I saw your light on, I had to take a chance and come over to apologize. If you hate me and have already called to put up a twenty-foot-high chain-link fence around your property, believe me, I truly understand. I'm so sorry for earlier, and sorry I disturbed you now. Thanks for listening. Good night."

She turned to leave, grateful to have gotten through this with some dignity intact.

"Wait," he said.

She turned around again.

"Can you come in and have some coffee?" he asked.

"Oh, it's late, almost midnight," she began, not wanting to put him out. Warning bells clanging wildly in her brain only stressed the lateness of the hour.

"I'm up. You're up. That part's okay," he said. "I think we've both gotten off to a bad start here, so I'd like to make amends, too. You wouldn't want to ruin my neighborly gesture."

This was the moment for mature female behavior. Janice felt more like running for the hills, than exhibiting mature female behavior.

"Thank you," she said. "Coffee would be nice."

He opened the door wider, and she stepped across the threshold into the kitchen.

"Have a seat," he said, gesturing to a table and chairs. "Instant okay?"

"As long as it's decaf," she replied, sitting.

"It is." He poured water into a kettle and set it on the old stove, turning a dial. Flames burst to life. "I'll be back in a moment."

Janice sat on the edge of her seat and wondered how she would get through this. He was a new neighbor, she told herself. He deserved an offer of friendliness. He deserved a little mature behavior from her. So far only Amy had managed to make a good impression and that was a sad statement on the Parkers.

Janice could do this. She could.

Slowly she sat back in the chair and let the silence envelop her. She couldn't remember the last time her house had been quiet like this. Yes, she could. Mother's Day. Since Tom's death, her in-laws took all the kids for the Mother's Day weekend. They wanted to spend time with their son's children, their only link to him now, and they wanted to give her a break, too. She liked her in-laws.

The kettle rumbled, breaking the quiet. It began to whistle. Janice rose to turn off the stove.

"I'll get it," Michael said, coming into the kitchen. He had dressed in jeans and a shirt. Somehow changing only emphasized in her mind his former near nakedness.

Janice sat back down, saying, "It's so quiet in here. I've been enjoying it."

"Sometimes it's too quiet," he said, pouring the coffee into cups.

"I'd like to be on the other side of that fence for once," she admitted, then chuckled. "I am."

He grinned, while bringing their coffee to the table. "I hope you don't mind if I don't go over to your side."

"You're excused. Thanks," she said, accepting a cup from him.

Their fingers touched. Janice didn't know which heated her hand more—the hot cup or his hot touch. Every nerve in her body said the latter.

"How do you like Marshfield so far?" she asked. "Barring widows with attitudes and screaming kids."

"Now did I say that?" He made a show of looking aggrieved. "I'll have you know I didn't even think it."

She smiled. "I did. I think I've been as bad as the triplets. The triples, as Amy calls them."

"There's a real trap in answering that comment," he said. "If I say you're not, then I sound like I don't like your kids. If I say they're not, I sound like I don't like you. Either way, I'm in trouble. I think I'll pass. The weather's been very nice, hasn't it? Not too warm for May and not too humid."

She laughed. "Okay, you're absolved."

"Thank you." He grinned.

He looked so boyish and charming. She bet he had women swooning at his feet. Of course a man like this, a perpetual bachelor—one who really focused on looks, for she didn't for a moment believe he didn't—was not a man in whom she should have an interest. A perpetual bachelor couldn't be faithful for long and certainly couldn't cope with a child not his own, let alone six of them.

Ergo, she didn't have an interest in Michael Holiday.

She ignored the voice that called her a liar. She asked, "How's the writing going?"

"Slow." He made a face. "I like pure quiet when I write, but somebody plays a horn around here that bothers the heck out of me."

Janice set down her cup. She coughed sheepishly. "The Addams family strikes again. That would be me."

"You? You play?"

"No. It's my son David. He's in the band and plays a baritone horn. He plays quite well, really. He's even won awards. I guess that doesn't come across the backyards."

"No, the playing's fine. It's just that I can't quite figure out *what* he's playing, and he's playing during my best writing time. I'm sitting there listening instead of paying attention to my column. Oh, brother." Michael ran a hand down his face. "I sound like another complainer."

"It's okay. I'll speak to David about moving his practice to earlier in the afternoon." She laughed wryly. "God, and here I thought you were safest from David."

He laughed. "Doesn't look like it. By the way, what music *is* he playing?"

"'When I'm Sixty-Four,' a Sousa medley and 'Watermelon Man.'"

He gaped at her. "You're kidding! I couldn't recognize a one."

"I usually can't, either, until I go to a school concert," she admitted. "He plays in bass cleft—that's the counterpart. We parents sit there at shows and say, 'Oh, so *that's* what that is.' It's fun."

"I bet."

Janice wouldn't have been surprised if his voice held sarcasm. Instead it sounded wistful.

She was kidding herself, she thought. The bachelor liked kids? Not hardly. She sipped her coffee, then looked around the kitchen. It needed work.

He must have seen her gaze, for he said, "I'm going to redo this kitchen. Sometime. Are there any good renovation companies in Marshfield?"

"Several. I do the books for two, and they're both expensive but honest," she said. "You'll get topnotch work from either one." She mentioned their names.

"Thanks."

"This is really nice," she admitted, after drinking some more of her coffee. "I'm usually talking homework or breaking up fights over TV time or having tea with Amy and her stuffed animals. Sometimes I think I've forgotten how to speak to adults."

He smiled at her. "You're doing fine. And you're welcome here anytime you want to talk to an adult."

"Thank you," she said, knowing she'd never take him up on the offer. She'd be nuts if she did. She glanced down at her coffee cup, to find it nearly empty. She wished it was full again, but the hour was late and although Heather and David were responsible kids, she didn't like to leave them long, especially when she hadn't told them she'd gone anywhere. They'd been sleeping—all the children had—when she'd gotten the impulse to apologize. A very good impulse now, but her repair work was fixed. She rose. "Much as I've enjoyed this, I have to go."

"How about another cup of coffee?" he asked. "We've barely talked."

Be adult, she reminded herself. "I'd love to, but I have to get back. Again, I'm sorry about the party. I was a chubby kid, and I guess I'm still a little sensitive."

"You? You were chubby?"

She chuckled. "Yes, me."

"I can't believe—" He stopped abruptly. "No, I won't go down that road again."

"Better not," she agreed.

He stood and put out his hand. "Thanks for apologizing and for the welcome to the neighborhood."

"Sure you want to thank me for that?" she teased. Forcing herself not to hesitate, she took his hand in a firm shake.

The touch shot through her, bringing that tingling sense of anticipation. His hand was so warm that her brain immediately conjured images of him touching her breasts, her thighs...more intimately.... Her skin actually *felt* the strength of his fingers and the heaviness of his palms on her body.

Janice swallowed and shoved the sensations away. She had salved her conscience and done her neighborly duty in the process. That was more than enough today. She took her hand back before she got into more trouble. Pointing to the kitchen door, while walking around the table, she tried to speak. "I'll, ah... Good night, Michael."

"I'll walk you out," he said.

"Oh, that's okay," she began, panic shooting through her.

"I'd be happy to."

She made herself smile. "Thank you."

Any other reaction would only signal that he disturbed her. While she doubted he would ever have a true interest in her, she didn't need to show her newly acquired, schoolgirl retro attitude. She and Michael Holiday weren't even on the same page about what a relationship should be. He was dead-end and no future, and she was Ms. Permanence. She knew herself well enough to know that. Relationship differences didn't even count the kids, and their reaction to a man in her life. She couldn't think of herself until Amy was grown up and gone. Not really.

But above all, Janice was scared to death to get out in the man-woman social world again.

Michael held the door open, and she had to duck under his arm to go through. Her shoulder brushed against his chest with the lightest of touches. Shock waves rolled through her.

Janice shot out the door.

Breathless, she pulled up and waited for him, repeating her mantra of "cool, calm and collected." Deodorant had nothing on her.

"It's a beautiful night," he said, when he joined her.

Janice looked up at the moon, full, huge and a beautiful pale yellow. It seemed to gaze down on her, smiling as if endorsing her walking with a man. The thick, velvet sky behind the moon seemed to cloak her clandestine meeting. She returned her gaze to the earth, her mind truly calmer. Her heart still beat with anticipation.

Michael put his hands in his pockets as he walked alongside her. He asked, "Have you ever seen the mountains of the moon?"

"No." Surprised, she glanced up at the moon again. "I didn't even know there were mountains on it."

"There are beautiful, haunting mountains, believe me. If I can ever find my telescope again, I'll call you to come out and see them. The kids would probably like it."

She stopped and gazed at him in amusement. "You're very brave, Michael."

"What the hell," he said. "You only live once. Maybe I can really scare your triplets and secure my ghost reputation forever."

"Don't go too far," she warned. "They could actually like it."

"I know what *I* like. Their mother."

Janice gulped. She had no clue what to say that would be dignified, suave, smooth and repressive. There had to be *something* in the English language to cover it.

She was even more unprepared to deal with his kissing her. His mouth settled firmly on hers, no apologies, and he pulled her into his arms. Brother, could he kiss! His lips played over hers, enticing her to respond. They were warm, not thin. Gentle, not soft. Needful, not frantic. She braced her arms against his biceps, ready to push herself away. Yet the feel of his muscles under the thin shirt had her clinging instead. The kiss was long and sweet, almost innocent. Eventually his mouth coaxed hers open. She wanted to resist. She tried to remember all the reasons she should. Not one surfaced. She could only feel and taste, mate her tongue with his. His body against hers was like heaven, reminding her that above all things she was a woman. He tasted so good, his mouth like forbidden chocolate. And he desired her. She could feel the tightness of his body, taste the wanting behind his kiss.

Suddenly, they parted as if an explosion had gone off between them. Not a bird's chirp nor a breeze's ruffle broke the silence as they stared in shock at each other.

Finally, Michael said, "Janice...I..."

She put her finger to his lips, stopping him from searching for words. "No. It was a lovely kiss." She took her finger away. "Let's not spoil it with apologies. Just know it will never happen again."

"It won't?"

"No," she said firmly. "It won't."

She walked away from him, proud of herself for handling the aftermath. She had been mature and very collected. She had also been a second away from pulling him to the ground and letting the kiss take her where it would. Okay, so she'd nearly had a glitch, but she had come through the fire. She had been *good*. And better still, in control.

As soon as she slipped through the fence, out of his sight, she ran for all she was worth through her own backyard. Her heart pounded with both an unsettling fear and an overwhelming high. She gasped for breath. For all her female bravado, she was damn scared of that kiss.

She opened the back door and went inside her safe, secure house.

Heather stood in the middle of the kitchen, wearing her nightgown and bathrobe. Her arms were folded across her chest, and her eyes blazed with anger.

"Where were you?" she demanded. "Do you have any idea what time it is?"

Janice stared at the teenage version of her own mother, who had confronted her exactly this way whenever Janice had come in after her curfew in high school.

Oh, God.

Chapter Three

Another reason never to involve yourself with a woman who has children is that you might like the kids more than you like her.

—Michael Holiday
Man Can Definitely Live by Bread Alone

Michael sat in the little chair, his knees up to his chin. He hoped the molded plastic would take his weight without breaking.

"Would you like cream or sugar?" Amy asked, passing him a minuscule teacup. She added quite solemnly, "I like five sugars in mine."

"Really?" he said. "I'd like to try that."

The sugars were imaginary, so his health was safe. Amy doled them out with her dinky spoon. Michael watched the empty spoon tip over his cup, fascinated with the precise way Amy dealt out childhood magic. When she was done, he thanked her. He stirred his "tea" properly. He didn't want to make a mistake. Mistakes killed magic.

"Pooh Bear likes his tea with ten sugars," Amy said, spooning out the condiment for the cheery-looking, stuffed yellow bear sitting opposite her. "That's why you're so fat, aren't you, Pooh? It's just shameful."

Michael hid a smile at the scolding.

Amy had come over with her invitation to tea and a determination not to receive a no. She had wheedled and pleaded, assuring him it was okay with her mother. Michael had finally caved in. He wasn't quite sure he'd agreed because he couldn't resist Amy or because he actually wanted to experience a kid thing again.

Or because he wanted to see Janice.

He hadn't seen her since that kiss and her kiss-off afterward. She had thrown out a challenge in her cool dismissal. So far he had resisted the purely macho urge to respond and show her how wrong she was about that kiss being their last. That he wanted to scared him. He didn't, not really.

No, he was here today because of an irresistible little charmer who offered a peek at a world where bears drank tea with ten sugars.

"I like your hat," he said to Amy. "It looks just wonderful on you."

"Thank you." Amy touched the straw brim of the old-fashioned Gibson Girl hat. "You don't think the yellow flower is too much?"

"Never." He glanced around the backyard, with its orderly beds. "You match the garden. Did you plant the flowers?"

"Some. Mostly, my mother did." Amy's speech was precise, too.

So Janice was a gardener, Michael thought, even as he wondered how she found the time. He wished he hadn't discovered something he had in common with her. The more diverse they were, the better.

"Tell me a daddy story now," Amy requested, drawing his wandering attention.

Michael pondered. He rarely saw his father anymore and

hadn't all that much when he had been young. "My dad took me swimming in the ocean. Oh, but the water was cold and fierce! The waves crashed against the sand. They were over my head. But my dad picked me up and held me as he walked into the water."

"Oh! Was it scary?" Amy's eyes were round and wide with awe.

Michael grinned. "Yes. But my dad just kept walking until my toes touched the water. The waves out in the ocean were more gentle. They tickled my feet. I saw a school of fish go by, and then some dolphins. Seagulls flew over our heads—"

"Amy? Have you seen…"

Janice paused on the threshold of the back door. She stood, staring at him, clearly surprised to find him having "tea" with her four-year-old.

Michael smiled and saluted her with his cup. "I was just telling Amy about being at the shore."

Janice didn't smile. "I'm sure she enjoyed the story. Amy, honey, you didn't tell me you asked Mr. Holiday to tea."

Michael frowned. He turned to Amy, who looked indignant.

"Oh, yes, I did, Mommy," the little girl said. "I asked you if I could play with Michael in the backyard."

Janice looked flummoxed. "Yes, I remember your asking, but I thought you meant Michael Canuzzi from two doors down."

"Well, I can't help it if you got the Michaels mixed up," Amy replied, taking a sip of her tea. Clearly, she was in a hoity-toity mood.

"She's got me there," Janice said ruefully.

Michael had wondered how she would react and reluctantly admired her for her humor. He wished she had screamed or scolded or generally acted like a fishwife. He didn't need help in finding her fascinating. He said, "I'm sorry, Janice. When Amy assured me you approved, I didn't realize there was a mix-up. If I had, I would have refused."

"No, it's okay. Although Amy and I will talk later about her leaving the yard to ask you." Janice looked pointedly at her daughter.

Amy said nothing for a long moment, then she smiled triumphantly. "But Michael Canuzzi lives outside the backyard. You didn't say nothin' when you thought I asked him."

Janice herself said nothing for a long moment. Michael laughed. He couldn't help enjoying her entrapment by a four-year-old.

"Wait until you have kids," Janice muttered.

"It'll be a long time if I have anything to say about it," he agreed.

"I came out, young lady, to tell you I'm finished hanging your new curtains," Janice said to her daughter.

Obviously, Janice didn't want to reply to him. He supposed in her position she wouldn't. She had six children, while he, about the same age as she, had none. What could she say? What could either of them say?

"Mommy got rid of my baby curtains," Amy said proudly. "Come and see my new ones."

"Oh, I don't think I should," Michael began. It was one thing to enjoy Janice's predicament. It was another to rub her face in it.

"Please, Mommy, please," Amy wheedled, running to her mother and wrapping her arms around Janice's knees. "You make such pretty curtains, I want Michael to see them. Please."

"I'm sure Michael has work to do—"

"It'll just be for a minute. Please!"

"It's up to him—"

"Come on, Michael," Amy ordered, letting go of her mother's legs. She didn't wait for his reply, saying as she went into the house, "And bring Pooh. He'll want to see my new curtains, too."

"Of course," Michael replied, knowing defeat when he saw it. He wiggled out of the child's chair, which clung to his hips before letting go with a slight *pop*.

He retrieved Pooh and tucked the stuffed bear in the crook of his arm, glad a little magic still lingered.

Amy had already disappeared inside, but Janice waited for him. "Don't mind the house," she said. "It's always a perpetual wreck."

While the occasional pile of things cluttered a bookcase or table, Michael found the house generally neat, but above all, comfortable. His mother's house had always been immaculate—and devoid of character. This house reminded him more of his grandparents' place, where a kid could be a kid, not a robot.

In the television room, a boy sat on an ottoman in front of the TV screen. He wore a Phillies baseball cap stylishly backward on his blond head. He held a video-game controller, his fingers flying over buttons. On the screen, things jumped and twirled and spun in response to his touch.

"David," Janice prompted, to get his attention.

"Yeah, Mom?" David never took his eyes from the screen.

"Come meet Mr. Holiday, our new neighbor behind us."

The boy never moved. "Hey, Mr. Holiday."

"David, pause it!"

The boy groaned and hit a button. The TV screen froze.

David got up and came over, his hand outstretched. "Hey, Mr. Holiday. Thanks for giving me back my balls."

"You're welcome," Michael said, willing himself not to even think double entendre. He shook hands with David, who stood as tall as Janice. Less boy and more man, David was in the first throes of adolescence. Besides his blond hair peeping out from the cap, he possessed small, even features nothing like Janice's. He must look like his father, Michael decided. He asked, "What are you playing?"

"Sega. It's Sonic." David's face lit up. "You play?"

"No," Michael admitted.

David's face fell. "Oh."

"Mommy! Michael!"

"The queen calls," Janice said, tapping Michael on the arm.

"Nice to meet you, David," Michael said. "And thanks for moving your practice time. I appreciate it."

Janice had clearly passed along the message, for David now practiced earlier in the afternoon. At least that's when Michael heard him.

"No problem," David said, already unlocking the figures on the screen and immersing himself in the game.

"Now you've met them all," Janice said, as they climbed the stairs.

"Yes. He's a nice boy," Michael replied, avoiding the piles of neatly folded clothes on the edge of some risers.

"He's a good kid," she commented, automatically picking up a pile.

From the plain, practical bras sitting on top, Michael guessed the pile was hers. Somehow he had envisioned her in Victoria's Secret satins, not K mart sensibles. He wondered if she changed the latter into something sexy when she wore them. She'd turned enough of his notions upside down already that he'd like to find out.

He wanted to apologize to her for the kiss, but resisted. She wanted no apology and he disliked the vulnerability one gave. Besides, why should he apologize? He'd enjoyed the kiss, and so had she.

"I should warn you that Amy shares a room with Cat out of necessity," Janice said, stopping to drop off her armload of clothes on a hall table. "It's…unique because of that."

"Okay." Michael braced himself, following her through an open door.

The bedroom was literally split in half, a wide piece of tape running from one side to the other. It began at the ceiling, stretched down one wall, across the carpet and up the opposite wall.

The tape literally separated day and night. One side was all pink-and-white gingham frills, with dolls and stuffed animals decorating dresser and bed. The other side would have sent a ten-year-old Michael into spirals of ecstasy. Baseball bats, soccer and basketballs were piled in a corner, and the bedspread sparked a football theme. Even the two windows were diverse, one all-girl, the other all-boy— or rather tomboy.

"Oh, Mommy, they're real pretty," Amy said, touching the pristine, lacy curtains on her side.

Janice smiled. "I'm glad you like them."

"Aren't they pretty, Michael?"

"Very," he agreed, trying to keep his gaze on her side of the room. If he looked at both sides at once, he thought he was having a psychotic episode. He added, "Pooh likes them, too."

"Oh, yes," Amy said. "Except that he can't eat them. He doesn't like that because he wants to eat everything."

"You weren't kidding when you said the room was unique," he told Janice in a low tone.

"I do what one must to ensure the peace while encouraging individuality. Amy has door privileges on Cat's side, and Cat has closet privileges."

"Solomon couldn't have done better," Michael said, in awe of her ingenuity with kids. As long as one could tolerate the slight schizophrenia.

"Solomon had over a hundred children. The man understood."

This was why he would never make a good parent, Michael thought. He'd never have come up with such a solution for a tomboy and an ultrafeminine girl. He'd still be wrapped up in who got what room, let alone how to cope with opposing tastes.

He looked at Janice, who smiled in pleasure at her youngest's fussing. How had she managed alone? How did she think up these ways to deal with six children? Where did she find the patience and common sense? She was the most amazing woman he had ever encountered.

Package that with a body an eighteen-year-old would envy and a face an angel would covet, and no man could resist her. Add to that a cool denial of attraction, and even the most avid reader of *Man Can Definitely Live By Bread Alone* would be in trouble.

He wasn't in trouble. He would not take up the challenge of seeing whether she would kiss him again. Nope, he would just finish admiring curtains like a good boy, then wander home to write about four-year-old vamps.

Janice must have felt his perusal, or even sensed his thoughts, because she turned to glance at him. Her gaze held his for the longest moment, those fawn-colored eyes limpid. If she didn't want to kiss him again, then he was a—

Michael tore his gaze away. He wouldn't consider what

he was. He knew all too well, and it wasn't pleasant. "Amy, your room is very pretty, as pretty as you."

Amy grinned, her face rosy.

Janice began, "I'm sure, Mr. Holiday—"

"Michael," Michael said.

"See?" Amy said. "I told you I could call him Michael, Mommy. Now you can, too."

Janice cleared her throat. "Yes. I did want to talk to Mr. Holiday about this."

"There is no need to talk," Michael said. "I'm an informal guy. Besides, Mr. Holiday is my father. Please."

Janice firmed her lips, then sighed. Michael didn't know which he wanted to kiss more—the pouty expression or the resigned one. Both appealed to his senses. If he wasn't careful, he'd find himself as the Kiss Avenger yet. He decided retreat was the better move at the moment—for his own sake.

"I have to be going," he said. "I really should get back to work."

"But we were playing!" Amy exclaimed, her face stricken.

Michael swallowed, wondering how to get out of this gracefully.

"Michael does need to work, Amy," Janice said into the breach. "If he doesn't, then he can't pay for his house, and he will have to move away. Do you want that?"

"No," Amy whispered.

Michael wished Mom looked as upset with his departure. Janice just smiled.

"He played with you for a little while, but now it's my turn, okay? All my work is finished. We could make cookies, if you like."

"Okay," Amy said, instantly happy and Michael instantly forgotten.

For some odd reason, he didn't like it.

When they all trooped downstairs, they passed young David in the TV room, still playing his video game.

Michael frowned. The kid looked like he hadn't moved from his position. To Janice, he said, "Isn't playing video games bad for children?"

Janice looked at him, her expression frosty. "David's a straight-A student and polite to his elders. He doesn't steal or vandalize. He doesn't do drugs. He doesn't cause any trouble. With a kid that good, it seems a shame to take away something that gives him great pleasure."

"But isn't it bad for their socializing?" he persisted. "I know I read that somewhere."

"David has a number of friends he socializes with. They're all players, I grant you, but like David, they're good kids."

"I didn't mean to imply they weren't." Michael back-pedaled, knowing he was stepping all over it. "It's just that I heard playing too many video games isn't good for kids."

"Thank you. I'll keep it in mind."

The dismissal stung. "But—"

They reached the back door before he could continue. Janice held it open, looking pointedly at him. "Thank you for playing with Amy, Michael. I know she enjoyed it."

"Yes, thank you," Amy chirped from behind her mother.

"Thank you for inviting me," Michael said, holding out Pooh Bear. What the hell else could he do but go, in face of the twin dismissals? After Amy took the bear, he held out his hand for her to shake.

Her palm was so little, warm and trusting in his own. Michael felt something inside him melt, something that had been frozen for a long time. *Impossible,* he thought.

He had had nothing frozen emotionally within him. What a stupid sensation. Probably he had indigestion from his hurried lunch—or even indigestion from the imaginary tea. But no *real* problems.

Yet as he cut across the yard, he couldn't help feeling as if he were fooling himself.

He'd better get his life in order. He needed to.

JANICE PULLED UP the spurge that ran riot among her dame's rockets. Not that the four-foot-tall plants were particularly troubled by the weeds. Her sense of order was, however.

And not by her seedy-looking garden.

She doubted she would ever forget the sight of Michael Holiday sitting in a teeny tiny chair, holding a teacup, pinky finger correctly extended, and chatting with her daughter and Pooh Bear—as if he did it every day of his life.

Was this the same man whose column only yesterday discussed at length the advantages of taking off whenever one liked for a vacation in Aruba? She bet Michael was panting to have high tea with the bikini-clad women on the beach. She bet his Pooh Bear panted, too.

And then there were his remarks about David and the video games. How could he, not a parent, question her child-rearing practices? She watched over David closely, but had seen how the games challenged the boy in many good ways...and helped David get through his father's death. Maybe other children would lose perspective, but David hadn't shown a sign of it so far.

Next time she would make sure she knew which Michael Amy wanted to play with.

"What the hell am I doing?" she muttered in disgust,

realizing her straying thoughts had led to ripping out six inches worth of coreopsis in the next bed.

Gardening was supposed to be soothing, a few moments of peace that she snatched for herself. As her kids would say when they thought she couldn't hear them: *This sucks.*

She sat on her heels, ignoring the aching in her back and knees. Wiping the perspiration from her forehead, she wondered how to handle having a disturbing man living behind her house. Not that she wanted to do anything *with* him. She had made that clear.

Now if only she believed it.

"It's a beautiful Saturday morning for that."

Janice jumped. She glanced up to find Michael hanging over the back fence. He wore heavy cowhide gloves, and his face was flushed and sweaty, showing he, too, was doing yard work.

His eyes were so damn green, she thought. And they crinkled at the corners when he smiled. He was smiling now.

"Your dame's rocket looks very good," he added. "Do you deadhead them to force new blooms?"

Janice stared at him, shocked that he knew about gardening. "Yes. Yes I do. When I can, that is."

"Get the kids out to lop off the dead blooms," he suggested. "They can't do much wrong, if you're very specific."

Janice laughed dryly. "Ah, the voice of innocence. The one time I tried it, Cat decided she didn't like red roses, and she cut all of them off. And Chris wanted to see if the nippers would cut human flesh, so he tried them on C.J. and Amy. In ten minutes' time, I had a pile of ruined rosebuds and two screaming kids."

"Sounds like something Freudian."

"Freud would have been on the couch, getting psycho-analyzed, believe me."

"These Shasta daisies need reclumping, and your irises need dividing."

She sighed. "I know. They've been on my project list for a couple of years now. I'll get to them eventually."

"I'll do it for you," he offered.

"Oh, no, I couldn't allow that."

"Why not?" He disappeared, to come through the gap in the fence.

Janice watched him squeeze his way in and out of the opening. The fit was tighter than for her, and his jeans molded his rear during the process.

He had a very cute rear.

Just what I wanted to know, she thought in disgust. Aloud she said, "No, really. Michael—"

"I'm happy to do it," he said. He rubbed his chest. "I'm going to have to widen that. Or lose some weight."

He looked good to her. A little too good. Janice cleared her throat. "I'll take care of the garden—"

"You just said you've been backed up for years. I know this is the daisies' growing season, not the best time for dividing them, but if they're not done now, you'll lose them altogether. The entire inner ring is dead." He reached back through the fence and brought over a spade, then tiptoed around an enormous columbine. "Have Shovel, Will Travel."

He began to work on her overgrown daisies.

For the first few moments, she felt uncomfortable, as if she'd been invaded. Her senses slowly relaxed, however, as Michael did nothing more than dig and whistle happily. Janice began weeding again. The silent companionship of two people bent on the same goal satisfied something deep within her.

"You've got a lot of plants in your garden," he commented. Nodding to the columbine, he continued, "That looks terrific with all its blooms. You must use bonemeal."

"Yes," she said, surprised. "How did you know?"

"Perennials love bonemeal. A little in the fall and spring, and you've got a happy garden."

"I like color," she said, "rather than the greenery here when we first bought the house. The garden areas bordering the fence were already dug, so I took advantage of them. It was a way to watch the kids in the yard and do something constructive besides. I found that if I used perennials and got out here a few times in the spring and fall, the gardens pretty much took care of themselves the rest of the time. Annuals had to be completely replanted every year.... I never would have thought you were a gardener."

"I worked for a garden shop during my college summers. I liked it a lot and that's why I like a house with grounds. It's fun to watch things grow."

Oh, God, a nurturer, she thought. Even if it was with plants. She needed a diversion. "What were you working on at your place?"

He chuckled. "Cutting back the wisteria from hell. Amy's scared of it, you know. She says it's alive and tries to eat kids."

"You like my daughter, don't you?"

He smiled. "I'm not much for kids, but I like Amy. She's hard to resist."

A thought flitted through her mind, not a good thought. She knew nothing about this man. Well, she did, if his columns reflected his true nature. But what if they didn't? Of course, she would never trust a stranger with her children, not that Amy had ever been alone with him for a long period of time. Janice had spoken with Amy before about strangers. Maybe they'd better have another talk.

"There's a gorgeous butterfly bush, too," he added. "But no one's been ruthless with it for years. Like roses, they need to be cut way back every year."

"I discovered that myself." Letting go of her dark thoughts, Janice pointed to her own bush, now developing its greenery. Soon it would produce lilaclike flowers that butterflies couldn't resist. But lilacs reminded her of a problem. "My lilac bush on the side of the house didn't bloom well this year. It looks very healthy. Would you know why?"

He thought a moment. "If you have a lot of dead blooms from last year, try cutting them all off. They sometimes need deadheading for new growth to find space."

"I'll try that," she said, pleased to have a possible solution.

He bent, bunched his muscles and lifted the entire Shasta daisy clump out of the earth. "Voilà! Now where do you want the second half, after I get this split?"

She glanced around the crowded garden. "Gosh, I don't know."

"Don't worry. I'll find room. And if I don't, I'll take the plant. I've got some bare spots that need help."

"Okay." Janice grinned. Despite her parental worries over the appropriateness of Amy's friendship with Michael, she had to admit that, like the night in his kitchen, this adult talk renewed her senses. Oh, to not have to talk about who wore what to the mall, or Sonic versus Mario, or Little League baseball, or Pooh Bears and tea. To not police anyone. To talk about *her* interests, mutual adult interests. This was heaven, soul satisfying. Gardener satisfying, at any rate.

"I'm attracted to you," Michael said.

Her bubble shattered. Not burst. Burst was too fast, too

easy. Janice swallowed, trying to gain time while she gathered her control.

"I shouldn't be attracted to you, but I am. I can't deny it."

"Why are you telling me this?" she asked in a low voice.

"You live behind me. You're single. I've kissed you twice now, even though I barely know you. I think I should be honest with you, rather than deny a truth."

"I was quite happy denying the truth," she said.

"Ah. Then you admit you're attracted to me," he said, grinning a smugly male grin.

"No, I'm not attracted," she corrected. "I told you that."

"Liar."

She gaped at him. "I am not a liar!"

"Did I kiss alone that night?" he asked. "I thought those were your lips kissing me back. Or were they someone else's?"

She couldn't believe how quickly the conversation had turned. *Don't panic,* she thought. *Don't panic. Act adult.* "They were mine...but I told you that was the last kiss."

"Are you sure?"

"Yes, I'm sure!"

"You don't sound sure."

She rose to her feet, adult forgotten. "What the hell do you mean I don't sound sure? I'm *very* sure."

He arched an eyebrow. "Then let's test your theory. I'll try to kiss you, and you tell me no."

"No."

"I haven't even tried yet."

"Yes, I know."

"Chicken."

"I'm not chicken!"

"Then I'll kiss you." He didn't move. "Eventually."

"No."

"You won't know where or when I will. But I will. And you won't stop me."

She realized she was caught in an endless loop of denial. It was time to take the upper hand. "Why are you at all attracted to a woman with six kids?"

He looked sober. "I don't know. I just am. I know that much."

Somehow that scared her more than his wanting to test her resolve.

"Mommy! Michael! What are you doing?"

Amy ran out from the house, all fresh and clean and ready to start the day. Heather followed behind her little sister.

"Thanks for taking care of her bath," Janice said to Heather. She was grateful for the interruption. Damn grateful.

"Just don't forget you're taking me to the mall as a payback," Heather said, smiling.

"What are you doing, Michael?"

"I'm helping your mom in her garden," Michael said to Amy.

"Oh...can I help, too?"

"Sure. We need to find a place for these new daisies. A pretty place that needs white flowers."

"Okay." Amy started hunting through the garden.

Heather laughed. "Mom must be in her heaven, having someone to help her with her pet project. She's always talking about the garden until we have to beg her to stop. It's boring."

Janice vowed to bore her daughter right into the ground. The plants could get their bonemeal straight from the source.

"Well, I'm with your mom on this," Michael said. "Bringing something to life takes great skill and nurturing. I find it exhilarating. *Very* exhilarating."

Janice suddenly had the feeling he wasn't talking about gardening.

A challenge had been declared.

Chapter Four

Never, on pain of death, allow a woman to meet your family. She'll like them. They'll like her. And you'll have your worst nightmare come to life.

—Michael Holiday
Man Can Definitely Live by Bread Alone

"What a great house!"

Michael smiled indulgently as Mary Ellen Magnussen-Holiday, his cousin Peter's wife, poked around the downstairs rooms. Mary Ellen and Peter had called to bring over a housewarming gift for him, and he had asked them to stay for dinner.

He liked Mary Ellen. Peter's sudden marriage had been a surprising turn of events, however. The man had actually researched eliminating love from the human race at one point. Who would have thought Peter would even marry? Why would he want to?

"It's a big house for you," Peter said, frowning. "Why would you buy a four-bedroom house for one person?"

"Who cares?" Mary Ellen said, sitting at the kitchen table finally. "You're just too damn logical, Peter. I've warned you about that before."

"I keep telling you that one of us has to be," Peter said.

"Besides, I thought logic was one of the things that you love about me."

"Only when you're not annoying about it."

Peter kissed his wife in answer. The two thrived on their gentle sniping, that was obvious.

"I assume you're going to redo the kitchen," Mary Ellen said. "It's too dark and dreary in here, for one thing. And too old-fashioned for another."

"I am redoing it eventually," Michael said, getting out the salad necessities. "Although I want to do a lot of the work myself, I did get a couple of contractor recommendations from Janice."

Michael clammed up, silently cursing when he realized he'd said a particular name. It didn't matter. Mention of Janice landed like a bomb in the kitchen.

"Janice?" Mary Ellen and Peter asked, their voices perfectly timed together. Even more together was the arch in each one's eyebrow.

"She lives behind me," Michael said calmly. He had avoided her since gardening day. The undercurrents made him wary. "But don't get excited. She's got six kids, three of which are a set of triplets. Or is that a triple of triplets? What is the correct term?"

"Set, I believe," Peter said.

"Who cares?" Mary Ellen repeated her litany. "The poor woman! And her husband."

"She's a widow," Michael said.

"Ah...a widow." Mary Ellen's tone was speculative. Then she added, "Oh, no doubt she's safe from you. With six kids, she's probably safe from *everybody*."

Michael worked industriously on the salad. If he didn't, he was likely to give away his own forays into that forbidden territory called Janice Parker. He was far too attracted to her for his own good. Worse, he had been happy as a clam, digging around in her garden while chatting with her. And especially with his little helper, Amy. Janice's six kids hardly deterred him. Well, three did.

The lovely sound of horn music drifted through the back windows, left open on this fine, late June day.

Peter frowned. "What is that?"

"One of the kids in the back. David. He plays baritone horn in his school band."

"Boy, you know a lot about this woman and her family," Mary Ellen said.

"Not really."

"I know that song he's playing," Peter mused, going over to the window. "At least I think I do."

"That's the old Beatles song 'When I'm Sixty-Four,'" Michael said, proud to have figured out each song—now that he knew what they were. He sang a little bit for Peter and Mary Ellen, in time with David's counterpart, to help them recognize it, too.

Mary Ellen laughed. "That is it. By the way, who are your other neighbors, on either side of you?"

"My next-door neighbors?"

"Yes. Either side. Who are they?"

He wasn't liking Mary Ellen so much at the moment, because he had yet to say more than a passing hello to any of them. He cleared his throat. "There's an older couple on either side."

"Do they have names?"

Michael shrugged.

Mary Ellen got the point. She grinned evilly. "You don't know them, but you know the name of the woman—the *first* name of the woman—behind you. And the kid, too."

"One of them," Peter said, not looking away from the window. "And what he plays."

"Right. And what he plays. Interesting. *Very* interesting."

"It's easily explained," Michael lied, hoping he could come up with an easy explanation right quick.

"Why are there three children running from one bush to another in your backyard?" Peter asked, bringing salvation.

Michael glanced out the window and cursed. "It's the triples."

"Triples?"

"The triplets. Cat, Chris and C.J."

"More names," Mary Ellen said to Peter.

"More names," Peter agreed. "What are they doing in the backyard, sneaking around like a Desert Rat patrol?"

"They think I'm a ghost," Michael said. "Even though they're forbidden to come in the yard, they've been sneaking in anyway every so often, to listen under my window."

"How could you forbid children to enter your yard?" Mary Ellen asked, outraged.

"It's not me. It's the mom who's forbidden them." Michael glanced out the window. The trio was closer now. "Keep talking like you don't know they're here."

"But I want to know why they think you're a ghost," Peter said.

"In a minute. Talk weather."

"Lovely day, isn't it?" Mary Ellen commented, playing along. She went to the window to look out from behind the curtain.

Michael waved the conversation on.

"Lovely," Peter added, shrugging. "But I think it will rain tomorrow."

The triplets were just under the windows, trying not to step on his day lilies. They noisily shushed each other.

"I see you," Michael said in his best James Earl Jones imitation.

The three shrieked, clamped their hands over their mouths and ran like hell for the break in the fence. Michael grinned in satisfaction, having beaten the triples at their little game. So far the score was in his favor.

"Cool," Mary Ellen said. "Can I scare them next time?"

"They won't be back for a few days." He wondered whether he was doing the wrong thing by playing this game with the three. He hated to go to Janice and complain, getting them into trouble, yet he didn't want them wandering unguarded in his backyard. God knows what they would get into.

"Here comes another one, a little one," Mary Ellen said. "You can't mean to scare her, Michael. She can't be more than five."

"She's four." Michael smiled. "And no, I would never scare her. That's Amy."

He went to the back door and opened it. "Hi, Amy."

"Hi, Michael," Amy chirped in her childish piping voice. She smiled angelically, reminding him of a small cherub brought to earth.

"I'm glad to see you, but you know you're not supposed to leave your yard," he told her.

"I know." She looked unrepentant, as usual. "Can you play today?"

"Not today. I have company."

"Who?"

"My cousin and his wife."

"They could play with us, too. I'll make extra tea and Pooh can sit on the ground."

"We appreciate that, honey," he said gently, wanting to let her down easy. "But they're no fun, like you are.

They don't know how to play well. Why don't I come over tomorrow? I've got to look at those daisies we planted.''

"Okay.'' Amy skipped back to the fence.

Michael wondered if he should have left the kid-eating wisteria alone. Amy, like the triples, had become bolder since he'd cut it back.

"Oh, God,'' Peter said. "I think I'm in love.''

His own problem exactly, Michael thought. With *daughter*. Not mother. What he felt for the mother was something entirely adult.

"So we're no fun, eh?'' Mary Ellen began, giving him a sour look.

"Well, we know I'm not,'' Peter corrected. "Michael, what is this with these kids?''

"Hell, I don't know,'' he admitted, running a hand through his hair in frustration. Maybe it all had to do with Mother's Day. "Amy's adopted me as her best buddy, and the triples are intent on making my life a hell.''

"Don't forget your serenader,'' Mary Ellen said.

"Where's the sixth?'' Peter asked. "You said she had six kids.''

"Heather's probably at the mall,'' Michael replied. "I believe she lives there.''

"Another name,'' Peter said, grinning.

"I noticed.'' Mary Ellen shook her head. "The others sound okay, but you ought to make peace with those triples.'' She snapped her fingers. "I know! Let's ask them to join us for dinner.''

"Are you nuts?'' Michael exclaimed, horrified with the idea.

"My words exactly,'' Peter chimed in.

"No, I'm not nuts. Ask the family over for dinner. Feed

them hot dogs and hamburgers and chips, and the kids will get to know you better.''

"My worst fear," Michael said.

"And Peter and I get to meet Mom. I'm *dying* to meet Mom.''

"That ought to be your worst fear," Peter told him.

"What's their number?" she asked, picking up the portable phone receiver.

"I don't know," Michael admitted.

"We'll look it up." Mary Ellen started flipping through the telephone directory, which Michael, being new to Marshfield, kept handy on the counter.

"Mary Ellen, I don't think this is wise," Michael began.

"Of course it is. And neighborly, too."

"But I'm serving chicken marinated in current jelly and Worcestershire sauce," Michael protested. "And I don't have enough to feed seven more people."

"We'll send Peter out to the store for the dogs and burgers and extras," Mary Ellen said, running her finger down a page of *P*'s.

"We will?" Peter asked.

"We will. Aha!" She tapped the page, then punched in numbers.

"Mary Ellen, please!" Michael yelped.

She smiled at him, then held out the phone.

"Hello? Hello?" He heard Janice's voice faintly through the receiver.

Reluctantly he took the phone and held it to his ear. "Hello, Janice. It's Michael. From the back."

"Oh!" Even surprised, her tone could melt honey.

"I'm, ah...having some company this evening, and I wondered if you and your children could join us?"

"Well...it's lovely of you to ask, but we really couldn't."

Relief and disappointment ran through him. "I understand. Maybe another time."

"Give me the phone," Mary Ellen said. She took the
receiver out of his helpless hands. "Janice? This is Mary
Ellen Holiday, Michael's cousin."

"Mary Ellen!" Michael whispered loudly.

She waved her hand to hush him. "Please don't say no
to Michael's invitation. He's got so much food here that
we need help eating it, and it will save you from making
a meal. That's got to be a plus with your busy life...."

"Mary Ellen!" Michael tried again.

She ignored him. "Oh, no, we're family, hardly company. He's so new to the neighborhood that it would be
lovely for him to get better acquainted with his neighbors...."

"Mary Ellen!" Michael bleated, knowing this was one
neighbor with whom he'd already become far too well acquainted.

"It would be a sin to waste all this food. Please come
over. We'd love to meet you and your children."

"Oh, no, you wouldn't," Michael muttered, remembering the triplets using him for a merry-go-round.

"Oh, absolutely not...that's perfectly fine. We can send
a care package home for him. He plays beautifully. We
heard him earlier... Anytime is fine. We'd love having
you."

Mary Ellen was like a freight train when she got started.
Impossible to stop. Michael turned to Peter. "You married
her?"

"Love," Peter replied. "It's the only explanation I
have."

Mary Ellen hung up the receiver, saying, "I heard that
and don't you ever forget it's love. Now get that cute tush
of yours to the store pronto. We need thirty hot dogs, thirty

hamburgers and rolls for both. Get chips, about three bags, and pickles and olives. Kids should have some greens. Oh, and don't forget mustard, relish and catsup. Michael probably doesn't have enough. And soda. Tons of it. One isn't coming. He's got a practice or something, but that doesn't matter. We need food now.''

"Anybody got a truck?" Peter asked.

"Very funny. Now go."

"I have only one question. Where's a store near here?"

Mary Ellen spun her husband around and gave him a push. "I don't know. Get thee forth and find one. And hurry it up! She'll be here in about fifteen minutes. We've got to look like we did have all this food hanging around."

"It's impossible," Peter said.

"You thought you could cure the human race of romantic love. *That* was impossible. Anything else is doable. Now get out of here and *do!*"

"Wait a damn minute!" Michael roared, feeling like he had to grab the end of the runaway train to try and stop it.

Mary Ellen and Peter turned to him. "What? What?"

Michael stared at them. In some recess of his brain, he realized the train was long gone and anything he did at this point would make him look foolish. "The store is two blocks to the right and four blocks down. You'll need some money."

He handed over a fifty. Peter skedaddled. Michael sighed in disgust.

Mary Ellen clouted him on the shoulder. "Cheer up! This will be great."

"You haven't seen the kids in real action," he muttered.

Peter returned from his errand through the front door just as Janice came through the backyard with the kids, all except David. Janice wore a tank top and shorts. She looked spectacular with her hair hanging loose around her shoulders.

Mary Ellen gaped. "*That's* the mother?"

Peter looked at Janice, then leaned over and whispered to Michael, "No wonder you bought the house. You are a dead man—you know that, don't you?"

Michael groaned. That's what he was afraid of.

MICHAEL'S COOKOUT wasn't as bad as Janice feared it would be. David had marching-band practice, but the rest were having a good time. Even the triplets, lured by the promise of barbecued food, had left their perch at the edge of Michael's backyard and actually mingled. They clearly liked Michael's cousin by marriage, Mary Ellen, who was a charming hurricane. Heather seemed to be enjoying herself, not sullen or bored, the de rigueur attitude of teenagers. Little Amy reveled in being the center of attention between Michael and his cousin, Peter.

"Can we make one of these?" Peter asked his wife, while chucking Amy under the chin.

"Five or six, if you like," Mary Ellen replied.

Janice laughed. "Don't be that enthusiastic."

"Oh, heck, you're taking all the fun out of everything," Mary Ellen told her, grinning. "Hey, kids! I'm thinking of a color."

The triplets and Amy immediately entered into Mary Ellen's guessing game.

Janice smiled, not surprised now that she had been gently coerced into this cookout. Mary Ellen was infectious, a dynamo who simply didn't accept the word *no* for an answer. If Michael had had any extra food before he issued his invitation, then Janice had a million dollars sitting in the bank. She knew damn well she did *not* have a million dollars sitting in the bank. If she wasn't careful for the rest of the month, she'd wind up with an overdraft.

But more than a persuasive cousin-in-law had lured her here. She watched Michael at the grill, flipping hamburgers and slapping cheese on them. He looked hot and sweaty, harassed and adorable. The last was not a good sign, she thought.

Since the day he had helped her, she'd been working diligently in her garden. She hadn't seen him once—until today. Maybe she had mistaken an underlying challenge from him. What the hell did she know anymore about how attraction worked between man and woman? She had enough trouble keeping herself awake through the early newscast. She was pretty sure he hadn't liked being told their kiss was *the* last, yet obviously, he really hadn't intended to act on his threat to kiss her again. Maybe some male-ego element had been satisfied just by him threatening to kiss her again and leaving her fretting about it.

It had worked very well. She fretted. A lot.

"You have great kids," Mary Ellen said, sitting next to her after the guessing game ran its natural life.

"Thanks," Janice replied, smiling. She tried her best to instill manners in her children and often felt as if she'd lost the battle.

"I told Michael he needed to make peace with your triplets. A load of hot dogs ought to help."

Michael must have told her the "ghost" story. Janice laughed. "I'm not so sure about that."

"You know...it's a shame about the boys," Mary Ellen said.

Janice frowned, wondering what Chris and C.J. had gotten into. "I'm sorry if my sons have done anything—"

"Not your boys." Mary Ellen chuckled. "I mean the

Holiday boys. Peter...well, not Peter anymore—he has me. But Michael and his other cousins, Jared and Raymond.''

Janice clammed up, having a feeling she was about to gain some insight about Michael Holiday that he would never reveal.

''Their grandparents had a tragedy when the cousins were young, about the age of your three there. Their grandmother had an affair and then tried to commit suicide afterward,'' Mary Ellen explained. ''Peter says the boys loved their grandparents, and they all vowed never to love anyone. I think they've held to it, because only Peter is married, and that's recent.''

''How tragic,'' Janice said, her heart going out to Michael. The story shocked her, and she was surprised that Mary Ellen would reveal the details. ''Didn't their parents help them through it? I know I had many, many talks with my kids after Tom, my husband, died, to help them adjust.''

''I don't think they had anyone, really, who talked with them,'' Mary Ellen said. ''At least their adult lives don't indicate it. Peter's a behavioral scientist. At one point, he actually thought eliminating romantic love from the human race would raise it to the next level of civilization. When I met him, he was well on his way to finding an antidote.''

''But that's impossible!'' Janice exclaimed.

''I had to shoot him in the butt with an arrow on Valentine's Day to get him to figure that out. Jared, one of the other cousins, is a first-rate divorce lawyer. Raymond, another, is a very cynical sports-talk radio host. You only have to read one of Michael's columns to see he glories in his bachelorhood.''

''Yes, I've noticed.'' Janice wondered if the involuntary disappointment in her tone was obvious. She hoped not.

If Mary Ellen had heard, she didn't acknowledge it.

"It's funny how things affect us when we're little. I've always felt guilty that my own parents stuck out a rotten marriage until I was an adult. Now why should I feel bad about that? I don't know, but I do."

Janice thought about her own folks, loving to their children and good companions to each other. She owed them a lot for giving her a grounding to pass on to her own kids—and for helping her cope with them, too. What her parents had taught her had helped her to eventually forgive Tom when she discovered he had been having an affair. That secret had come to light with his death—in the woman's house...in her bed. Janice rarely thought of it now. Sometimes, though, it still hurt to know she had been betrayed by a man she trusted.

But if Mary Ellen was right—and Janice had no reason to doubt the woman—Michael hadn't had any help to get him through the bewildering changes in his grandparents' lives. She couldn't imagine any child vowing never to love again, yet the story explained so much about him.

Janice wondered if she represented the ultimate in commitment and that's what attracted him to her. If he could conquer her, he could get back at the people who'd hurt him as a child.

Move over, Freud, she thought wryly.

She noticed Cat, then Chris, each snitch a hot dog off the serving platter as Michael was busy loading freshly cooked ones onto buns and setting them down. Janice let C.J. get his own edible loot before excusing herself, to casually meander over to where the trio hid behind an oleander bush. They were stuffing hot dogs in their faces.

"If you touch one more of anything without permission," she said, watching in satisfaction as they nearly jumped out of their skin, "I will personally drag you home by your ears and you won't see the outside of the house for a week. We are guests here, and we will be polite. Do we understand each other?''

The three nodded.

''Good.''

''How did you know, Mom?'' Cat asked.

''I know everything. I'm a mother,'' she said. ''Now finish the evidence of your crime and go be the sweet, charming children I know you can be. Okay?''

The kids hesitated.

''*Okay?*'' Janice repeated a little louder.

''Okay.''

She went to the grill and waved some drifting smoke away from Michael's head. ''You look like you could use some help.''

''God, yes.'' Michael handed her a pair of tongs. ''Get that stuff off before it burns.''

Janice held up a blackened hot dog. ''Too late for anyone else, but great for me. I like them burnt.''

''You're only being polite.''

''I'm never polite. Ask my kids.'' She set the hot dog on a barely crisp bun. ''I hate toasted buns.''

''Me, too.''

Michael's glance sent a delicious shiver up her spine. *Ridiculous,* she thought. She knew so much more about him that only told her he was a total dead end on a personal level—and yet her body still reacted out of proportion to his look. She needed to get herself together for some nice guy who didn't panic about kids and commitment.

Who was she kidding? She needed to get her head out of the man cloud altogether. She wasn't equipped to handle them anymore.

''You're burning the cheese,'' she told him pragmatically.

"Oh. Right." He got the cooked burgers onto the buns she held out for him.

In the next lull, he asked, "What happened with the triplets? I saw you go over and speak to them."

"They borrowed some hot dogs when you weren't looking."

His eyebrows shot up. "When? Just now?"

She nodded. "Good thing you don't keep any state secrets. They'd be gone by now, too."

"I wonder if this means I've lost my scaring abilities, with them coming close like that. I don't know whether it's bad or good."

She chuckled. "I'd wonder, too. By the way, I enjoyed your column about Aruba the other day. I wish I was there."

He laughed. "Me, too, at the moment. Actually, it's too hot and humid there for me. And unless you stay at one of those all-encompassing resorts or at the beach itself, there's not much to do."

"Then why hold it up as an example of a great getaway?"

"Because it has a great-sounding getaway name. I used Aruba as a metaphor for just being able to pick up and go."

"You are the ultimate yuppie," Janice said, shaking her head.

"Thanks. Damn! The ultimate yuppie just lost a burger through the grill rods."

Like that day in her garden, they worked well together, quietly and efficiently. Janice wished they didn't. She had sympathy for this man now. She liked him. It was a very dangerous combination.

Except for a squabble over who got the catsup first, the kids were reasonably well behaved during the meal—to

Janice's relief. One never knew when kids would lose common sense, not that they ever had much. Amy sat between her and Michael. Janice didn't know whether to be relieved or jealous. Peter asked if he could study her children's behavior patterns, behavior being his field. Janice declined, not wanting her kids to be guinea pigs. Mary Ellen just grinned at her.

Underneath the surface casualness, Janice felt tension rising within herself. Worse, she couldn't keep from glancing at Michael. Even having Amy between them was no barrier to her wandering thoughts.

His face held a slight flush from the grill heat, and his hair stuck damply to his temples. His sharp features could have been carved in stone. Peter looked like Michael, yet his face didn't cause a twinge within her. When Janice glanced at Michael, it hurt to even breathe. The wildly colored golf shirt he wore couldn't hide the muscles in his shoulders and arms. A very slight stubble spread on his jawline, a five o'clock shadow that she knew would feel rough against her skin if he kissed her again.

He turned to her, and Janice realized he must have sensed her rising desire for him. His green eyes grew lambent, his lids half closed as he assessed her face. This man understood the facets of sensuality. He practically defined them.

Janice looked away and concentrated on her burned hot dog. She hadn't lied when she said she liked them that way, but it literally tasted like ashes in her mouth. She forced herself to eat it. She forced herself to finish her plate of chips and pickles. She forced herself to act natural and to help clean up afterward.

In the empty kitchen, she sighed with relief, feeling as though she had found a breathing space from all the sensations swirling inside her. The litter of paper plates demanded attention, and she threw herself into the task of scraping excess food off them before throwing them away. God only knew what she would do if she had to continue to be a waited-upon guest. She wouldn't be missed. Mary Ellen currently led the younger kids on a treasure hunt in the backyard. Heather was talking movies with Peter, who was probably reveling in that bewildering phenomenon, teenage behavior. Michael was cleaning the barbecue grill.

Janice sighed again, relieved to have the kitchen to herself. Sometimes the constant noise of humanity at her house got to her. This time, it was more than a need for peace and quiet that demanded a break. She needed to get her body and her head together before she faced Michael again.

The screen door slammed, startling her. Michael came into the room, far earlier than she was prepared to deal with him.

He walked right up to her. She shrank back against the refrigerator, trying to protect herself from the wildness in his eyes.

"Don't ever again tell me we had our last kiss and then look at me like you're stripping the clothes from my body, and in front of everyone!"

"I did not!" she began, with bravado.

"Wanna bet?"

He kissed her before she could stop him, a searing kiss that shook her to her toes. She wanted to pull away, but his mouth was a fire she couldn't control. His lips quested over hers, demanding a response she couldn't deny. He smelled and tasted smoky, with a trace of sweet relish and tangy mustard. So ordinary. So intoxicating. And just as she'd predicted and craved, his masculine stubble rubbed enticingly against her soft skin, almost burning her like a brand.

She curled her fingers around his arms and mated her tongue with his. His body crowded hers against the fridge, the enamel cold on her back as he pressed his length to her own. His hands spread along her ribs, then cupped her bottom, kneading her flesh. A shudder rushed through her at his touch.

This was what she had come for this evening, she thought. To feel his mouth on hers, his warm skin, his need. She was starved for a man's touch. She'd had offers since Tom's death, but hadn't felt the least urge to pursue them. This man didn't offer. He took knowingly. She couldn't stop him and didn't want to try. That he was all wrong for her didn't matter at the moment. She wanted what he demanded.

Voices outside broke through the kiss. The two of them separated and stared at each other.

"Don't say you don't want to be kissed by me," he told her in a low, shaky voice.

"I won't," she admitted, trying to hang on to some shred of her dignity. "But don't tell me you want a relationship with me any more than I want one with you."

He gazed at her, a mix of emotions in his expression. "I won't. I don't want to be involved with you."

"And I don't want to be involved with you." She refused to let her ego be bruised at his honesty and her own.

"So what do we do about this attraction?" he asked.

"Nothing," she said.

"Nothing!"

"Nothing," she repeated.

"Are you telling me to just say no?"

"Hardly," she scoffed. "That's a platitude for kids that doesn't work. But we're adults. We're not ruled by our out-of-control hormones, and we're not too young to understand the consequences of consummating our desire.

We understand there's more to this besides ourselves.''
She drew in a deep breath. "Mary Ellen told me about
your grandparents. You know how adult relationships affect kids. I'll grant you, it's been a long time for me, but
you don't want to be the first after my husband. I'll be a
disaster at best, believe me. And while I'm adult enough
to accept the consequences of a strictly sexual relationship,
my children aren't. I won't put myself ahead of them.
Think about it, Michael.''

He said nothing for a long moment. "I understand. I
agree.''

She mentally pushed away all doubts and regrets.
"Good. Now go get your telescope.''

"My telescope?''

"You once promised to show me and the kids the mountains on the moon. What better way to get through this
farce than gazing at a place I'll never get to?''

After another long look at her, Michael went for his
telescope.

Janice sagged against the refrigerator, shaking from her
speech. She'd gotten it all out. She had been brutally honest. She had done the right thing for herself...for her children. He'd accepted it.

She hated the kids.

She hated him.

Most of all, she hated herself.

Chapter Five

Don't allow a woman to rule your thoughts. If you do, she'll control you and the relationship. Simply purge her from your mind. All it takes is a little willpower.

—Michael Holiday
Man Can Definitely Live by Bread Alone

"Seeing you reminds me, I've got to call that neighbor of yours, Janice Parker. She still hasn't phoned me about my June accounts. She does my books for me, you know. And she does a fine job with them, even if she does have to draw blood from a turnip some months. That's four dollars and thirty-seven cents, with tax."

Michael handed over the cash to Mr. Wren, the hardware-store owner. Washers and caulk thread were expensive here, he thought. Next time he would drive to the national-chain home-improvement center. He'd pay less, and he wouldn't have to hear Janice's name, either. *They* wouldn't know her from Eve.

He escaped from the hardware store and headed down the block on his next errand. He had a half-dozen projects going at the house, none of them close to being finished since he liked to squeeze in a round of golf every so often. He really ought to call the people Janice recommended....

"Hell," he muttered. He couldn't get away from her in his own head.

Oh, hell, he thought again, as her lecture from the cookout night came back to haunt him. She had managed to hit every sore point about their relationship, and damn her for saying she no more wanted a relationship with him than he wanted with her. *He* decided what he wanted....

"Look at the moon and leave it at that," he muttered, then realized passersby on the sidewalk were staring at him. Women, especially mothers who exercised outside on their special holiday, were *not* what he wanted.

He went into the bank, his next chore. Things weren't better there.

"It's a pleasure to meet you," the woman bank manager said, shaking his hand. She was in her fifties and dressed in a dark suit. It gave Michael hope that she'd be all-business. "We're very excited to have a celebrity in our midst."

"Thanks," Michael replied, sitting in the requisite customer chair. He was never sure what to say when people called him a celebrity. Thanks seemed the most innocuous. He hardly felt like one.

"You live behind Janice Parker, don't you?"

Michael gritted his teeth together, then said, "Yes. Yes, I do."

"She's an incredible woman," the manager said. "Raising all those kids alone like that. I barely got through three. Thank God, mine are grown and I'm done. Do you have children?"

"No," Michael said, trying to be patient and polite.

The woman smiled. "Well, you're young yet. But don't wait too long or you won't have the stamina to deal with them."

"I'll keep it in mind. I'm here to open a household checking account...."

As he filled out the paperwork his new account required, Michael longed for the anonymity of the big city, where he could live next door to people for years and still not know their names. Instead, he had moved to Anytown, U.S.A., where everyone knew everybody—and mentioned it often. He wished he could banish mention of Janice. He didn't need to hear how wonderful people thought she was.

Too late.

That last kiss imprinted itself in his brain. He couldn't stop himself after she had gazed at him with her soul in her soft, brown eyes. The heat the kiss generated, the feel of her breasts against his chest, the incredible softness of her derriere, the way her hips pressed to his... He never should have kissed her. Hell, he should have grabbed that phone out of Mary Ellen's hand. The impromptu cookout had been a huge mistake. He'd known it, and yet he had allowed it to happen anyway.

Janice got to him. Somehow. Some way.

He refused to think about her anymore. She didn't want him. She had made that very clear. He really didn't want her. Well, he might, but he wasn't completely stupid.

He decided the best way he could symbolize his new resolve not to think of her again would be to fix that hole in the fence as soon as he got home. It *was* on his list of things to do, but the job had migrated to the bottom. He moved it to the number-one spot. Amy might be upset, but he couldn't help that. It really wasn't healthy for her to attach herself to him emotionally—nor he to her.

Even as he stopped at the lumberyard and ordered the needed boards, his brain refused to eliminate Janice from its confines. His heart sat heavy in his chest when he thought about Amy. He knew, however, that his decision was for the best.

Really. It was.

He arranged for the lumber to be delivered immediately, wanting to make the break right away. The lumberyard manager was delighted with the extra cash and promised to deliver it within the hour.

Michael beat the truck home. When it came, he had the repair boards taken to the site. After the men were gone, he got out his new hammer and nails, a housewarming gift from his cousin Jared. He went to the hole in the fence.

Amy was in her backyard, playing with a tiger-striped kitten.

"Where did the kitten come from?" Michael couldn't resist asking, even though he knew he shouldn't talk to her, since that would be encouraging her friendship. Satisfying one curious question couldn't hurt.

Amy ran to him, holding her kitten in her arms. "Heather's friend Jen's cat had kittens accidentally, and we got one! Accidentally means big mistake. My mommy told me."

Michael grinned wryly, wondering if Janice viewed him as "accidentally" as he viewed her. Probably. Yet it bothered him to think so. "It's a very pretty kitten. What's its name?"

"Michael," Amy said proudly.

Michael felt as if someone had just walloped him over the head with one of his new two-by-fours. "Michael?"

"Yes. I named him after you. He's a lot of fun, but my mom says he's a baby and has to sleep a lot. He's mostly mine, but the triples say he's theirs. They want to call him Stupid. Now *that's* stupid."

"I kind of like Michael, too," he said, looking at his namesake. The kitten snuggled in Amy's arms, already half-asleep. Never had Michael felt so flattered in his life. No one had ever named anything after him before.

"Oh! He's all purry," Amy said, wonder in her face. She suddenly thrust the kitten up in the air. "Wanna hear?"

Startled, the little thing hissed a protest and twisted in her hands.

"No, no," Michael said, motioning for her to hold the animal properly. "You let him sleep in your arms. I'll hold him later, okay?"

"Okay." Amy tucked the kitten against her again. It squirmed for a moment, decided it was secure enough and settled down for another snooze. Amy stroked it, helping the kitten along to dreamland. Then she asked, "Wanna play?"

The moment he dreaded. "I'd love to, but I can't." He gestured to the gap in the fence. "I've got to put the boards back in today."

Amy's eyes widened. She stood very still. "But if you put the boards back in, how will I come visit you when I want to?"

Michael coughed. Boy, she got to the crux of the matter right away. "Your mom can bring you around——"

"No!" Amy exclaimed, stamping her foot. "No! No! No! Mommy! Mommy!"

Screaming and crying in full-blown tantrum, she turned and ran to her house before Michael could stop her.

He hung his head and cursed soundly. He had made a mess of telling her about the fence repair. He knew nothing about handling children and it showed.

Janice emerged from the house with Amy holding her hand. The kitten wasn't with them. One Michael was safe, he thought. Tears streaked Amy's face, breaking his heart. Her mouth was open from her continual sobbing.

Janice's hair was pulled back at the nape of her neck, and her body looked like an eighteen-year-old's, the jean shorts and T-shirt she wore only emphasizing her youth. Damn, she looked far better than any image his brain conjured. Michael swallowed.

"Michael, what happened out here?" she demanded, clearly concerned for her daughter. "I can't get a straight answer out of Amy except for a 'Make him stop.'"

"She got upset when I told her I couldn't play today because I have to fix the break in the fence," Michael explained.

All expression washed from Janice's face.

She stared at him. Michael felt the cold glance down to his toes. Never had a woman made him feel so transparent.

"Make him stop!" Amy wailed.

Janice knelt in front of her daughter. She took Amy's arms to get the child's attention. "Amy, honey. Michael can't have a broken fence forever. You know that's not right. He has to fix it."

"But then he won't be my friend no more," Amy said, between tears. "I don't have a daddy, and now I won't have a friend."

"Amy!" Michael said in dismay, realizing how her mind worked. He squeezed through the hole in the fence, not caring when the wood scraped hard against his chest and back. He went to her and knelt. "I'll always be your friend. Fixing the fence doesn't change that."

"Yes, it does." Amy sniffed back new tears. "You'll go away."

"No, I won't. I'll be right here all the time."

Amy said nothing, clearly thinking over his words.

Janice rubbed her daughter's back. "Sure, Michael will be here, but Amy, Michael's a man, not a child like you.

He can't be your playmate all the time. He has lots of other things he has to do—''

"To pay the mortgage," Amy said.

Michael bit back a smile. "That's right."

"And he has to fix his fence," Janice added firmly. "It's really better this way."

"No, it's not!" Amy replied, looking rebellious all over again.

Michael tried a different tack. "You don't want your new kitten to get out of the yard and be lost, do you?"

Amy looked nonplussed. "No."

"If I don't fix my fence, he can get out and be lost," Michael continued. "We don't want that, do we?"

Amy shook her head. "No."

"Besides, I'll look pretty silly running around the neighborhood yelling, 'Michael! Michael!' Everyone will say, 'But there you are.'"

Amy giggled. Suddenly, she flung her arms around his neck. "You really are nice, Michael."

"Yes, I am," he said, looking straight at Janice and emphasizing the words.

Janice's expression didn't change.

He found himself caught up in the thin, child arms wrapped around his neck, the touch of her lingering tears at his cheek. He wondered how the hell he'd ever considered mending the fence. Amy was far too precious to set aside.

Only now he had her approval for the fence mending.

She disentangled herself from his hug. "Come in and see where Michael sleeps now, Michael." She giggled at the double names.

He recognized that a refusal, even a hesitation on his part, would put Amy right back in the emotional quicksand. Hard knocks come soon enough, and she had already had more than her share. Today softness was essential. "Sure. If it's okay with your mom."

"Thank you," Janice muttered. Then she smiled at her daughter. "It's okay, but if Michael's sleeping, you let him sleep. Remember what I said about picking him up too much. I *will* send him back to Jen's house."

"I won't," Amy promised. To Michael, she added, "You better promise, too."

"I promise," he said solemnly.

They went into the house together, Amy holding his hand. But Michael was far too aware of Janice only a footstep away. Her scent, a mixture of flowers and woman, swirled through his nostrils. Sunlight glinted off tiny highlights in her dark hair. He couldn't honestly say Janice was the most beautiful woman he had ever met, yet she had something indefinable that reached into his soul.

Michael paused on the threshold of her house, this last thought startling him.

"Come on, Michael," Amy said impatiently, tugging on his hand.

He shook the notion away. He must be getting a cold; his head was clogged. That was all that was wrong with him.

Inside, the kitten was sound asleep in a box in the kitchen. Little Michael looked wiped.

"Playing is hard work for a kitten," Amy said, tucking the bright quilt around the furry body.

Michael the human smiled at her maternal fussing. She was worth a hundred columns, he thought.

A cheer went up from the other side of the house.

Michael raised his eyebrows.

"That's David and his friends," Janice explained. "They're playing a video game in the television room."

Michael looked through the hallway, where he had a

clear view of the room she mentioned. He could see several boys, David in the center of them, his hat on backward again, playing video games. From their tense bodies, Michael had no doubt they were in the heat of battle.

"It's a beautiful day outside," he commented. It was a beautiful day, not too hot yet for June. "Why aren't they out there?"

"They will be. Would you like some coffee?" she offered. "I'd like to talk with you."

"That sounds ominous."

She chuckled. "No. Not really."

"Okay."

She waved him into a seat at the table. He ought to be fixing the hole in the fence. He ought to be doing a lot of things, none of them having coffee with Janice.

He sat.

As she poured coffee into mugs, he said, "Everyone in town seems to know you. Have you lived here all your life?"

"Sometimes it seems that way. We moved here before Heather was born. I do business with a lot of people, too. I guess that's why everyone seems to know me. Believe me, they know you more."

She had roots here, long-established ones. A man who fooled with her did so without impunity from the town. She was too well respected for that.

She placed his cup in front of him, then sat in the opposite chair.

"Thanks. That reminds me," he said. "Mr. Wren is looking for his June books."

She wrinkled her nose. "Dan Wren is always so impatient."

Amy wandered out of the room, bored with watching the kitten sleep.

"I know what you're doing," Janice said. "About the fence. I think it's a very wise choice."

"You do?" Somehow, he didn't like her agreeing with him.

"Yes. In fact, I got the kitten because I intended to stop Amy's visits with you, although a war is developing between her and the triplets—"

"Wait a minute," Michael interrupted. "Why were you stopping her visits with me?"

"Because her attachment to you is becoming unhealthy," Janice said.

"Unhealthy!" Coming from her he sounded like the disease of the week. "I do wash my hands upon occasion."

"I'm laughing out loud, you're so funny," she replied dryly. "You know I mean that she's adopting you as a father figure. That's not good."

"I understand the responsibility," he told her. "I do see it, I assure you."

"I don't think you're prepared for it, though."

"Obviously, I'm not going to be given a chance."

"Nope, you're not. I have to think of Amy."

He cupped his hands around the mug of coffee, its heat oddly cooling his temper. When he finally felt the urge to break the mug dissipate, he said, "This has nothing to do with Amy's feelings. You're trying to protect yourself from me."

Janice looked ready to fling her own mug at him. He braced. Instead, she just said, "Don't flatter yourself."

"And don't kid yourself."

"Oh, I'm not. I won't have Amy hurt…or worse."

"Dammit, now you make me sound like a deviant or something."

"Well…I don't know anything about you, do I?"

Michael opened his mouth to bellow at her nonsense, but he was interrupted by one of David's friends.

"Could I have a drink, Mrs. Parker?" the boy asked, looking nervously from her to Michael.

"Sure," Janice said, smiling sweetly.

Michael burned.

"David!" she called out. "John needs a drink."

"Could you get it, Mom?" he replied. "I'm on the last level."

"David!"

"Mom, please! I can't pause now!"

"He can't. Honest," John confirmed.

Janice shook her head. "John, honey, what would you like? We have orange or cranberry juice. Or water. Or Kool-Aid."

"I'll have cranberry juice," John replied, surprising Michael. He would have thought the boy would go for the kid drink.

Janice fixed the cranberry juice for John, who then left the kitchen. Michael got back to the subject at hand.

"Have I *ever* done anything to any of your children that would even make you *think* I'm a lowlife of the worst sort?" Michael asked, clipping off each word in his fury.

"Well, no," Janice admitted.

"Thank you for that."

"I'm sorry you're unhappy, Michael, but a person can't be too careful with her children," she said.

"I understand that."

"And you have made advances toward me."

"Yes, you. The *adult*," he emphasized, then looked heavenward. "I can't win here. Now I sound like I'm a deviant with you."

"What's *deviant*?" one of the triplets asked as the three chose that apt moment to invade the kitchen. Cat was easy to distinguish, but Michael couldn't tell which boy was which.

"It means someone who doesn't behave normally," he replied, not even trying to guess who was Chris and who was C.J.

The trio looked at him accusingly.

"You're safe from me, guys," Michael assured them, feeling like the entire family viewed him as the ogre of Marshfield.

Janice chuckled. "Mr. Holiday is not about to fly around the room or rattle his chains. What do you three want?"

"Popsicles."

"You know where they are. Don't make a mess and put the sticks and wrappers in the trash when you're finished."

"We *know,* Mom."

"Then why don't you ever do it?" Janice asked.

Not bothering to answer, the kids trooped to the refrigerator, got their Popsicles, then took off. There was a column in all this, Michael thought. He just wished he could see it.

"Okay," Janice said, when they were alone—relatively—again. "I might be too harsh—"

"Might be?"

"*Probably.* Most likely... Ninety-nine and forty-four one-hundredths percent sure."

He stared at her.

"Don't ask for more. I don't know you well enough yet. I hope you do understand my point of view about the father figure. That is where my concern truly lies. I won't have Amy left in the lurch because you get tired of the game."

"I like Amy," he said. "A lot. I don't leave friends in the lurch."

"Only women."

He took a big gulp of coffee, not caring that it almost burned going down. He made his next pronouncement succinctly. "This is not about Amy. *You're* chicken."

Her eyes widened. "I am not!"

"You're doing a damn good job of hiding behind your kids."

"I'm *concerned* for my kids—"

"So you accuse me of nonsense."

"I'm not accusing..." She waved her hands. "Forget it! I only wanted to say I agree with you about fixing the fence. You *are* going to fix the fence, right?"

He thought about the chore. All his good reasons for doing it were still valid, but it galled him that she thought he was... God knows what she thought, because even she couldn't seem to make up her mind. But it definitely galled the hell out of him.

"I'm so glad we're in agreement about the fence," he said sarcastically, while biting back the irrational urge to say he would leave the damn gap open for the rest of their lives. "In fact, I'll go fix it now."

He got up and left.

Less than an hour later, Michael slammed the last nail with the hammer three final times, ensuring the symbolic barrier imprisoned Janice's "sicko" neighbor.

Lovely.

"MOMMY? Where's Michael?"

Janice turned to Amy, leaving off her vegetable chopping for a moment.

She wished her daughter wasn't so attached to their neighbor. She wished she had handled the whole thing better with him. Instead, she'd sounded like an ass. She wasn't afraid of him. She was just being sensible about the nature of their relationship.

"Honey, Michael had to go home a long time ago."

"But Michael lives here now, remember?" Amy said. "Only he's not in his box."

"Oh, the cat." Janice smiled, relieved. Yet another "Michael" to confuse her. "He's in the house somewhere, I'm sure. Why don't you look around for him?"

"I did," Amy said, her mouth turning down with worry.

"He's probably hiding," Janice assured her daughter. "It's been very exciting for him to be with a new family. He just needs a little time to himself, to help him adjust. He'll come out when he's ready. Maybe he just went to use the litter box."

She hoped. So far, Michael hadn't needed to use it.

"I'll look again," Amy said. Patience had never been one of her virtues.

Janice sighed. She wondered yet again at the wisdom of bringing a pet into a houseful of children—especially such a young pet. The kids had begged for years, so why had she given in now?

Michael the human, that's why.

She did want to distance herself from him. Every time she was around him she threw herself at him. And she was concerned about Amy's attachment to him. One way or another, the child would be hurt. Not her. *Amy.* If Michael took offense with the way Janice protected her daughter, then she would accept that. Only why couldn't she get the memory of him having "tea" with Amy out of her head?

She wished she could accept the fence repair as well. Having that break closed felt like a slap in the face. Why should common sense on his part hurt her so much?

Another unanswered question, she admitted. Now, thanks to her daughter's insistence on naming the cat after Michael, she had a constant reminder of him. Why couldn't Amy have picked "Spot"?

"Mommy, Michael's not here!" Amy wailed, running into the room.

Janice sighed and left off her chopping. "Okay. We'll look for him together."

She searched the house with Amy, rousing the boys to help when she and her daughter couldn't find the kitten on their first tour.

"He's not anywhere, I don't think," David said, when he and his friends gathered in the kitchen. "We looked, Mom. Honest."

David's usual "look" consisted of one quick glance, reserved for clothes on the floor and other things she nagged him about. But Janice believed him this time. He seemed puzzled that a little kitten had eluded him.

She put her hands on her hips and frowned. "Do you think he could have gotten out?"

The kids all shrugged.

"Well, let's check anyway," she said. "He might have. The triplets have been in and out the doors all day."

They began in the front and backyards, everyone calling the kitten's name. Amy crawled under bushes in her zeal. They went next door, and farther. Janice hoped they would find the kitten soon. She started to worry.

The new, nearly white boards in the weathered back fence glared at her. She hated them, hated their cold rebuke, hated the way things were working out with her newest neighbor.

"Get a grip," she muttered, disgusted with herself.

Michael Holiday was an impossible choice for any kind of relationship. She could see it, feel it, hear it, taste it— yet none of that mattered a damn to her wayward body. He had only to look at her and she burned.

She was acting like a love-starved widow alone too long. If she were ever to get involved again, she needed to pick a nice guy. If she kept her husband's betrayal in mind, she wouldn't pick anybody. No man was trustworthy, and she ought to remember that.

Still, the fence lured her. She got to wondering if a kitten could have squeezed through somehow. No one they talked with had seen a trace of a kitten in the neighborhood. She looked at the fence again. *Nah*, she thought. Kitty Michael couldn't be at his namesake's.

"David!" she called.

Her son popped out from the side of the house, where some old bushes might tempt a cat to hide. "Yeah?"

"Take Amy and check inside the house again, okay?"

"Okay!"

The kids went inside. Janice walked along the flower beds, part of her noting how the daisies Michael had separated for her were reviving nicely. They might even bloom this year.

Forget it, she thought.

Behind a clump of day lilies, she found a board curved away at the bottom, the wood having curled through moisture and time. The kitten, if he came this way, could have easily squeezed through the small opening. Janice straightened and eyed the top of the fence.

"With my luck, he's over there."

Groaning, she wondered what to do. She hated the thought of going around and knocking on the door. She had no desire to see the man after their earlier "discussion."

She eyed her old, sturdy Japanese maple. Although it was only about fifteen feet high, some of its branches reached over the fence. Maybe she could get in and out without "big" Michael even knowing.

She hoisted herself up on a branch, then got one leg over the top of the six-foot-high fence. Thank God it wasn't a stockade, she thought in amusement. The straight-cut tops hurt enough against her bare legs. She got her other leg over, letting go of the branch one hand at a time to grab on to the boards. She balanced for a moment on the fencetop, while trying to ignore the way it dug into her butt. Then she took a deep breath, hefted herself up and dropped down onto the overgrown flower bed behind a thick holly tree in Michael's backyard.

"Not bad for an old lady with six kids," she admitted, congratulating herself. All the exercise and time on her bike had paid off yet again. Only one little problem...

How would she get back over? From here she couldn't reach any branches from her Japanese maple, and Michael's trees were like the holly, too prickly and with no overhang.

She'd worry about that when she had to, she thought. Right now, she'd better find Michael the cat before Michael the human found her. After carefully checking for the human version, she stepped out from her hiding place and called the kitten in a low voice.

"Michael! Here, kitty, kitty, kitty. Michael..."

She moved along the fence, through the underbrush. No cat. Old Mr. Hobarth had planted trees and bushes galore, and they were now a tangle of leaves and branches. She picked her way among them, cursing under her breath the whole time. The damn cat could be anywhere in this, and she'd never find him.

"Michael, where the hell *are* you?" she asked, in a loud stage whisper.

"Right behind you, Janice."

Chapter Six

Never tell a woman the truth about yourself. They get all gooey-eyed, and you're sunk. They'll never go away then.
—Michael Holiday
Man Can Definitely Live by Bread Alone

Michael watched as Janice shrieked and whirled around.

"You scared me!" she accused, holding a hand between her breasts.

"This is a nice surprise, especially after our discussion a little while ago," he said. "By the way, most people knock on the door."

She looked away and shrugged. "We can't find Michael the kitten. I thought he might have gotten over here."

"I take it he hasn't been found yet," he said, knowing Amy must be upset.

Janice looked back. "Not yet."

"I haven't seen him. However, the bigger question is how you got over here." He wasn't sure whether he was annoyed or glad to see her. "I thought I had already fixed the gap."

Her expression turned rueful. "You did. I hopped the fence."

"You *are* in good shape. And don't yell at me for that."

"Okay. But you make it sound like I pole-vaulted. I just climbed my little maple, got on the fence and carefully fell off it. That I didn't scrape myself or worse is a miracle."

"Probably." He waved a hand toward his yard. "Although I didn't see young Michael, I haven't been looking. You're welcome to. In fact, you only had to come around and ask."

"Well, I was saving time."

A likely story, he thought, surmising that she had wanted to avoid him. That notion amused him, gave him a sense of power. Something ought to. He still smarted over her "concern."

"I'll even help you look for him," Michael volunteered.

"Thanks." She seemed anything but thankful.

She called the kitten several times in a sweet voice, stretching up to look between branches and bending low to check under thick leafy bushes. Michael followed behind. He called, too, feeling a little psychic, since he'd told Amy he had to put the fence back to *not* look silly doing this. More to his liking, following behind Janice meant he could admire the view she presented. And she presented a great one. Her shorts clung to her derriere.

Reminded of the first time he had seen her on Mother's Day, he said, "I haven't noticed you working out in the backyard anymore. Is something wrong?"

She straightened. "It's a rare treat to be able to exercise without interruption. Mother's Day was nice so I did it outside. Usually I carve out ten minutes here and there during the day. I do ride my stationary bike while watching television."

"I see." Which meant except for rare treats, he couldn't watch at all. Too bad. She held a certain speculative excitement for him when she exercised.

When she did anything. That was the problem, Michael

thought. She could breathe and he wanted her. Even now the simple, innocent act of looking for a lost kitten wreaked havoc with his emotional and physical equilibrium. He wanted her. He wondered if she felt the same.

On some level he understood her caution with him, but it got on his nerves. He couldn't mention their run-in. He wouldn't.

"You owe me an apology from before," he said. So much for couldn't and wouldn't.

"I hope so," she replied, unfazed.

He liked her coolness. She challenged him in so many ways. "So when do I get it?"

"I don't think you do."

He stepped closer. "Why?"

"You and I want two different things," she said, backing up against the fence.

He might have believed her if she had stood her ground, but the space she tried to widen between them showed what a liar she was.

"Do we want different things?" he asked, closing the distance, suddenly in no mood for teasing and stalling.

He kissed her.

Her mouth turned to instant flame, surprising him and confirming her attraction with her intense response. He expected rejection or coaxing, but not this...honest need.

As if she realized her boldness, she started to push him away a little, but he pressed her lips slightly open. She moaned in the back of her throat, then mated her tongue with his. No one could mistake her reaction. He certainly couldn't—especially when her arms wrapped around his neck.

He pulled her to him and kissed her with every bit of finesse he had ever learned. Or tried to. Somehow, all the sophistication went out of his head with her in his arms. He felt as if he were a schoolboy with his first girl again.

He kissed her cheeks, her forehead, her eyelids. He buried his face in her hair, his senses invaded by the sweet, woodsy scent of her shampoo.

"Were you looking for this?" he whispered, touching her breast.

"No." She arched herself into his hand. Her nipple seemed to throb against his palm. "I...oh, Michael..."

He loved the way she said his name like that. All shivery passion. He wanted to please her. That need cut through the reticence, the fear he felt at his own response to her. His pleasure mattered little now, when it usually mattered a great deal. He slipped his fingers under her T-shirt, finding her skin smooth and tight over her stomach.

"You feel so good," he murmured, taking the weight of her breast in his palm.

Janice clung to him, her hands tugging at his hair, almost pleading with him to continue. He intended to. She was all fire, consuming him....

"Meow."

The tiny squeak at their feet was followed by another. Michael groaned at the interruption and looked down.

Sure enough, his feline namesake looked up at him with wide, inquiring blue eyes.

Janice leaned against him for a moment. "This is insanity."

With those words, she extricated herself from his embrace. She smoothed her top. Michael watched her, watched signs of the privilege she'd granted disappear.

"We need to talk about this," he said, running a hand through his hair. He remembered where that hand had just been and the memory jolted through him, igniting his insides all over again.

"I agree that we need to talk," she replied, making his suggestion sound ominous. She bent and picked up Michael the cat. He snuggled against her breasts.

Lucky Michael, Michael thought.

"Mommy!"

"Mom, where are you?"

The children's voices held puzzlement and panic as they carried over the fence.

"I'm back here," Janice called out, staring at him.

Michael got the message: discussion postponed. Dammit.

"Did you find Michael?" Amy asked, her voice now just on the other side of the boards.

"Both Michaels," Michael said.

"Oh! Hey, I can see you. Look in the space here." A pinky finger wiggled through a small knothole in the fence.

Michael, ignoring Janice, bent and grabbed at Amy's finger. The child pulled it back, giggling as she did.

"Watch you don't get a splinter," Janice warned.

"Party pooper," Michael replied, feeling defiant for some reason. He pressed his eye to the fence hole. All of a sudden, Amy's eye loomed large as she peeked through the fence from the other side. She and he were practically glued eyeball-to-eyeball.

Looking away, Michael chuckled, while Amy pealed with glee.

"Do it again, Michael!" she said.

He did. Kids got such joy from the smallest things, he thought. He remembered he and his cousins just running in and out of the waves whenever his grandmother took them to the beach. They would laugh and yelp and race until their hearts were full. He had had so little of that in his life then, and he hadn't had it since.

His grandmother's affair had changed all that for him. For all of them.

"Michael, your eye is so sad," Amy said.

"How can it be?" he asked. "I'm looking at you, kid."

But the magic moment was gone for him.

"David, here. Take Michael," Janice said, handing the kitten over the fence to her son. Michael the kitten squeaked in panic.

Young male hands reached out and took the feline, the exchange smooth. At least David was out in the sunlight, Michael thought. He had begun to wonder about the boy's attachment to video games. Janice could say what she wanted about excellent grades and friends and all that, Michael still wasn't sure she was right.

"Michael, you bad boy," Amy scolded.

Michael the human rocked back on his heels and chuckled. "Your mom would agree."

Janice clamped a hand over his mouth. She whispered in his ear, "Shh! Don't let them hear you."

Her breath sent jolts of heat through his body again.

Not able to resist, he licked her palm. She snatched her hand away and glared at him.

He grinned, unrepentant. Adults had their own special brand of magic.

"Take the cat in the house. I'll be around in a moment," she called out to her kids.

"I'll boost you over," Michael said.

"No, thank you," she replied primly.

He stood and laced his fingers together to make a cup. "*This* way." Lowering his voice, he added, "I won't turn into an animal. I promise."

"Come on, Mommy!" Amy called.

Janice eyed him for a moment. The lure of a quick exit outweighed the disadvantage of his closeness. She stepped toward him, put her right foot in the stirrup of his hands, one palm on his shoulder and one on the fence. Her fingers almost caressed his skin.

Better still, her breasts were level with his gaze. And he was gazing.

Michael swallowed. She was perfection and a torment.

He boosted her, nearly keeling over backward when her breasts dipped, then jutted forward practically in his face. The rest of her body rose, lithe yet strong, as she straightened, letting go of his shoulder. She *was* tormenting him, he thought, the junction of her thighs now in his face. Sweat broke out on his forehead. He had a tremendous urge to lean forward and kiss her intimately.

She'd probably fly right over the fence if he did. And he *had* promised to be a gentleman. Dammit.

Janice sat on the fence for a moment to get her balance, then swung one leg over. He wished she'd straddle him like that. First the cat, then the fence enjoyed her charms. In his next life, he wanted to be Janice's chair. God knows, his stuffing would be singing with joy.

She swung her other leg over and jumped. He heard a thud and a barnyard curse on the other side of the fence. The kids giggled.

"What happened?" he asked, hoisting himself up to look over.

Janice sat in a patch of dame's rocket. The lavender crucifer flowers waved gently over her head.

"I didn't jump out far enough," she said.

"No kidding."

"Michael!" Amy yelled happily, waving to him. "I see you."

"I see you." He waved back at her, bracing his elbows so he could hang on the fence.

David waved. "Hey, Mr. Holiday."

Michael smiled. "Hi, David."

The boy had a tan, which surprised Michael. Maybe David got it from the glow of the television.

Janice got up and dusted herself off. She tried righting a few plants, but the stalks were nearly broken through.

"Try taping or binding at the break, then stake them," Michael advised. "They might hold for the rest of the season. Even if they don't, they'll come up next year."

"I know." Janice looked up at him. "Thank you, Michael, for your help."

"Thank *you*," he said, meaning it. He'd be damned before he apologized for their kiss—and more.

Janice's face flushed bright red. He liked it, liked knowing he could make her blush. It meant her emotions were aroused by him. His certainly were by her.

She didn't reply, just turned and took the kids with her to the house. Amy and David each sent him a last wave.

Michael watched mother, son, daughter and kitten go. He had the oddest twinge of the oddest emotion.

It felt like envy.

JANICE DROPPED OFF Charlie Hesler's balance statement for the month of May. She explained what she'd calculated and why to the computer-store owner. Charlie looked blankly at her. Janice made herself explain patiently again. Charlie had tried to do it himself with his own software, normally just a lot of time for a store owner. In Charlie's case, it was a recipe for disaster. He didn't understand accounting at all, and no amount of lectures got through. Eventually, she emerged from the computer store into the hot afternoon sunlight.

June always had those unexpected two weeks of intense heat, she thought, while trying to ignore the sweat trickling under her blouse and suit jacket.

She could have worn casual clothes, and many wouldn't have questioned her. But she always wore a business suit when she was doing business for two reasons. The first was presentation. If she looked businesslike while she talked business, people gained more confidence in her abilities. Second, and more important, if she looked all-business, it helped dispel any notions that she was a widow on the prowl. More than one man in town had propositioned her, their conclusions about her widow's "needs" clear. If she wanted to survive financially, if she wanted to do business, then she had to deal with a lot of the same men. The more she ensured their notions about her were mistaken, the better everyone got along—and she didn't have to punch anyone in the nose to get her point across.

So why didn't she punch Michael in the nose when he kissed her? Especially when he took liberties?

Because she was stupid.

Yup. Nothing else explained her throwing herself at him the way she did. No amount of mental lecturing by her sensible side helped, either. She'd swear the lectures made things worse. Something did, because she was less in control around him than ever before.

She ought to have her head examined. She ought to, but she wouldn't. The whole thing was too embarrassing to admit. She already knew the answer anyway. She *was* a woman with needs who had responded to a man. She only needed more time and a wiser choice in men.

The little town park down the street beckoned to her. The triplets were at baseball practice, and Amy played at a friend's house for the afternoon. Heather didn't need to be picked up at the mall for another hour, and David was safely holding down the fort at home. Janice decided to snatch a little more rare time for herself and walked into the park. She settled on a bench under the shade of oak trees.

She removed her jacket and folded it neatly on the bench beside her, then unbuttoned her blouse collar. Wondering how the colonials had survived in their long coats and dresses, she flipped off her heels and pressed her feet in the cool grass.

She sighed in relief and closed her eyes. The breeze ruffled the leaves above her. It touched her braided hair and open throat, bringing coolness across her skin. The scents of earth and trees and flowers melded together in a freshness that calmed her senses.

All her daily problems dropped away. She could see herself in a meadow...lying on her stomach...rested, lazy...Michael by her side....

"You look like you're in heaven."

Startled by the voice—*the* voice—Janice snapped open her eyes. Michael stood before her, as if she had conjured him. "I didn't even hear you."

He grinned wryly. "I guess not. Where were you?"

"In a meadow. A *quiet* meadow."

"Sorry to burst your daydream." He didn't move.

Janice felt the very air between them change, become more charged. Some gate of awareness inside her had opened, and she didn't know how to close it.

"We really need to talk," he said, sitting next to her.

She wasn't ready for this, she thought, then calmed herself. She hadn't been ready for a lot of things in her life...six kids, a set of triplets...but she managed. She would manage now.

"We know we're attracted to each other," he began. "Or do you intend to deny it?"

"Nope." She forced herself to lean back on the bench

slats. She even rested her elbow on the top one. *Cool,* she thought. She would be very cool.

"Okay." He eyed her curiously. "You said once before that we should do nothing."

"That's my story, and I'm sticking to it."

His gaze narrowed. "You haven't so far."

She gulped. Maybe she was being too flip about this. "Okay, so I've had a setback or two."

"Lady, you couldn't have gotten a piece of paper between us."

She glanced around the park. Except for some mothers watching their children at the swings, the place was deserted. Most people didn't have the erratic working hours she and Michael could carve out for themselves. Another thing in common she didn't need to remember.

"This won't go in a column, will it?" she asked.

"Nope."

She wasn't sure whether to take him seriously or not. "I hope it won't. I still believe this is a temporary aberration on both our parts and will eventually go away."

"I'm beginning to wonder about that," he said.

"Are you telling me," she asked carefully, "that you have a serious interest in me?"

He said nothing for an agonizing moment. "I think the physical attraction is serious."

Hardly a ringing endorsement, she thought, having the urge to punch him in the nose. Boy, but she harbored a violent streak. "Physical attractions come and go. That's nothing to follow through on."

"Maybe."

"No maybe about it. Let's forget the social problems of having sex nowadays and face a few personal facts between you and me. You feel nothing for me beyond the physical." He had a very nice physical, but she'd never tell him that. "I have kids whose feelings I have to take into consideration. And I have to set an example of good behavior for them. If I follow an impulse, I'll be hypocritical as hell telling them not to follow theirs. Second, I don't trust men generally. Men can't take the pressure of daily life. My husband was unprepared to deal with triplets. After them, he didn't want any more children, but I got pregnant with Amy."

Michael sucked in his breath. "He didn't want Amy?"

"No, he didn't. Oh, he said all the right things after she was born, but he never once held her. And he died in another woman's bed. He left me with a mess, frankly, because he couldn't cope with our life. You, a bachelor, would run like a scared rabbit at the first true taste of my life. And third, the most important of all...I'm just too damn tired to handle the emotional ups and downs you'd bring to the relationship table. So thanks. I'm flattered. But I'll skip it anyway."

"Gee, I sound lovely," he commented.

She chuckled. She couldn't help it. "I like you, Michael. I wish I didn't."

"Okay, so I scare you. I understand completely, and I know you're no prize, either. No offense."

"Some taken, but I get your drift." Truthfully, she was no prize, not with her family situation.

"I think we may be making a mistake by denying ourselves," he said, shocking her and yet not shocking her. "It seems the more we say no, the more intense our encounters become. I think if we...for lack of a better word...indulge ourselves—"

"Those were pretty bad ones," she told him.

He sighed. "I know. Okay, here's better, I hope. If we give in to our attraction for each other, the attraction will run its natural course. We can then both walk away. It's a mature response to our situation.''

"Oh. I'm sure it is, in the sophisticated world you come from.''

"I'm not from a sophisticated world.''

"It's more sophisticated than mine, which consists of doses of Barney and Animaniacs. I'm a little vulnerable to be mature about all this. Nice try, Michael. I know it's not going to work for me.''

"I'm not your husband,'' he said.

"No, you're not. Tom was a better man than you are.''

"But you just said he cheated on you!''

She nodded. "We married young and had a lot of kids before he was ready. I've had time to think about what happened to him. I can understand it. I can even forgive it now, in some ways. But it's taught me that even the best-meaning men can't be trusted. You've made a career out of avoiding commitment. You're about as bad a risk as they come for me. Sorry, I'll suffer in silence.''

"You are as willful as Amy.''

"Thanks. That gives me hope.''

He shook his head. "I can't deny I don't want a commitment. Like you with men, I don't trust women. My parents divorced when I was young, and I was their Ping-Pong ball to get at each other. Mary Ellen told you about my grandparents. The only person I trusted then not to hurt me was my grandmother. She betrayed me as much as she betrayed my grandfather. I'm an adult now. I understand she had reasons, maybe even good ones, for seeking another man. But I learned from it. Women are as guilty as men about breaking their commitments. I'm honest enough not to make any.''

The poor man, Janice thought, her sympathies rising to the surface. She was wary of men, but Michael's distrust was ingrained from childhood. Now he hid his hurts behind "honesty."

She reached across the back bench slats and took his hand. "You were a hurt little boy, weren't you? Oh, Michael, I do understand."

His eyes widened, and he pulled his hand away. "Wait a minute. Wait a damn minute! You make me sound like a psychiatrist's dream."

"I think you are."

"I told you about my childhood to show you that you're not alone in your distrust. That it's a good thing, that you see relationships clearly, for what they are—ultimately flawed—because you don't want to be emotionally involved. There's no need to go all Mother Earth sympathetic on me."

She smiled, feeling very in control of this discussion. One of the good things around Michael Holiday. "I think there's every reason to sympathize with you. Michael, I think more than a temporary lover, you need a woman friend."

He stood. "What the hell happened here? One minute you're the Ice Queen and the next, you're Mr. Flipping Rogers!"

"I think that should be Mrs. Flipping Rogers," Janice said, amused by Michael's consternation. He hadn't expected her offer of friendship. Frankly, she hadn't either. But she could be his friend—and he sounded as if he needed one badly. No one should be as armored as he against the better half of mankind.

"You're enjoying this, aren't you?" he asked.

"You are fun."

"You're the most puzzling woman I've ever met."

She smiled. "Good. I like to be different."

"I bet you do."

"This is real suburbia, Michael. We have our underlying currents that run very deep and take unexpected turns. Watch when you start meddling in the waters." She stood up. "I have to go. The kids will be home from school soon."

He just stared at her.

She flushed, wondering if she *could* have a friendship with this man. She hoped so. She had said she would. "Thanks for clearing the air with me."

She walked away.

Chapter Seven

Accept a woman's invitation to dinner at her home with great caution.

—Michael Holiday
Man Can Definitely Live by Bread Alone

Someone had been in the backyard.

Michael stared at the disturbed bed of an old lily patch under his kitchen window. The newly broken stalks told him someone, or more likely, some ones, had left in a hurry.

"I ought to write mysteries," he muttered, although this clue was easier to read than a Dick and Jane primer.

Notes of a baritone horn floated over the summer air. Michael hadn't heard David practice for a while; the heat and humidity had kept windows closed for air-conditioning. David stumbled over a passage and Michael frowned at the rarity. Well, at least the boy wasn't playing video games.

It was David's siblings Michael fumed about. A certain *set* of siblings. He had no doubts over who his lily-breaking culprits were.

He went to the fence, suspicious that his repairs had been demolished. The new boards still stood in splendor.

"Well, hell," he muttered, confused.

He inspected the entire fence line for a new break. He found none, even after tapping the boards to see if any had shifted loose. Nothing.

So how, he wondered, had they gotten in?

"Michael! Are you there? I heard someone there."

Amy's piping voice broke the near silence.

"Yes," Michael said, smiling. "It's me."

"Come to our peephole," she said. "We can talk."

He chuckled and went over to the missing knot. Sure enough, Amy's eye was waiting for him.

"Hi, Michael," she said, in that chirpy little voice he liked so much.

"Hi, Amy girl. How's little Michael? Has he been behaving himself and not running away?"

"Oh, yes. He's been real good. The triples play too hard with him sometimes, but I tell Mom and Mom yells."

He bet Mom yelled. He'd rather have Janice angry and yelling at him than amused and a "friend." The last thing he wanted from her was friendship. Worse, he, not her husband, was the bad guy. Women knew where they stood with him in relationships. He didn't lie, and he didn't betray. Maybe he didn't stay, but he never hid that from a woman.

God, how the hell had that conversation turned totally around? His Mother's Day goddess had more damned facets than he could handle.

"When are you going to play with me again?" Amy asked.

Michael pondered the question. Janice would blow a gasket if he played with Amy. "Anytime you like."

"Can you come over now?"

The afternoon sun hung low in the sky, signaling the

coming dinner hour. He could spare the time until Amy had to eat.

"If it's okay with your mother." Michael grinned, pleased to put the decision on Janice's shoulders. He'd like to see how much of a "friend" she intended to be.

"Wait right there," Amy commanded.

Her eye disappeared, and he heard her run across the yard. Sitting down, he leaned back against the fence and closed his eyes.

Janice.

He didn't know what to do with her. He admitted it freely. Somehow, she had turned his well-structured life into a pity party. Dammit, he was a mature adult who tempered his impulses with common sense. He tried to show her that, but she took it the wrong way. Completely the wrong way.

He didn't understand her. He didn't understand himself. He remembered his cousin Peter calling him for advice when in the throes of attraction. Maybe he needed advice. Not from Peter. Peter had lost his battle with Mary Ellen.

Jared.

Jared was a winner, Michael thought. He should talk with Jared. A divorce lawyer had to know more about man-woman relationships and how to avoid them.

"My mom says you can come over," Amy said suddenly through the fence. Her voice was huffy, as if she'd run all the way.

Well...he had expected a "no." He had sort of hoped for one. He liked Amy and her charms, but facing Janice the pitier was more formidable than facing a fire-breathing dragon.

Dammit, was he a man or a mouse?

Mouse, he thought.

Screwing up his courage, he said, "I'll be over in a few minutes. I have to walk around."

"Hurry up," Amy told him.

She was a bossy little thing, he acknowledged in amusement. Now why did he take it from a four-year-old and not an adult?

Because Amy was cute as a button.

Man, he was in trouble.

Even as he questioned the wisdom of going to "play" with Amy, he walked around the block.

Amy stood waiting for him at the end of her driveway. She grinned widely and ran the last few feet to him, throwing her arms around his legs.

"You came!"

Help me, Michael thought, feeling a pain slice through his soul. This child gave love so innocently, so freely. He would never hurt her. *Never.* Janice had nothing to worry about here. "I told you I would."

"I know. I'm real glad to see you." Amy let go of his legs. "I learned a new game we could play."

He took her hand as they walked up to the house. "What game is that?"

"Candyland!"

Michael chuckled. He doubted he had played the game *since* he'd been Amy's age.

The moment he saw Janice inside the house, he paused. She could never be a friend, he thought, his blood pumping thickly through his body.

She sat at her desk in the corner of the kitchen, working in front of the computer. Despite the hunch in her slender shoulders and the intense look on her face, she *was* beautiful. All womanly curves and experience. To his amusement, she reminded him of David playing one of his video games. But mostly, she just took his breath, knocked him out and turned him to hot, seething mush inside.

Not a good sign for his emotional health. Not a good sign at all.

He had it bad, he thought. Nothing she had said the other day—nothing his common sense told him, either—made a difference in his reaction to her. Something on her lap moved. Michael the kitten yawned and stretched. He scooted around, then settled into a sleepy ball of fur again.

Lucky, lucky, Michael. Michael the human decided that if he wasn't careful, he'd find himself wishing he'd come back in another life as Janice's knickers. One man hadn't exactly covered himself in glory over that one, and he was not about to make it two.

She tapped a few keys, the spreadsheet on the screen rippling in response. She frowned at the results.

"Mommy, we're ready to play Candyland," Amy announced.

Janice turned in her chair. She smiled at Michael. He smiled back, feeling as if he'd received approval from a goddess.

"Hi," she said.

"Hi." Okay, friends wasn't what he had in mind, but maybe he could live with it.

Who the hell was he kidding?

Janice turned to Amy, while stroking Michael the kitten. "I'm sorry, honey, but Mr. Wren called. There's a mistake in the work I did for him." She glanced at Michael. "Which *he* forgot to give me." She looked back at Amy. "I've got to correct it and drive it to him tonight."

"Mommy! You promised!" Amy exclaimed, looking ready to explode in a temper tantrum.

"I know I did, and I'm very sorry. You and Michael can play without me."

Amy stamped her foot. "No! You play, too!"

Fortunately, they were interrupted by an odd odor emanating from one of the pots on the stove.

"Uh-oh," Michael said, letting go of Amy's hand.

Janice yelped and jumped up, sending the kitten sliding from her lap. Michael reached the stove before she did, and he removed the offending pot from the heat. He took off the lid. Tomato sauce still boiled angrily inside.

Janice cursed.

"Get me another pot," Michael said. "We'll salvage what we can from this one. It looks like the bottom burned."

Janice groaned. "It did. That's what I get for trying to do six things at once, my usual state."

"Mommy burns food a lot," Amy told him, smiling angelically.

Michael grinned at her. She'd be announcing more family secrets any moment now.

"I do. I did my usual thing of putting the heat up to get it going. Then Mr. Wren called, and I forgot about it," Janice admitted, opening the drawer in the bottom of the stove and handing him up another pot. "I think it's my new weight-loss program."

Michael tried to rid himself of the image of her on her knees in front of him, even if it was for something as mundane as retrieving a pot. She rose to her feet, thank goodness. He transferred the decent sauce left to the new pot, then sniffed it carefully. Burned tomatoes still lingered in the aroma, but not badly.

"What was it going to be?" he asked, shaking the sauce pot.

"Just a simple pasta sauce. Looks more like disaster sauce now."

Michael took the burned pot and set it in the sink. He

poured hot water in it, to let it soak. "Look, you go back to work and I'll take care of dinner."

"Thanks, but I couldn't allow that."

She stood so close he could feel her body heat. She was making him crazy, he admitted, wanting to kiss her. He swallowed and said, "You need to get your work done. Amy and I will fix this for you. Won't we, Amy girl? It'll be a new game for us to play. 'Let's cook dinner.'"

"Okay," Amy said, looking dubious but at least willing.

Janice protested more, but Michael just ignored her, shuffling her back to her computer. He tried to ignore the satiny feel of her skin under his hands. That wasn't so easy. He managed to get her settled in her chair again.

"Work," he said.

"But—"

"Shut up and work."

She gave him a look that would have frozen stone.

"Be quiet and work?"

"Much better," she informed him and went to work.

With a smile, he got spices out of her cabinet, then sat Amy on the counter, away from the stove. The little girl smiled in pleasure as he began to repair the sauce. He wasn't sure if enough was left to feed the Parker family and decided to stretch it, just to be sure. He found carrots, onions and green peppers in the refrigerator. He designated Amy his official "adder." He sliced the vegetables and she dumped them off the cutting board into the pot. They ate a raw carrot while they prepared the meal. While the new sauce cooked on a very low simmer, he and Amy went to work on the burned pot.

"Boy, Mommy, you really burned it," Amy told her, when they finally rinsed away the last of the old sauce.

Janice chuckled ruefully. "I certainly did. When I burn something, I don't fool around."

She had burned him, Michael thought, and he hadn't even been looking when she had. This woman cooked and counted and cuddled cats all at the same time. She did whatever needed doing—and with love. He couldn't imagine his own mother ever handling all Janice did. The experts claimed that women held families together. That hadn't been his own experience—until now.

Eventually, a sweeter bouquet replaced the burned odor. Michael decided to save Janice a step and put on the *rotella* pasta. Heather eventually wandered into the kitchen.

"That smells really good," the teen said. "What is it?"

"Pasta sauce with vegetables," Michael said.

Her face fell. "Vegetables!"

Janice laughed. "I keep telling you they won't kill you."

"It'll just seem that way," Michael added.

"*I'm* going to eat them," Amy announced. "I helped make 'em, didn't I, Michael?"

He smiled and tugged a lock of her hair. "I never had a better vegetable dumper in my life. You plopped them in there so well, Paul Prudhomme would have been proud."

"Who's Paul Puddle?" Amy asked.

Michael chuckled.

"Okay. I'm convinced," Heather said, picking Amy off the counter. "If you made it, I'll eat it."

Amy beamed.

Unsure of just how much a crew of seven ate, Michael got some fresh green beans he'd noticed in the fridge and blanched them, adding a touch of garlic. Janice's kitchen was well stocked with fruits and vegetables, surprising him. Didn't kids live for junk food? Whatever, he found it kind of nice to cook for more than one. And he was certainly off to a good start in the "friend" department, helping Janice out when she was in a bind. He kind of liked that, too. No one had needed him before.

"Mommy? Can Michael stay for dinner?" Amy asked.

Janice looked up from her computer, her expression a telling mixture of appalled embarrassment.

"That's okay, Amy," Michael said, saving Janice. "I should be getting home."

"Please stay, Michael," Janice said, giving him a genuine smile. "We'd love to have you stay. You saved the meal, after all. I absolutely insist, and I won't take no for an answer."

He smiled back. "All right. Thank you."

"Good." She looked at her daughters. "Set the table, girls. And Amy, thank you for having such wonderful manners."

Amy beamed. To Michael, she said, "You can sit next to me."

"I'd be honored." He drained the pasta into a colander.

Everyone was called to dinner. David took the news of a guest without a ruffle. The boy was unflappable, Michael decided. The triplets, Cat, Chris and C.J., did a triple-take when told the news.

"*He's* staying?" the three asked dubiously in unison.

"Yes, he's staying for dinner," Janice said. "Kids, we *will* be polite."

She gave the triplets the parental evil eye. The look was unmistakable—and one crossed it if one dared. Michael had a feeling the nine-year-olds would be undeterred.

"I never haunt meals," Michael said, trying to make light of their reluctance to have him at the table.

The triplets said nothing more. Instead they sat across the table and stared at him, unblinking. At first he ignored them, but those unwavering gazes began to grate on his nerves. Other than Michael's disconcerting feeling of being under three microscopes, the dinner began without a hitch.

"Michael!" Janice exclaimed, after her first forkful. "This is marvelous."

He grinned with satisfaction. "I'm glad you like it."

A fork clattered on a plate. Cat said, "*He* made this?"

Janice nodded. "Yes. It's terrific, isn't it?"

"I hate it," Cat announced. The boys nodded their agreement, their own forks clattering to their plates for emphasis.

Michael froze. The insult from the three couldn't have been clearer.

Janice calmly took a bite, chewed and swallowed. "Too bad. You don't eat dinner, you go hungry for the rest of the night."

"We could have cereal," Cat suggested.

"Nope. Pasta or nothing. Your choice."

"But, Mom!"

"No buts," Janice said. "Make a decision."

Not wanting to be the source of a standoff, Michael cleared his throat, about to speak up on the triplets behalf. Janice skewered him with a glare that would have frozen over hell itself. Michael shoved a string bean into his mouth to shut himself up.

"You guys are stupid if you don't eat it," David suddenly said. "This is pretty good!"

Michael wanted to hug the boy. David could play his baritone any damn time he pleased. Michael decided he'd buy David ten new video games, too. What a great kid!

"Hey, dorks, even I like it," Heather added. "And you know I hate vegetables."

Ten trips to the mall on him, Michael vowed, grateful for the vegetable-hater's endorsement.

"Thank you, Heather," Janice said. "Please remember to refrain from name-calling at the table in the future."

Heather flushed and went back to eating.

Michael smiled at her encouragingly. Fifteen trips, just to make up for the embarrassment factor. Another great Parker kid!

"I'll get ice cream 'cause I'm gonna eat all mine," Amy said, then sneered to the triplets. "And you *won't!*"

That did it. Cat picked up her fork again, although she grumbled. Her brothers followed suit. Cat speared a carrot and held it up to her nose, sniffing it suspiciously for five long seconds.

"Cat," Janice warned.

Cat ignored her mother and sniffed a moment longer. She gingerly took a bite, then shuddered. But she swallowed. "Whatcha put in this? Gasoline?"

"*I* burned the sauce, young lady," Janice said sternly. "Mr. Holiday very kindly fixed it for me."

"And me, too." Amy piped up, clearly wanting her due. "I helped him."

Janice smiled. "Yes, you did."

Cat and her brothers remained unconvinced, although they ate. But they sniffed every piece of vegetable and pasta before they put it in their mouths. Michael watched them surreptitiously. He had to admit he was fascinated with how the three skirted their mother's warnings about rudeness. He had a column in this, he thought, although he normally skipped children in his writing. Maybe he had been missing a whole new angle of humanity to explore.

Janice asked each of the children how his or her day was. The kids' responses ranged from one-word answers to voluminous stories about every minute since they'd woken up that morning.

Amy fell into the last category, causing Cat to remark, "You're not suppose to tell *everything*."

"Shut up, you big baby!" Amy shouted back.

"You shut up, dweeb-head!"

"Excuse me!" Janice exclaimed. "We do not speak this way at the table."

"She 'rupted me!" Amy accused.

"I did not!"

"Yes, you did!"

Michael expected the food to fly across the table at any second. He noticed David and Heather just kept eating, as if nothing were out of the ordinary. Neither of them seemed fazed by the world war about to "'rupt" any second now.

Only it didn't.

"If you want ice cream for dessert, you will stop *now*," Janice said.

The tension left both little girls' bodies faster than lightning from a cloud. They looked at her, stricken, clearly afraid she meant her threat.

"I'll be good," Amy vowed.

Cat nodded agreement.

"I thought so."

Everyone resumed dinner. Michael admired Janice's effectiveness. Even conversation settled to normal. Except for the occasional food sniff, Michael thought the meal was going well enough...

Until he saw Chris and C.J. begin to fiddle with their green beans. At first Michael thought they were avoiding eating them in the hubbub around them. Then he saw them furtively pick up a green bean with their fingers. Janice, busy talking with David about some upcoming band event, didn't notice. Neither did Cat or Heather, who talked about a mutual friend's stupid little brother.

The boys stuck their string beans up their noses.

Michael's jaw dropped. The boys waggled their heads, string beans bopping off their upper lips. Michael couldn't believe their audacity. But the evidence was before him. Four string beans in four nostrils.

"Ugh!" Amy squealed. "Mommy! Mommy! Chris and C.J. stuck their string beans up their noses!"

The boys ripped the string beans out while Amy complained. Janice and the other kids turned to them, too late to see.

"We did not!" the two said together. The outrage in their voices was so genuine that Michael almost believed them. And he had seen the string-bean stunt with his own eyes!

"Yes, they did," Amy insisted.

Janice turned to him. "Did you see them, Michael?"

Michael glanced at the boys, who shrank in their seats. He had been put on a knife edge. If he told, the triplets would hate him forever. If he didn't, and Janice found out, she would be very annoyed with him. The decision was easy.

"I didn't notice," Michael lied.

Janice gazed at him for a moment, then turned back to the boys. "I will give you the benefit of the doubt for once. But I swear I *will* send you all to the etiquette school, where they'll make you dress in a suit and tie, and dance with girls taller and meaner than you in front of everyone. You will be taken to a fancy hotel where you will have to drink tea with your pinky out, girl-style, and you will not be allowed to stick a string bean anywhere. You will die the slow death of boy embarrassment, and I will laugh with pleasure. I love you, but don't press your luck. Understood?"

The boys nodded.

"Now eat *every* string bean on your plate."

"Mom!"

Michael grimaced, wanting to plead the boys' case because he didn't know if he could handle it, either.

"Is there a problem?" Janice asked her children sweetly.

The two boys looked at each other, then shook their heads. They began to eat. Very reluctantly.

"Ha-ha," Amy said, clearly gloating.

"That's enough," Janice admonished her. "Finish your dinners, everyone."

Michael obeyed, like the good boy he was. He didn't look at Chris or C.J. once.

Family dinners were not for him. *Definitely* not for him.

"MOMMY, I CAN'T FIND Michael anywhere!"

Janice groaned to herself. She really wished the triplets had won the cat-naming contest. "He's probably sleeping somewhere. He'll come out when he's ready, honey."

"But I looked everywhere," Amy protested. "Come look, Mommy. Please!"

Knowing it was easier to look for a cat than to argue with a four-year-old, Janice pressed several computer keys to save her spreadsheet work. "When we find him, you must leave him alone to sleep, Amy."

"Oh, I will, Mommy. I just want to know he's okay."

"And I don't want to be rich and lazy," she muttered, dubious about her daughter's ability to stick to her promise.

As they hunted for the kitten, Janice thought about the human with the same name. Thinking about Michael Holiday had become almost constant—especially after the dinner fiasco of the other night.

Her face reddened once more when she remembered the

kids' behavior and her inability to control it. She had no doubt the whole thing had proved an eye-opener for Michael. She ought to be grateful, not mortified for her children.

She hadn't seen him since—or heard him in the backyard, a place where she seemed to gravitate to. Well, she had to look after the Shasta daisies he had separated. Okay, so they were thriving like a frog in a pond, but she had needed to look.

Still, this avoidance was what she wanted. It was what she needed. Talking common sense and then following it. Now she was on the proper path of her life.

So why did she hate it so damned much?

Janice realized that the kitten's possible hiding places were becoming fewer and fewer. David cinched the truth when he commented he had noticed little Michael near the back door when he'd been taking out the trash after lunch.

"Mommy," Amy whispered. "He got out once before."

"I know, honey." Janice wondered if Michael the cat would turn out to be a footloose and fancy-free roamer when he reached maturity. God knows, the other made a living from it. "Okay. We'll check outside."

"I bet he went to see Michael," Amy said. "He likes Michael."

Janice bet the kitten had, too. That would be her luck. The little gap hadn't been fixed from the last time. She hadn't given it a thought. Probably the human Michael hadn't, either.

"You go in with David, and I'll go look," she told Amy.

"I could look."

"I know you can, but we'll have to walk around, and that will take more time and Michael could run away. I'll hop the fence again and be back in a little bit. Now go with David.''

"Okay." Clearly, getting her kitten back mattered more than "helping" to Amy. But Janice didn't feel like walking around the block twice with the little girl and an anticipated squirmy kitten she would insist on carrying.

Janice waited until Amy was back in the house before she scaled her tree again. She went "over the wall" in easier fashion this time.

"Michael," she whispered, searching through the bushes. "Here, kitty, kitty."

"I have no clue why I bothered to fix that fence."

Janice straightened from a butterfly bush and turned. Sure enough, the wrong Michael stood behind her, sending her awareness level up about ten notches on the scale.

He grinned wryly. "Lose something again?"

He wore a sleeveless tank shirt and khaki shorts, his body lean and bronzed by the sun.

Janice cleared her throat. "Amy can't find the kitten in the house. We think he might have gotten outside, and I thought I better check here. He did come here once, you know," she added lamely.

"I remember. Very clearly."

Her awareness level climbed right off the scale. *Get a grip,* she chanted in her head, then got down to business. "Have you seen the cat?"

"No. But I just got back from playing golf. He could be here."

"Okay." She wasn't hanging around now. "Well, if you do see him, just call and I'll come get him."

She started to walk past him, but he took her arm, stopping her. Janice wanted to shrink from him, scream and run, but she couldn't move. He didn't scare her. The heat of his fingers on her skin, and how quickly and how much she wanted more of his touch, frightened her.

Scents rose up all around her—roses, lavender, earth, male.... Male most of all. The sun kissed her flesh, heating it further. She tasted salt on her upper lip. Michael stood like an earth god before her.

"It's happening again," he said in a low voice. "This attraction between us."

"Yes," she replied, her own voice low, too.

"We can't be friends."

"No." She had tried. The evening of the dinner, she had tried to show that she meant to be friends. But she had been too aware of him, of wanting his approval of all her children. The effort had been useless.

She forced herself to concentrate on reality. Her kids were a great reality.

"I'm sorry for my children's behavior at dinner," she said, hooking onto a lifeline that would scare him off. "They were incredibly rude to you."

"I suppose Cat couldn't believe a ghost could cook," he replied, letting go of her arm. "But you're changing the subject, and the subject is us."

"There is no us."

"Unfortunately, I think there is. I think we're very attracted to each other, and that's why we can't stay away."

Somewhere, her brain admitted she could have had David check for the kitten in Michael's yard. Or called Michael to do it himself. But no, she *had* to hop the fence. "We've had this discussion before, and it's useless."

"I think our mouths say one thing and our bodies another."

"You just want sex," she said. "Although I have no clue why you want it with me."

He leaned closer. "You sell yourself short...way short.

You're a beautiful woman, Janice. You've forgotten that in all the mothering you're doing.''

She started to reply, but he kissed her. His mouth was electric, sending jolts of pleasure right through her. Janice swirled her tongue with his, the taste of him a lure she could not resist. She gripped his shoulders, feeling his muscles beneath his skin. God, but she had missed the way a man moved under her hands.

But this man...he sent her senses spinning way out of control with only a touch.

"See?" he whispered, when the kiss ended. "You want me."

She pulled away from him. "I ought to smack you."

Michael stared at her, the big dumb man clearly in shock. "What? Why?"

"Men are incredibly egotistical and stupid. I'd forgotten that, too."

"How the hell am I egotistical and stupid?"

He was breathing, wasn't he? Aloud, she said, "You expect me to lie down like a lamb because I'm attracted to you."

"That's not what I said!"

"Sure it is. Sorry. I pass." She walked away. To hell with trying to climb back over the fence. She'd just walk around the block. She'd expected to do it with the kitten anyway, and it would be good for her health. Maybe she'd walk off her urge to kill. That was good for her health, too.

"Dammit, Janice!" Michael began from behind her.

She ignored him. Michael the kitten ran out from a bush. Janice picked the feline up. "Can't you find someone else's yard to run away in?"

The kitten squeaked at her.

"Next time I may just leave you here with Mr. Sex Machine."

The kitten meowed in protest.

Janice laughed wryly. "You said it all, kid."

She was out of the yard in two more steps. The human Michael didn't stop her.

THE LAW OFFICES of Davis, Hansen & Davis, reminded Michael of a silent tomb—quiet and hushed and empty of life. Well, what did he expect at eight o'clock in the evening?

"Do you even go home?" Michael asked his cousin.

Jared Holiday laughed. He looked enough like Michael to be his brother. He *was* the closest thing Michael had to a brother, the two of them of the same age and having grown close over the years.

"I go home once in a while," Jared admitted. "What can I say? I love my work, and I love *to* work."

Michael shuddered. Dealing with weeping, prospective divorcées hardly seemed like the ideal job to him. "Better you than me."

"Why aren't you working?" Jared asked. "I know you like to write in the evenings."

"I can't write," Michael said, cursing to have to admit the truth. "I sit in front of that damnable computer and I've got nothing to say. I'm going to be in trouble real fast if I don't get moving again."

"*You* have nothing to say?" Jared gaped. "You yack almost as much as Ray, and he's got to do it for four hours on the radio five days a week. Okay, so you're having writer's block. It was bound to happen. Hell, you've done a column for so long, I'm surprised you haven't had it sooner."

"I hope it's only writer's block," Michael muttered. He

wished he could believe it, but knew deep down in his heart that his trouble had a different source. "You've seen men do a lot of stupid things over a woman...."

"A lot," Jared agreed. "And I've made them pay for it, too."

"What makes them do it?" Michael asked.

"The great bachelor is asking questions about men's behavior? I can't believe it."

"Me, neither," Michael replied in disgust. "But I am."

Jared frowned. "Is this a ploy for a column, to get you past the writer's block? Michael, I can't divulge anything for use in a column."

"No. No columns."

Jared peered at him, his expression speculative.

Michael shifted uncomfortably. "It's...personal."

"Who is she?" Jared asked.

Michael stood, the question startling him. "I don't know what you mean."

"The hell you don't."

Michael sat and sighed. He hadn't come here to shoot the breeze with his cousin, so he might as well make a full confession. He put a dollar on Jared's desk. "I'm hiring you."

"Why?"

"So you never tell a soul, especially Peter or Raymond—God, not Raymond—what I'm about to tell you."

Jared picked up the dollar. "Boy, I can't wait to hear this one."

"You're right. It's a woman," Michael said. "With six kids."

Jared burst into laughter. He laughed until the tears ran down his face. "You? Six kids? God. Oh, God. That's rich!"

"It's like I'm being controlled by someone else," Michael continued, trying to ignore Jared's laughter. "I've got a hundred reasons not to see her—and I'm trying not to, believe me—but when I do, I can't think straight. What the hell is wrong with me?"

"I don't know, but it's priceless. You and a divorcée with six kids."

"Widow."

"Oh, brother." Jared shrugged. "The only thing I can tell you is stay away from her."

Michael vaguely remembered giving his cousin Peter similar advice when Peter began to be involved with Mary Ellen. "It's easy to say, but impossible to do."

"What does she want?" Jared asked.

Michael paused. "Me. I'm sure of it, even though she denies it.... No, I take that back. She doesn't deny it, but she says she'd doesn't want to get involved with me."

"Maybe that's the truth, Michael. She really doesn't want to be involved with you."

"If you kissed her, you'd know different."

"Maybe I ought to."

"Don't even think it," Michael snapped, instantly angry with his cousin.

Jared raised his eyebrows.

"See?" Michael said, waving a hand. "I have stupid, impulsive behavior. All the things I've preached against for years."

"True. I would think the six kids would scare you off." Jared made a face. "Hell, they'd scare me off. They'd scare anybody off."

"The triplets do."

"Triplets! My God, Michael, what the hell are you playing at?"

"I don't know." Michael ran a hand through his hair in frustration. "But the youngest...I'm in love with little

Amy. David, the oldest boy, is easygoing, except that I think Janice lets him play video games too much. And Heather, the oldest, is beautiful like her mother. She and I get along.''

"Man, you hang yourself from the rafters now."

"That bad, eh?"

"That bad."

Michael decided to find the nearest rope.

Chapter Eight

Stay home for the holiday. Everyone just gets too damn emotional.

—Michael Holiday
Man Can Definitely Live by Bread Alone

"Janice? I hate to ask this, but can I borrow David for a while this afternoon? I'm working on my kitchen, and I need someone to hold up cabinets for me."

Michael's voice over the telephone line surprised Janice—and shook her right down to her toes. She'd never expected him to call. Naturally, why would he? Except for cabinets.

"I'm sorry, Michael," she began, pleased to hear her voice calm. "David's not home right now. Actually, none of the kids are. They're at my in-laws today. It's Father's Day."

"Oh. That's right. You didn't go?"

"No." She smiled. "My in-laws like to spend time with their grandchildren on Mother's Day and Father's Day. They feel it keeps them in touch with their son."

"I understand. It's a wonderful sentiment, and it's very gracious of you to let them go."

She hadn't much choice, really, she thought. Besides,

she liked her in-laws a good deal and felt she owed them. The holiday weekends were all they asked of her. And they did give her blocks of free time, something she wasn't about to refuse. Still, while Mother's Day felt like a gift from them, Father's Day tended to be a day of memories, good and bad. Right now, she was feeling the bad ones. But that wasn't Michael's problem. "Can David help you tomorrow?"

"Tomorrow I'm leaving for New York for a few days. Thanks, but I'll manage. If you hear screams of agony coming over the fence, just send the ambulance to my house."

She shouldn't, she thought, feeling an urge to help him. Yet she would feel awful if she didn't. The other day she had reacted badly to him, an occupational hazard in his presence. Maybe she could show a little maturity. It'd be a change. "Can I help you instead of David? I'm as good a holder as he. Well, nearly as good."

Mother guilt was a tremendous force. Besides, she'd behaved in more moody fashion with this man than Heather would with a boy. Some maturity would help. And she preferred being busy to brooding.

He hesitated one telling moment. "Are you sure?"

She glanced at her computer screen. It was only work. "I'm sure."

"Thanks."

"I'll be around in a few minutes."

She nearly talked herself out of helping him as she walked around the block to his house. He was waiting at his front door for her. He looked as good as she remembered. Better. Janice drew in her breath and screwed up her courage.

"Hi," he said, turning the mundane greeting into something special.

She smiled. "Hi."

After he let her inside, he said, "I really appreciate this. It's more involved than I expected."

He said nothing about their last meeting. She was glad. They talked enough about their attraction and it seemed to get nowhere.

She walked into the kitchen. Cabinets sat everywhere, beautiful birch wood gleaming and ready to be fastened onto the stripped walls. "Weren't you going to hire a contractor?"

"For some outside work. Siding's more complicated than I can handle. I like to do as much as I can myself." He grinned. "Otherwise, I'd have to work, and I avoid that as much as possible."

She chuckled. "Don't tell me, but Tim Allen is your hero."

"Yes, only I hope I do better than him with the actual improvement work."

This wasn't so awkward, she thought, proud of herself. She could be a mature adult; now she only had to be consistent about it.

"We need to make a plumb line," he said, taking out a tape measure.

"Okay."

Janice took one end of the measure and stood where he told her, holding the tape where he indicated. He stood above her on a ladder and held up his end of the tape measure.

She tried not to think of the symbolism of the tape running straight from him to her—or his body so close to her own.

He reached down and marked off a spot near her breast. Janice swallowed, the room feeling suddenly hot. Then he dropped a chalked, colored string, holding it from his top mark. When the string stopped swinging, he had her just press it against the wall at the baseboard. He snapped the string, which left a straight chalk line running down the wall.

That done, she moved over several feet. He moved with her, taking the ladder. Again, he climbed above her, measured, then marked a spot on the wall by her breast. She wondered if it would be easier for her to just press her breast to the wall and say, "Here."

Boy, she was desperate if she could turn a simple chore into a scenario for sex. Okay, so she was desperate.

She tried conversation to distract herself from his closeness. "We know why I'm alone on Father's Day, but what about you? Why aren't you visiting with your father rather than hanging cabinets? Oh! I'm sorry. Maybe he passed away."

"No." They did the snapping-of-the-chalked-string routine. He said, "Move down again."

She did, bracing herself for the breast mark. Why did he have such lean, strong hands?

"I talked to my dad earlier today. He lives in Pittsburgh now. My mother's in Arizona with her third husband."

"You are spread apart from your family. Your parents, anyway. What about your brothers and sisters?"

"I've got a half sister I've never been close to. She's my mother's fair-haired child. I told you before that my parents divorced when I was little. Amy's age, actually. And you know already about the custody fights. Needless to say, I don't find either of the parental holidays particularly exciting."

Janice didn't know what to say. She could only envision the monumental adult battles that had tugged Michael one way and then the other until he was finally dropped for another marriage and another child.

He chuckled. "Don't worry. I'm well adjusted."

She looked at him in disbelief. "About as well as the triplets are."

"That's scary."

"No kidding." The more she heard about his childhood, the more it explained about his attitudes as an adult.

The sensual spell he held over her lessened as her heart filled with compassion for him. He must have been such a lost, unhappy little boy who had grown up to be an emotionally walled-off adult. She had sensed it from the beginning. Women must have broken themselves trying to get through that wall he had around him. She had to be careful that she wasn't counted among them.

They hung cabinets for the rest of the afternoon. Janice found the job wasn't bad, since she had only to hold the bulky things in place until Michael got a couple of screws in the wall. She discovered the "breast" marks were where the bottom of the cabinets had to be aligned.

She liked seeing his kitchen come to life. She was even envious. God knows, her own kitchen begged for an overhaul—which probably wouldn't happen in her lifetime if she were truthful with herself. But like that morning in her garden, she and Michael worked well together. Very well.

"How about dinner?" he suggested, when they got the fourth cabinet in place.

"Well..." she began, feeling wary again. She had risked enough just being around him like this. All the blood in her veins sang with awareness.

"Pizza?"

That cinched it. "Deal. If I can have mushrooms and pepperoni."

"My personal favorite." He named a national chain, but she stopped him.

"Vito's is better. And cleaner. He's a local guy with his own pizzeria."

"You call," Michael said.

"Okay."

She ordered the pizza for them. He suggested beer to wash the pizza down. She couldn't say no. It turned out he stocked the same brand in his fridge that she preferred to drink, the few times a year she did drink beer. She wished he didn't. The less they liked the same, the better.

Michael paid for the pizza. *Good thing,* she thought. She had no cash on her, just house keys. They cleared a couple of places on his cluttered table and began eating. She took a bite of her slice, sighed in sheer joy and closed her eyes to savor the taste of fresh mushrooms and spicy pepperoni in a tangy sauce on crusty flat bread. She opened her eyes to sip her beer, the yeasty liquid mingling with the other flavors in her mouth. She closed her eyes again. God, but it was so good.

"You act like you haven't eaten in a week," Michael commented, amusement in his voice. "Or maybe that isn't a good thing to say, after the last time at the mayor's house."

She opened her eyes and grinned at him. "You're forgiven. I haven't had this in a month. More. I can't afford pizza very often with my wolves. We make our own. It isn't nearly as good as Vito's." She leaned closer to him. "Don't tell anybody, but whenever I run an errand in town, and I have no kids with me, I sneak into Vito's sometimes and get a slice."

He paused in his eating. "Janice. That's awful."

She laughed. "Hey. It keeps the weight off. I don't mind, truly, and now it's wonderful. I time my visits to Vito's for lunch, to help the weight cause. I never have beer, of course. But this reminds me of college. Man, that was a great time—now that the midnight cramming for exams is done.''

Michael laughed.

''I sneak into the ice-cream shop, too. I'm a rotten mother—and proud of it.''

''You're hardly rotten, but I eat too much takeout.''

''You?'' She gaped for a second, astonished. ''You cook like a dream. Why would you want to eat out?''

He shrugged. ''It seems useless to cook for just one person. And a whole lot easier to get takeout. Even that's tiring after a while.'' He took another bite of his pizza. ''But it'll be a long time before I get bored with this. Thanks for introducing me to Vito's.''

''Thanks for treating me.''

''Thanks for helping me with the cabinets.''

''We are so polite,'' she said, giggling.

''Aren't we, though.... What do you do for fun, Janice?'' he asked.

''Me? Nothing.''

''Come on. This town's got to have something.''

''Oh, the town. Well, it's got a few bars, if you like that sort of thing. And a couple of restaurants. The movie theater is by the mall—''

''But *you* don't have any fun in them.''

''Oh, we get to the movies a couple times a year,'' she began.

''Janice! That's with the kids. What about you?''

''Me?'' She could hear the squeak in her voice and cleared her throat. ''I get around.''

He smiled wryly at her. ''You sneak pizza and ice cream.''

''Believe me, there's a joy in that, as pathetic as it sounds,'' she said, laughing.

''But you don't do anything else for you.''

"I do what I can, but it's not easy," she admitted. "I've been lucky in many ways, even if I am raising kids alone. I'm grateful for much more than I regret. Many, many people can never say that."

He just shook his head. She caught his implications. He would never understand that she found contentment and satisfaction in raising her kids, all six of them. They weren't a chore—although they could be a trial at times. That she waited for things for herself didn't matter. She would catch up eventually.

She reached across the space separating them and put her hand over his. "Michael, you have a poor view of family life. It's understandable, given your childhood. What you see as sacrifice I know is satisfying love. I'm very happy with my life, even though it's not easy for me. I'm a better person for the adversity. If you had children, you would truly understand what I'm talking about." She grinned. "But I will admit that after I get Amy through college and out into the world, then it's gonna be party time for me."

He laughed and squeezed her fingers. "I want to be around, just to see that."

A tingle of anticipation ran up Janice's spine. His fingers around her own imbued her with a heightened awareness, bordering on recklessness. This was dangerous. She wanted to throw all her common sense out the window— and herself at him.

She took a deep breath and extricated her hand from his with some naturalness and grace. She hoped. She took a bite of her pizza. Unfortunately, her stomach churned with anxiety and the pizza went down like a blob.

Damn! Why did he have to be so attractive? Couldn't he have fat jowls or droopy bags under his eyes? How about a generally dissipated look? Bloated features, blotchy skin, mousy brown eyes and hair? Instead, Michael had to be tanned and square jawed and magnificently green eyed. Leave it to Mother Nature to make such a human god.

"Do I have sauce on my chin?" he asked, frowning.

"No. Why?"

"You're looking at me like I've got some kind of disgusting thing hanging off me."

Hardly, she thought. Heat flooded her face. She couldn't stop the flush, nor will it away. Worse, her face became painfully hot. She knew it was a dead giveaway. She knew she ought to deny staring at him at all. "Actually, I was just thinking you look too damn good for my own good."

His pizza slice halted halfway to his mouth. "You were?"

"Yeah, I was." She started eating again, feeling oddly nonchalant for having admitted the truth. Maybe because she dealt with most things head-on she was more comfortable dealing with her reactions to him head-on.

"You do this to make me crazy, don't you?" he asked. "I don't know what to do with you."

"Nothing," she told him. "And I'm not trying to make you crazy. It just seemed senseless to lie when I'm blushing like a schoolgirl with her first crush."

"I thought you were blushing because I had something awful hanging from my nose and you didn't want to tell me."

She burst out laughing. "God, no."

Michael threw his pizza back in the box. "Now that I've killed dinner..."

She took another bite of her slice. "You'll have to say something worse than that at the dinner table before I'm grossed out. You've been to my dinner table, although no one passed peas through his nose. David did that once when he was little.''

To her surprise, Michael looked almost guilty. Something clicked in her brain. ''The boys *did* stick string beans up their noses that night. Why didn't you tell me?''

''Because the alternative was looking like a baddie with all three of the triplets. And I don't need any more help there.''

''Michael! How am I supposed to instill discipline when you are aiding and abetting the criminals?''

''I thought you did a great Solomon's job that night,'' he said defensively. ''They were punished quite well by having to eat all their string beans. And so was I by having to watch them do so.''

She laughed, humor at the irony of her punishment taking the place of annoyance.

''Truthfully,'' he continued, ''if I were a bad guy, those three would spend their lives trying to get my goat. They are getting in the yard still, despite my fixing the fence.''

She bristled. ''I'll stop that immediately.''

''No, you won't,'' he said, surprising her again. ''I want to come to terms with the triples on my own, not by being a stoolie. Besides, I'm an adult. I ought to be able to keep kids out of my yard without running to Mom.''

''You are innocent.'' She smiled. ''Okay, you handle the triplets. This ought to be fun.''

''Thank you for your support.''

''Oh, you've got it if you need it. I can't wait to see if you do. But I wonder how the kids are getting in your yard. I know the kitten's getting in through a warped slat. By the way, you have a warped slat.''

''Gee, thanks.''

She took a final sip of her beer. ''Let's go see if we can

find out how my three are getting in. Maybe if you fix that, you won't have to deal with the problem at all.''

"Good thinking."

They went out his back door, to find the deepening shadows of twilight bathing his yard. The willow tree hung heavy with its curtain of leaves. The oaks and maples towered over their heads like leafy mountains.

"The humidity went down," Michael commented. "I'll have to turn off the air-conditioning when I go back in."

"You can shut yourself away with that," she agreed. "Nice though it is. I wouldn't survive without central air."

"Me, neither. I'm no pioneer stock."

"We're wimps and we love it."

"Amen."

This was so nice, she thought, knowing she needed the adult companionship. Michael's companionship.

They headed for the fence between their properties. Janice paused, however, when she spotted an intriguing bush. White trumpet flowers, at least six inches across, gleamed brightly in the growing blackness. They seemed to give off their own light.

"What is that?" she asked curiously. She detoured over to the bush, which grew in front of an old stand of lilacs. "It looks like a cross between a lily and a hibiscus."

"It's a moonflower," Michael replied. "It blooms every night, then the flowers die in the morning. New flowers bloom the next night again. It'll do that until midfall."

"It's gorgeous."

"I can give you some if you like. It makes a seedpod from every flower, so I'll always have plenty of seeds. Moonflowers are perennial, too."

She bent to sniff an opening bloom. Its spicy scent reminded her of sandalwood. "It's glorious."

"It is."

She straightened. "I still want it."

"Do you?"

She gazed at him, having the feeling he wasn't talking about moonflowers anymore. "Yes."

"You amaze me," he said. "I try not to figure you out, but I can't help myself. And I don't succeed. How can a woman with six children look so calm and serene? How can you switch gears so smoothly? How can you be straightforward with your feelings? How can you then ignore those feelings?"

"I'm an open book, Michael."

"And the pages keep turning. How is it I've told you more than I've told any woman? How is it that you've gotten under my skin like no other? I don't trust women. I have good reason not to...so why have I trusted you with things I never have before?"

"I ask myself the same question," she replied in a low voice. "I don't trust men, either. I've learned not to. I shouldn't be attracted to you, yet I am. Maybe we understand each other on some subconscious level and that's what holds the attraction."

"Maybe."

He reached for her. She didn't pull away when he kissed her. He tasted like pizza and beer. He tasted like something she had denied herself too long.

She wrapped her arms around his neck and mated her tongue with his. His chest crushed her breasts and his thighs wedged between hers. He pressed against her intimately, sending shock waves of pleasure rippling deep within her body.

His hands roamed her back before cupping her derriere. They were strong and sure, yet exciting and new. He could kiss her for eternity, and she would never tire of it. But she wouldn't have eternity with any man. She would not have eternity with this one.

He kissed her neck and throat, his tongue laving her skin and driving her insane with want. Her entire body was a force he was driving in only one direction.

He kissed her mouth again, his lips twisting and turning hers wildly as their kisses grew more heated. Their passion took her off her feet, made her desperate for more. She couldn't remember the last time she had felt raw, a primitive female, guided only by the urge to satisfy herself and mate.

She moaned in her throat and kissed his cheeks, his jawline. She ran her tongue along the cords of his neck, delighted when his breath shuddered in and out of his lungs. She loved the idea that she could make this sophisticated man lose his control.

His hands reached up and cupped her breasts, his thumbs rubbing against her nipples.

Janice shuddered and moaned, pressing herself impossibly closer. She slipped her hands under his shirt, letting her fingers find every hard muscle and bone of his back. His hot skin burned her palms, imprinting the feel of his flesh in her brain. She dug her nails in slightly. His lips turned frantic on her shoulders. He pushed her shirt and bra up. He kissed her breasts, suckling one, then the other. No sophistication, just simple raw, primitive male need. For her.

Janice's legs melted away in her passion. She sagged against him, unable to bear her own weight. Desire was a two-way street, and she wanted him with as much compelling need as he wanted her. She had told herself good reasons to stay away from Michael Holiday. She had tried. But couldn't she take a moment for herself? Couldn't she have the wrong man even if just for one night in her life?

Couldn't she make a choice based on momentary need, rather than logic?

She knew he would walk away tomorrow. If they made love, she could guarantee it. She didn't care. This was tonight, and tonight she wanted a man she shouldn't have. Just for herself. She could walk away tomorrow, too. She would have to.

"Michael," she whispered. "Make love with me. Please."

MICHAEL COULDN'T BELIEVE the intimate plea came from cool and serene Janice Parker, yet he didn't question it.

He should—for her sake alone. But he had lost the ability to think logically with Janice touching him, kissing him, pressing hip-to-hip with him.

She moved against him eagerly. From somewhere deep inside him, he found a moment of control. "Janice. Are you sure?"

"Yes." She kissed him, her mouth incredible silk. "Yes. I'm sure."

He kissed her fervently. Her lips held that unique cool fire that so enticed him. His hands went everywhere, ensuring himself that she was truly here, in his arms. That she wanted him as much as he wanted her.

"We should go back inside..." he began.

"No. No, here. Make love with me right here in the garden."

She pulled him down to the soft grass and earth, her urgency clamoring through his own veins. He gave up thought and just touched and tasted. She lay underneath him, her hands caressing his shoulders and back, her mouth pulling him further into her spell. She never ceased to amaze him—and now...now she was woman incarnate. He had sensed the tremendous passion inside her, but he never thought it would arise so quickly. Like lightning.

She tugged at his shirt, taking it off him. Cool evening air brushed across his hot skin, somehow adding to the innocent seduction. For it was a seduction. Every fiber of his being sensed that he would be a changed man after making love with Janice. Yet the prospect didn't frighten him. Her palms traced the hair on his chest over and over, driving him slowly insane with her explorations.

He took off her shirt and bra, revealing her flesh. Her breasts surprised him, smaller than he expected for a woman with six children, yet her nipples were noticeably larger. The combination sent his senses spinning. Her taut stomach reminded him of velvet over steel, another incongruity that made her unique to him.

He kissed her breasts, nipping and sucking until she was like a wild woman under him. Her hands clawed at him, giving him a sense of power. Not over her, but with her. He found the snap of her jean shorts. She didn't stop him as he unfastened the garment and pushed the last of her clothes down her gorgeous legs. His fingers lingered on her slim thighs and tight calves.

She kicked off her sandals and pulled him to her, kissing him with such need that he felt as if he were the only man on earth to her only woman. He spread his fingers over the junction of her thighs. She was already moist, ready for him. The honest reaction of her body pleased him more than any studied seduction would.

He fumbled while trying to remove his shorts one-handed. Female hands took over the task and gracefully slid the clothes off his body. Her fingers caressed his hips and thighs, circling ever closer to his hardened flesh. When she finally touched him as intimately as he touched her, he thought he would shame himself. He wondered if she would compare him to her dead husband. He wondered if he would please her as well or better.

Her hands urged him forward and he could no longer resist.

He slid into her heated depths without thought. He was simply man and she was woman. Yet this union held so much more than he could define. He held himself still, savoring the way they fit together so marvelously... savoring the sensations being with her like this created.

Janice's sigh held much satisfaction, and she kissed his shoulder. Her contentment already at their joining nearly undid him. Finally, he thrust into her. She raised her hips to meet him, her body strong, sure and totally feminine in her movements.

They came together in ancient rhythms created by nature itself, rising higher and higher in the comforting darkness. The trees overhead sheltered them. The lilac bushes protected them. The grasses cradled them. When they met together in one last bursting thrust, their cries of satisfaction were swallowed by the very air around them.

And as they drifted back to earth, the moonflowers next to them opened in full bloom.

"OH, MICHAEL. That was so wonderful."

Of all the words Michael hoped to hear from Janice in the aftermath of their lovemaking, those were the best. He lay with her in his arms, in his little Garden of Eden, and wanted nothing more than the bone-draining contentment that he now had.

He chuckled. "You were the wonderful one."

She had been, more wonderful than any man had a right to expect. He shouldn't question her motives for wanting to make love with him. He knew he shouldn't, yet something compelled him to ask, "Why did you change your mind?"

She smiled against his bare shoulder. "Because you were right all along. I couldn't fight how I felt forever. Tonight I realized the futility of trying."

Her answer hurt. He knew it shouldn't, yet he couldn't say what else he wanted from her.

"Michael, we...I didn't think about this until now... please tell me your health is good."

He smiled and kissed her. "It's very good in all ways. I'll give you my doctor's report if you like."

"No." She tightened her arms around him. "I'm glad it's good. And so is mine."

He hadn't worried about her at all, already knowing her personal situation. But he wanted to reassure her on another point. "Janice, you have nothing to regret about tonight—"

"Oh, I don't regret a thing. And I don't expect a thing, Michael. Don't worry. It's okay. Everything is okay."

A major part of his contentment thudded to earth. He raised his head. "What do you mean, you don't expect a thing?"

"Just what I said." She chuckled. "I do understand our lovemaking has no strings attached to it. I needed you tonight and you needed me. It's as simple as that. I don't want or look for anything more." She reached out and grabbed her clothes. "I better go. The kids will be home anytime now."

He let her dress, her response stunning him speechless. He didn't like what she'd said at all. "Janice, I think we should talk about this."

"No need, Michael." She put her hand on his arm. "No apologies. Don't spoil it for me now. You were wonderful tonight. You gave me something special, just for myself.

I'll cherish it always. And I won't give you a single regret. I promise. Look! The moonflowers have bloomed. Remember, you promised to give me some seeds from them.''

She was gone before he could stop her, running from the yard like some elusive wood nymph.

Michael slowly dressed, while wondering if he had imagined making love with Janice. Again she had done the unexpected. She amazed him. She confused him.

He gazed at the fully opened white blossoms of the moonflower. They gleamed with promise. He had been right about one thing: he was a changed man.

He felt used.

Chapter Nine

Never compare one woman to another. The result can be disastrous.

—Michael Holiday
Man Can Definitely Live by Bread Alone

The heavens opened and poured rain on the day Michael left for New York.

"Mom, *please* take me to the mall," Heather begged. "I can't stand being cooped up here!"

Janice ignored her daughter, too busy trying to settle the triplets into a board game. The three squabbled over which one, an unusual happening since the two boys normally deferred to their leader sister. Clearly, they were growing independent from each other.

Oh, God, she thought. *Another "phase."*

"Mommy, can we have a tea?" Amy whined behind her. "You promised!"

"It's my world and you're welcome to it," Janice muttered under her breath. Louder, she said, "Give me a few minutes, Amy."

"But what about the mall?" Heather wailed.

"I don't want Parcheesi!"

"I don't want Game of the States!"

"I want to go outside! Who cares if it's raining!"

Thunder split the darkened sky and lightning slashed all around the house in an ear-deafening explosion.

The kids screamed and Janice jumped. Her heart pounded in fright. Michael the cat scooted from the room, his tail a thick burr.

Janice took a breath to calm herself. "Anyone want to go outside now?"

No one answered.

"Sensible children," she praised. "Okay. Now that we've settled one question, let's find something we can all do together. How about a game of Go Fish?"

"Okay!"

Go Fish was no ordinary children's card game with her set of wheeler-dealer triplets playing, as well as little Amy, whose hands could barely hold her cards. Janice just plain acted silly. Clowning around was worth it when it meant having contented kids. Even Heather started laughing halfway through the rounds.

This was her life, Janice thought. Games of Go Fish interspersed with child refereeing. Opportunities for reaffirming herself as a woman were few and far between. Regret rose up in her heart, but she forced it away.

She would regret nothing from last night. Making love with Michael had been dreamlike, as if the fairies had sprinkled magic dust all around them. That feeling enabled her to not dream more than she should about Michael Holiday. She hadn't even wanted to leave the yard for a bed, knowing that if she didn't seize the moment and make love on the spot, she would have lost her nerve altogether.

She was so glad she hadn't.

She had promised herself to expect no more than Michael was capable of giving—only a moment—and she had walked away with grace, knowing the score up front.

Inside, she hugged herself, feeling free and joyous and maybe just a little like forbidden fruit. That only added to her internal excitement. She had needed the lovemaking on so many levels. She wasn't worried about getting pregnant. After six children, she knew her body's rhythms well and knew she had been safe. Michael had assured her of other safety concerns, and she trusted him. The timing for intimacy had been perfect.

But her one taste only had her craving for more. The cliché about horny widows and divorcées was dead-on with her. Only she didn't want any man. She wanted Michael.

No! Her heart had to wall itself off, she thought. Anything else was a pipe dream, if not emotionally devastating. She would now move on.

"Mom?" David hurried into the kitchen. "You better come and look in the television room. There's a bunch of water coming in."

Janice shot out of her chair and raced for the den. Her heart pounded more fiercely than when the lightning had struck. Sure enough, one corner of the den ceiling had a steadily growing *drip, drip, drip* splattering the top of the television set.

Janice immediately turned off the set. "I hope no water got inside it or this will blow up." She reached behind the back of the set and pulled the plug. "Okay. That's better. Heather, go get towels and the furniture polish to clean off this wet spot on the wood. Kids, go get a bucket. David, let's you and me move this TV out of the way."

As everyone scrambled to help, Janice sighed. Yep, this was definitely her life...and Michael would definitely want no part of it. Even she didn't at times like this.

"What do you think happened?" David asked, after they'd pushed the television away from the leak.

"I think that lightning bolt hit something it shouldn't, like the tree outside." She paused. "I hope not, although I wonder now if that was the crack I heard. I'll go out after the storm and look."

David's eyes grew round. "Wow!"

Janice grinned, unable to resist teasing him. "Maybe God's telling you to stop playing so much of those video games."

"Maybe God was telling me I should have skipped that cave I went into," David countered, unrepentant. "I was getting creamed by Weebovees in there."

She chuckled. "You're too smart for your own good. But games are out until the water problem's resolved."

"I need to practice my horn more, anyway."

"There you go."

The mop-up crew returned. They got the television cleaned up and the bucket set under the drip. After the storm stopped, Janice and the kids went outside to see what had happened.

She moaned when she looked at her roof. A corner had been smashed by the pine tree that normally stood next to the house. Lightning had split off part of it, which had come down right on the edge of the roof. Or the roof could have been weak or rotted there, making it susceptible to even a light bump.

"Of all the luck," she muttered, wondering what this would cost her. Far more than she had, no doubt about that.

"Cool," David said, fascinated with Mother Nature's wrath on their house.

"Can I climb on the roof and look?" Cat asked, jumping up and down. Chris and C.J. jumped and clamored with her.

"No way," Janice said.

"Mom, what do we do?" Heather asked, while Amy just wrapped her arms around Janice's legs.

"Good question, honey." Janice stared up at the hole in the roof and smoothed Amy's hair. At the moment she felt overwhelmed and out of her element. What did she know from roofs? She wished she had another adult there, a companion with whom she could share the disaster. Someone to give her support. Drawing a deep breath, she said, "I guess I call the insurance company and someone to fix this as soon as possible."

In her life, there was always something she had to deal with. *Always.*

MICHAEL WALKED INTO his publisher's offices, finding them a rabbit warren of cubicles, with books and shelves and desks crammed everywhere.

The offices reminded him of New York City itself. Crammed with buildings, cars and people, it had a frenetic energy he had never encountered anywhere else. Sophisticated New York was such a far cry from suburban Marshfield.

The assistant editor before him was a far cry from Janice Parker. Young, with stylishly short, blond hair and a body that was filled out nicely, Rebecca Lawrence was exactly the sort of woman he'd once dated. A total yuppie, she understood the nineties' rules between men and women. She wasn't some damned-elusive Earth Mother who shouldn't know them at all and yet played them better than he did.

"We're really thrilled that your book is with our house," Rebecca said. She wore the requisite white blouse and short skirt that hugged her curves and showed off her legs. Her makeup enhanced her cornflower blue eyes. "I did some of the editing for *Man Can Definitely Live by*

Bread Alone, and I laughed all the way through it, Mr. Holiday.''

''It's Michael. Please.''

She smiled. ''Michael. It's funny but so valid, too.''

''Thank you.''

''Mr. McCann is in conference right now, but he's asked me to show you what we're doing and to go over the tour we've preliminarily planned for you with our staff publicist. We think you'll be extremely pleased.''

As Rebecca followed through with her words, Michael *was* pleased with what his publisher was doing for his book. He was less pleased with the niggling thoughts about what he had left at home.

How the hell could Janice have just walked away like that?

For a week she had been firm in her stance that she had no interest in exploring their attraction to each other. And then she'd seduced him! Not that he'd been an unwilling partner. But she had initiated their lovemaking. Worse, she'd practically patted him on the head afterward, told him he was a good boy and walked away.

Well, he felt that she had.

They had more than ''just sex'' between them; she had to know that. He should have confronted her right away.

With any other woman, he would have been relieved with the walk-away reaction, but not from Janice.

Why not from Janice?

He didn't understand himself, and he certainly didn't understand her.

Rebecca smiled at him as she and the publicist walked him through the fifteen-day, fifteen-city publicity tour they planned for him to make around the middle of August, when the book was released to bookstores.

Now Rebecca was a woman he understood. Around

twenty-five, single and living in the most cosmopolitan city in the world, she was the ideal date of his *Man Can Definitely Live by Bread Alone* readers. Her expectations in a relationship would be the same as his. She wouldn't expect more. And he could bank on that. Unlike a certain other woman.

"Have you seen the new play that just opened at the Schubert?" she asked him. *"Seven Hearts and Flowers?"*

"No," Michael admitted. "I haven't been to the theater in a while."

"You haven't?" She shook her head. "We'll take you tonight. The play's just wonderful. It's incredible the way it takes on politics and a dying neighborhood. Really, it matches anything off Broadway for satirical skewering."

"Sounds good," Michael said politely, while privately preferring the glitzy *Sunset Boulevard.*

"You're right. *Flowers* is great," the publicist said. "I'm so sick of musical remakes."

"Oh, me, too," Rebecca agreed. "I think that's a dead theater form...."

The two began discussing musicals and their feelings passionately. Michael listened for a while, then tuned them out, the conversation seeming way beyond him. He felt like a country yokel, a notion he'd never had before when visiting New York.

He wondered if Amy was having tea with Pooh. He wondered if the triples had gotten into his yard. God help his lilies if they had. He wondered if Heather was at the mall and if David was playing video games right now. He glanced at his watch. Eleven in the morning; definitely to both. Mostly, he wondered what Janice was doing. What was she thinking and was she thinking of him?

Charles McCann, vice president of the trade-paperback

division and Michael's editor, rushed into the conference room. He shook Michael's hand.

"God, I'm sorry, Michael," Charles said. "My wife, Ellie, called me just as my meeting broke up, with a family problem that couldn't wait. My youngest daughter got into my desk at home and drew pictures all over three manuscripts. Ellie thought she better alert me. Fortunately, we've got copies here. I gave Meredith a lecture, but I think it lost something over the telephone."

Michael chuckled. "How old is your daughter?"

"Three. If she wasn't so damn cute, she'd be in deep trouble. *Deep* trouble."

"I know what you mean. My neighbor's little girl is four. She's very cute and she knows it."

Charles's eyes twinkled. "Columns worth, but that's not your specialty, over which I'm sure you're sighing with relief."

"I don't know," Michael said, smiling and far more interested in this conversational topic than the musical as a dying theater art form. "I'm finding children a whole new, tempting arena."

"Let's get your book off the ground before you change gears."

"I've gone over the advertising and marketing strategies we've planned for Michael," Rebecca said, smiling at her own efficiency. "We're still working on the logistics for the book-promotion tour. I've also made a reservation at Chez Laguna for lunch. You'll like it, Michael. It's the hottest restaurant in the city, and it specializes in a mix of nouveau French, California and Chinese cuisines."

Michael blinked at the combination, boggling in its New-Agey precepts. Where was a Vito's Pizzeria when one needed it?

The hell with this, he thought, becoming disgusted with

his maudlin musings. Forget Janice. *She* clearly wanted it that way. Forget the kids and suburbia. He'd been playing with fire as it was. This publisher visit had come at exactly the right moment to remind him of who and what he was.

He smiled intimately at Rebecca. "I'm looking forward to it."

"IT'S NOT THAT BAD."

Lou O'Hara gazed down from his ladder, smiling as he made the pronouncement. The contractor had come over within hours of Janice's call.

"Can you tell what happened?" she asked.

"Sure. The branch fell on your house."

The kids all giggled. Lou grinned at them.

Janice smiled wryly. "Okay, I walked into that one. I mean, was the roof weak there to begin with?"

"It's a little soft. I hate to tell you, but you'll need a new roof eventually. The tiles are curling, and they might have let some water under them, which might be how the branch did as much damage as it did."

Janice groaned. A new roof!

"I'll check the rest of it," Lou said. "But from what I can see, you should be able to get away with this one for a few more years. You should just be aware that it's showing its age."

"Thanks," Janice said gratefully.

Lou was her age and she had known him for several years. A nice man, he had been divorced this past winter. His daughter was in David's class and a son was in Cat's, plus he had two other, younger children. Janice admitted objectively that Lou was a good-looking man, dark haired and brown eyed. Some woman would snatch him up in no time, she thought.

The triplets clamored to climb the ladder and look around.

Lou pursed his lips. "It's not a toy, guys."

"Oh, we know," Cat said. "Can we still look? We won't do anything else. We promise."

The boys nodded in agreement.

"I'll take each of you up on the condition that you understand that it's this one time only and you promise that you will *never* go up on your own. I'll trust you to keep your promise because you look like good kids. If you keep your word, maybe you can help me fix your mother's roof. From the ground."

"We promise! We promise!"

"Okay. Ladies first."

Janice watched, concerned, as Lou helped Cat up the ladder. Cat peeked over the edge of the roof, her eyes round with wonder. She came down docilely when he told her her time was up. Chris and C.J. went up in turns, although C.J. was visibly shaky when returning to terra firma.

Amy stood reluctantly behind Janice.

"What's the matter, baby?" Cat began, taunting her sister.

Lou intervened. "I can't let Amy up. It's against the law to put four-year-olds on a ladder."

Amy grinned. "That's okay."

Clearly, she was glad to get out of the ladder climb on technical grounds. Only the adults knew it was a fib.

Lou grinned back at Amy. "It sure is okay. But you can help me do some other stuff. I like to have lots of helpers."

"Okay."

Janice smiled. Lou scrambled back up the ladder. She noticed he had wide shoulders and slim hips, his jeans outlining well-muscled thighs. His tanned, corded forearms spoke of long hours of hard work out-of-doors. He, like her, had been married. He, like her, had children and understood them. He was the sort of man in whom she ought to be interested—if she were to be interested in any man.

Unfortunately, her insides didn't even emit a twinge of sexual heat at his good looks and compatibility.

Lou eventually came down from the roof, after a thorough examination. "There's one or two more soft spots where the water is getting around the tiles, but we can tar them up and keep this roof going for a while longer."

"Wonderful," Janice said, relieved at his assessment.

"Let me work up an estimate for you. Your insurance company should cover it, less the deductible. If you get your homeowner's policy, I can tell you exactly how much is covered."

"Come in for coffee or an iced tea," Janice invited. "I'll get the policy for you."

"Thanks. I'd like an iced tea."

Lou settled into her kitchen easily, taking a seat at the table. She found her homeowner's policy and handed it to him, then fixed him a glass of iced tea. Amy nearly hung over his forearm while he flipped through the sheets of papers.

"I can't read yet," she said.

"This isn't fun to read, or I'd read it to you," Lou told her. He took off his cap, a baseball-style one that advertised O'Hara Improvement, and put it on Amy's head. "There. It's yours."

Amy raised her face, since the cap came nearly over her eyes. She squinted at Lou. "It is?"

"Yep." He gave it a tug, making her giggle. "If you can't go on the roof, you get a hat."

"Yeah!" Amy cheered.

Lou read through the rest of the policy, then began filling out his own estimate form. Amy stayed around him, her chin on the tabletop as she dreamily watched what he was doing.

Janice smiled at her youngest. Amy really wanted a father figure, she thought. Too bad it couldn't be the one she liked most of all.

The mournful sound of a horn drifted through the house.

"David's getting really good," Lou said. "I'd say he's improved since the spring concert when he had that solo."

"Yes, he has." His knowledge of her son's accomplishment surprised Janice, then she remembered. "Your Alison's in marching band, too."

"Yeah. Clarinet. They were really good last year, weren't they?"

Janice nodded and sat across from him. "I think they'll take it all this year in band competitions. We've only lost six seniors, so the core of kids is still there." Their school was a combination junior-senior high school, making all the attending students eligible for band.

"I think you're right." Lou sighed. "I really miss hearing her practice now that I'm divorced. I miss a lot of things, but it's better. I love Mary, but we fought all the time and counseling didn't help. Our fighting was hurting the kids. Now at least they have some peace."

Sad as his words were, it sounded as if he had moved on from the marriage itself. Janice and Lou talked some more about band and school and other mutual child-rearing problems. This man was no Michael. He didn't move her sexually at all. But Michael, for all the attraction he held for her, didn't trust women. He wanted no commitment, nor was he interested in ever making one. If it was just herself involved, she would probably do something stupid like fall in love with him. God knows, she wanted to. She admitted it. Maybe she was more than halfway there. Michael was a man over whom a woman could be stupid....

She refused to be stupid. She was too old and too tired for it.

More importantly, she had the kids to consider. They couldn't form attachments to men she was involved with, only to have them broken when the man walked away. If she were to involve her kids, it had to be with a man who understood what he was getting into.

Michael had opened a door for her, one left closed almost too long. He had reminded her she was a woman with a woman's needs. She would always be grateful to him for that. She would always harbor a secret spot for him in her heart, for what could never be.

Lou finished his paperwork. He patted Amy on the back, then smiled at Janice. His gaze flickered down, then back again.

Janice decided right then and there that if Lou, or a good man like him, opened the door for a date, she would walk through it.

It was time she moved on.

"WASN'T THAT JUST marvelous!" Rebecca gushed about *Seven Hearts and Flowers* as they left the theater.

"I'm still trying to figure out what the title means," Michael admitted. "I didn't see any hearts or flowers."

Rebecca laughed throatily. "They were symbolic of the seven families trapped by the landlord's political ties, which kept them from getting restitution."

"But I thought there were only six families."

Rebecca curled her hand around the crook of his arm, sticking close to him in the exiting crowd. "You're forgetting old Mrs. Greenlaw."

"But she died in the first few minutes of the play."

"Yes, but she was the seventh tenant."

Michael wondered if he was becoming too pedestrian in his old age. But the whole play had been too obscure for him, evidently having pointed jabs at inner city government.

Rebecca huddled closer to him. Her perfume invaded his nostrils. It didn't do a thing to arouse him. In fact, it was downright cloying. Michael grimaced.

"There's a wonderful Thai, faux European coffeehouse in the village," she said. "I know it's still open. Everyone goes there. I think you'll like it."

"Okay," Michael said. What the hell. He wasn't ready to go to the hotel yet. Maybe a Thai, faux European coffeehouse would put the play in perspective. He decided it would have to put *anything* in perspective. How could a Thai, faux European coffeehouse not?

Rebecca hadn't been kidding when she said "everyone" went to the coffeehouse. The place was so mobbed with people it looked as though the entire theater district had dumped itself on the place. Most of the patrons were in their twenties, like Rebecca. The guys looked Chandleresque, while the young women were Rachels in the making. He felt like Tom Selleck in the cast of *Friends*. Out of his element.

He and Rebecca squeezed onto a broken-down sofa together. Rebecca ordered an espresso with ginger and mocha cream from a perky waitress. The waitress frowned when Michael ordered a coffee.

"Decaf? Latte? Honey? Coconut?"

"Just black," Michael assured her.

"You're kidding!" the waitress exclaimed.

"No. Just black."

She shrugged and wrote it down. "Okay."

After she left, Rebecca said, "I'm sure you save your adventurous side for more important things than coffee."

His adventurous side seemed more tied up with a widow. Now that was dangerous, but Rebecca wouldn't understand. "Simple pleasures hold more promise. Besides, all that stuff is fattening as hell."

Rebecca laughed. "You're just like your book. I think you could be the next Dave Barry and take just about any topic to explore in your own unique way. Has Charles talked with you about another book?"

Their coffees arrived. Rebecca's frothed like a dog with rabies. Michael gratefully sipped the good old, familiar, plain black liquid.

"No, Charles hasn't," he said finally. "I think I'd like to do one."

One with kids who torture adults. Especially torture in triplicate. That would be good.

She shook her head. "Sometimes Charles is lackadaisical. I would love to work as soon as possible with you on another project." She leaned close. "I think you and I would work well together. *Very* well."

Clearly, she saw him as a stepping-stone up the corporate publishing ladder. She was the kind of woman he had recommended his readers look for. Ambitious, intelligent, sensuous, unencumbered and uncomplicated, Rebecca had career goals she wanted to fulfill first. She looked for a man to compliment her current life-style, not become a central fixture in it.

Michael sensed the sexual undercurrents of their conversation. An idiot could sense them, he thought. He ought to be more interested, however. What the hell was wrong with him?

A spotlight was turned on, illuminating a small stage in one corner of the coffeehouse. A guy with blond dreadlocks sat on the single stool and plucked the strings of a Spanish guitar. Then he began to chant.

"The bird flew into the meadow,
I watched it.
The bird flew out of the meadow,
I watched it.
It died;
I watched it."

People clapped. Rebecca applauded, too, after setting down her cup. "That's Sad Bill. He really captures the essence of using allegory in describing life."

Michael thought the guy just didn't want to be bothered burying a dead bird. He wondered if a person had to be above a certain age to develop a healthy cynicism about spontaneous poetry.

"Sad Bill" launched into a series of questions about tugboats disintegrating once they finished pulling cruise ships into the dock.

Michael admitted there had been a time in his life when he would have been nodding in agreement, too. Like right out of college. Now he just felt...

Old.

The notion landed with a thud. But unfortunately, it had a rightness to it. *No,* he thought. Maybe he was a little unhip, but thirty-six was hardly old...

Rebecca leaned into him. Her breasts brushed against his arm. Her perfume bombarded him again. Michael found one easier to ignore than another. Unfortunately, it was the wrong one.

"This is wonderful, isn't it?" she said in a low voice.

"Yes," he said, suddenly determined to enjoy himself. "Yes, it is."

And if the opportunity presented itself later in the night—and it would or he knew *nothing* about women— he wouldn't turn it down.

To hell with elusive widows who made love like a dream. This was his life, and he was much safer in it.

OKAY, MICHAEL THOUGHT two days later, pulling his car into his driveway.

So the opportunity had thrown herself at him and he had turned it down without a single regret. In fact, he had walked all over Manhattan yesterday afternoon—from Central Park nearly down to Wall Street—just trying to sort out the reason why he had.

During his stroll he had come to several conclusions, all generally earth-shattering.

He was old.

He was cynical.

He wanted more than sex from a relationship.

Or rather, he wanted a widow who had six children. Knowing all the entanglements, he still wanted her in more than a momentary way.

"God," he muttered, pressing his forehead against the steering wheel. He chuckled wryly to himself. He should have listened to Jared, to himself, and just walked away.

That was impossible now. Possibly, it had been impossible for a long time. Something had changed. He didn't know how or when. Maybe when he moved to Marshfield. Maybe even before that.

He got out of the car and dumped his bag in the house. Noting that everything was fine—depressingly empty, actually—he walked out to his garden. The evening air felt good on his face.

He had put down roots here, following some secret yearning for a place of his own, he realized. He'd harbored a yearning, too, to have more than just himself in his world. In this house.

The twilight still provided enough light for him to see that his lily bed under the kitchen window had recovered well from the triplet trampling of last week. No new trampling was to be seen.

Michael smiled. No doubt the joy was gone without him home to torment. He would have to do something soon about those three.

He'd have to do something sooner about their mother.

He decided to do it now. He walked around the block, while summoning the courage to say what he had to say…and the right words in which to do it. He pondered openings, knowing that how he started would make all the difference in whether she accepted him or not. What-ifs plagued him.

What if she laughed in his face?

What if she rejected him?

What if she felt the same as he?

Amy answered the door. She threw herself at him with a shriek of joy. "Michael! You're back!"

Michael lifted Amy in his arms and hugged her. Nothing was sweeter than this child's love, he thought. It would get him past the triplets. It had to.

"How's my Amy girl?" he asked. "And how's my buddy, Michael? Has he been behaving himself and not running away?"

"Oh, he's been good." Amy grinned. "But he scratched Chris for pulling his tail."

"That'll teach him. Maybe." He glanced beyond her, through the open door and into the empty foyer. "Is your mom around?"

"Oh, no," Amy said cheerfully. "She went on a date with Lou."

Michael's heart slammed against his chest. A date! And who the hell was Lou?

Chapter Ten

Jealousy can be an indicator that you're on a path to commitment. Therefore don't indulge yourself in the emotion.

—Michael Holiday
Man Can Definitely Live by Bread Alone

"Who the hell is Lou?"

Janice spun around to find Michael standing behind her in her garden. Well, not exactly behind her, she amended. He stood on the other side of the fence.

Her stomach tightened as she stared at him. She hadn't seen him since he had returned from New York several days ago. If she was honest with herself, she would admit she had come out with her morning coffee hoping to glimpse him. She preferred the white lie of wanting to assess her weeding needs. God knows, the garden needed weeding.

She realized Michael's eyes blazed with green fire and his mouth sat in a grim line. He looked angry. At her.

Janice swallowed, sans coffee. "I beg your pardon?"

"I *said*, who the hell is Lou?"

"Oh. Lou O'Hara. He fixed my roof."

"Your roof?" Michael glanced up at the roof in question, his expression turning to puzzlement.

"The pine tree split during the storm we had while you were gone," she explained. "A branch hit a soft spot on the roof and crashed into a corner. I had a leak. I called Lou. He came to fix it."

"And then he took you on a date."

Her jaw dropped. "How do you know I was on a date?"

"I came over when I got home. To see you. Only you were on a date."

"You came to see me?"

"Didn't Amy tell you I was over?" He made a face. "Of course Amy told you. Amy tells the world everything."

"She said she saw you, but I assumed it was back here." Amy had told her, which was why Janice had been "assessing" the bejesus out of her garden. "Why did you come to see me?"

"Where the hell else was I going, after we made love?" he asked, sarcasm dripping in his voice. "Of course I was coming to see you. We had a lot to talk about. Or I thought we did. Obviously, you had more important things to talk about with *Lou*."

Anger came over the fence at her in waves. She didn't have to be psychic to detect the emotion in him. Why was he so angry with her? Hadn't she given him the kind of relationship he wanted from a woman?

She walked over to the fence and repeated her thoughts out loud. "Why are you angry with me? You have no interest in me—"

"The hell I don't!" He waved a hand. "See? You can't trust women—"

"Wait a minute!" She pressed her own hands to her temples. "I'm confused. You've made it real clear you don't want a permanent relationship with *any* woman. You should be happy I'm not looking for more from you.''

''You're a hypocrite,'' he said.

''Me!''

''Yes, you. *You* tell me over and over that you have no interest in just sex. Then you have a one-night stand with me. And right after you do, you go out with someone else. What is it with you, Janice? Don't you practice what you preach? Because you preached it plenty.''

His words whirled like maddened dervishes through her mind. He couldn't mean he wanted something more permanent with her. Not him. Not *the* Michael Holiday.

''Are you saying—'' she began, then interrupted herself. ''No. You can't be saying you want a permanent relationship.''

''Haven't you been listening?'' he snapped, yanking on the fence top. ''God, but I hate this thing. I don't know what the hell I'm saying. I don't know what the hell I'm doing. I only know everything I thought is now turned upside down. Especially about you. Who the hell is Lou?''

''I told you. My contractor.''

''Oh, *your* contractor. You go out on dates with contractors right after making love with writers. What's the matter? Is my profession not macho enough for you?''

''I think you've gone nuts.''

''The hell I have!''

Janice realized his voice was loud—loud enough to carry to the neighbors' windows. Thank God for air-conditioning, which kept everyone's windows shut. Still, this wasn't the time or place for such a discussion.

''I'm coming over there,'' she said. ''You can explain this to me in something other than the Greek terms you're using now.''

"Good. I've been telling you we need to talk. About damn time somebody listened to me."

Janice vowed to smack him senseless when she got to his house. Maybe if he started with a clean slate in the logic department, she'd finally get some sense out of him. Right now, he sounded by turns jealous, petulant and one-hundred-and-eighty degrees reversed from his stance about women. She *had* to know what he was talking about.

Inside her house, she called out, "Kids! I have to go see Mr. Holiday for a little bit. I'll be back soon. Heather, you're in charge."

"Okay, Mom!"

"Can I go? Can I go?" Amy said, running into the foyer.

Oh boy, that would be a kicker, Janice thought. She pushed Amy's hair from her little face. "Not this time, honey. I need to talk to Michael alone, okay?"

"No!" Amy stamped her feet. "I want to go, too!"

Janice gritted her teeth together, then said, "No. Not this time, Amy. If you throw a tantrum, you will not see Michael for three whole days. Now, go have Heather brush your hair."

Amy's look was mulish, but she said nothing more. Janice took advantage of the child's silence to make her escape.

Janice walked around the block, conscious of her neighbors. She wondered what they thought, then put it out of her head. She couldn't help what they thought. She could only help what she thought of herself. Besides, she was just going over to a neighbor's.

Michael was waiting for her at the front door. He turned away as she reached it, although he said, "Come in."

She opened the screen door and went into his house. Its

interior was as cool as he was. Firming her lips, she said, "Now what is all this about?"

He shrugged. "You tell me."

She threw up her hands. "You accost me in my garden. You yell at me. You tell me we need to talk and *then* you clam up! I don't think so, Michael."

"*You* tell me you won't make love, then you do, then you kiss me off and go out with some clown named Lou!"

"You sound jealous," she accused.

"Maybe I am. How could you do that?" he asked. "Didn't our lovemaking mean a thing to you?"

"Of course it did." Her head pounded. Hope rose in her heart. "It meant so much…everything. But I'm not about to be foolish. I have to protect my heart, Michael."

"Is that what this Lou guy is about? Protecting your heart?"

"Giving it a chance, I guess. He's a nice man, divorced with four kids."

"So you have a lot in common with him?"

She nodded.

"I can't compete with that, Janice."

"Do you…" She swallowed. "Do you want to?"

He glanced away. "I came home from New York determined to continue our relationship. I can't make any guarantees. I just know I'm not scared off by the kids and what goes with them."

She forced herself to think logically. "I can't believe I've done anything to create this metamorphosis in you, Michael. You're only wanting a relationship with me because I haven't been a conquest."

"Is that what you think of me?" he asked. "That I'm a playboy king who needs to make some sick emotional conquest of a woman?"

"Well, your columns are all about avoiding love and marriage."

"The columns! I'm going for a laugh, and you're taking it as gospel. I advocate avoiding women altogether. Don't you read the news? It's unhealthy to jump from bed to bed. Have I *ever* advocated that?"

"Well, no."

"Thank you."

"But why change the avoidance position? What triggered that?"

"You," he said simply.

Janice said nothing. She felt overwhelmed, pushed and prodded, generally confused and oddly hopeful. She must be dreaming this conversation, she thought. That was the only explanation that made sense.

"So what's the story with *Lou?*"

Obviously he was obsessed with Lou. She decided to deal with that issue first. "Lou is a very nice man. That's *all* Lou is, okay?"

"Are you...are you seeing him again?"

"No."

Michael smiled. "Good."

He reached for her, but she evaded him. "Oh, no. You've got some 'plainin' to do, Ricky Ricardo. I feel like you've been speaking Spanish with me."

"Well, maybe a little," he conceded. "I had an epiphany in New York."

"Epiphany?"

"I can't think of a better word. There was this girl—"

"Whoa!" Janice glared at him, her body freezing at the mention of a "girl." Her stomach churned and her vision faded. Steam built up deep inside her. "What *girl?*"

"She was an assistant at my publisher's, assigned to keep me happy."

"How *happy?*" Janice hated happy.

"Just to show me around the offices and escort me to dinner and the theater. Business entertainment, Janice. It's done all the time, and that's *all* it was." He grinned. "You're sounding jealous. Are you?"

"No. Keep talking."

He made a face. "Okay. She was the kind of woman who doesn't look for, want or expect a permanent relationship with a man right now. She's normally the type of woman I would be interested in. I wasn't interested. Janice, she made me feel old."

She snorted in amusement. She didn't want to, but she couldn't help herself. "Poor baby."

"Thanks," he muttered. "I realized I wanted a whole lot more than she was offering. And I wanted it all from you."

"Talk about hypocrites!" she exclaimed, her anger bursting to the surface. "You are a hypocrite of the first water, Michael Holiday."

"Me!" He gaped at her.

"Oh, come on," she snapped. "You're yelling at me about a simple dinner with a nice man, while you're out there gallivanting around with some sweet, young thing."

"*Gallivanting* is a nice word, but that's not what I was doing at all." He glared back at her. "Mine was a business evening—"

"Sure it was."

"*Yours,*" he continued, "was a flat-out date! There's a huge difference."

"Semantics. So did you sleep with her?" That question burned through her.

"No, I didn't sleep with her. I told you, I wasn't interested." He paused. "You really are jealous! Thank God! That means you have feelings for me, too. You said before that you had to protect your heart. Is that what the date with Lou was about?''

"Yes."

He pulled her to him. "Janice, I think I love you."

She stared at him. "You do?"

He laughed. "What else would explain my not running the first time I laid eyes on the kids?''

"The first time you laid eyes on them, they had you trapped. I had to rescue you."

"Well, I wasn't running."

"True." She wrapped her arms around his waist. "Michael, I'm scared, but I'm half in love with you already.''

He kissed her. Their mouths melded together with a rightness that Janice felt straight down to her toes. The need for each other was overshadowed by a deeper emotion that reassured her and scared her at the same time.

"I want you," he whispered. "Here. Now. But we can't.''

"Yes, we can. For a little while."

She took his hand and led him to the stairs. He took her to his bedroom...and into his bed.

"My body..." she began, thinking of the evidence of four pregnancies as he pulled her clothes off. "It's marred.''

"It's what you are," he said, kissing the silvery pink lines on her abdomen. "It's perfection."

She gave herself up to his touch, his lips, his body. Their lovemaking held a sweetness and a poignancy that she had never felt before. He thought he loved her. He'd turned down a younger, unencumbered woman for her.

Maybe it was a start.

"YOU'RE PRETTY GOOD for an old man."

Michael chuckled, content to have Janice's naked body

snuggled along his in the aftermath of their lovemaking. She hadn't disappeared directly after, like the first time. But he knew she would soon—very soon—out of necessity.

"You liked that, didn't you?" he said, flexing his fingers into the soft flesh of her derriere.

She laughed, her brown eyes sparkling with contentment and mirth. He had put those emotions there, he thought, and it meant a great deal to him that he had.

"Yeah, I liked that. It makes me feel like a teenager."

"Great," he grumbled. "I feel old and you feel like a kid. What's wrong with this picture?"

"Not a thing." She sobered, however. "What do we do now?"

He kissed the top swell of her breast. Her flesh tasted so sweet. "I can think of several things."

"Me, too. But I have to go soon." She chuckled. "Amy wanted to come over with me."

"Oh, God." Michael laughed. "That would take some explaining. What I want is simple. I want to see you. I have to. I want to trust you." It took a lot for him to admit that, but he wanted her to know how he felt about her. "I guess we date now."

She laughed. "Isn't that like shutting the barn door after the horse escaped?"

"Probably. But, hell, if you're doing dinner dates with contractors, you can do dates with me."

"I think Lou and I already figured that out. He's still in love with his ex-wife, and my interests were...elsewhere."

"Me," Michael said, grinning.

She kissed his mouth. "Give the ego a rest, dear. But the dinner was a nice start for both Lou and me."

"I wanted to be your first nice start," he said, wishing he'd never taken that damn trip to New York.

"Oh, you started something," she assured him. She kissed him. "You started the best part."

"Good."

Reluctantly, she pulled away from his side and sat. "I have to get back."

"I know. If you don't, the triples will be climbing my rose trellis to look for you." He leaned over and kissed her slender back, marveling at her satiny skin. "Shall I pick you up tonight? Seven?"

"Okay." She shrugged into her clothes. "Boy, I can't wait to explain this to the crew."

"Want me to go with you?"

"No. They'll be fine." She turned and looked at him. "I want to trust you, too, Michael."

"You can," he assured her.

She nodded.

He lay in his bed after she'd left, savoring the lingering scent of their lovemaking. He didn't know where their relationship would lead him, but he would follow it to the end.

THAT EVENING, Michael knocked on Janice's door with trepidation. Fence hopping and around-the-block running were entirely different from a date. He was damn nervous. His very first date with a girl hadn't left him this anxious. Yet knowing how little Janice got out, he had planned a perfect evening for her. Perfect. Once everything went right he would be more sure of himself.

He hoped.

Michael heard one of the triplets shout, "I'll get it!"

"No, I will!" another one yelled, and the pounding feet raced to the door. Dismissing the momentarily crazed notion that a *Jumanji* stampede from the *Jumanji* movie was bearing down on him, Michael straightened his tie and wiped a trickle of perspiration from his brow. Man, the evening was humid.

Well, it was a good excuse for sweating.

The door swung open. Chris and C.J. were yelling at each other.

"I called it first!"

"No, I called it first!"

"Liar!"

"Guys," Michael said firmly, although he still couldn't tell them apart. "Stop yelling and tell your mom I'm here."

The boys clammed up instantly, a miracle. They stared at him. Michael wondered if Janice had told them about the date. She had said she would.

"Tell him to come in!" Janice yelled from the bowels of her house.

The boys said nothing, just stepped back from the door.

Michael opened the screen and entered. It automatically shut behind him, and he closed the front door, keeping the blessedly cool air inside. Heather walked into the foyer. She said hello, then muttered loud enough for him to hear, "*She* has two dates, and I haven't had any yet."

Michael felt like a second strike had just been swung, and he hadn't even known he was up at the plate.

Cat strolled into the foyer and, bold as brass, said, "I like Lou better."

Strike three. Michael resisted the urge to walk back to the dugout, namely his house. He had made a commitment, and part of that commitment was dealing with these children. "Lou's a nice guy. By the way, next time you sneak into my yard, be a little more subtle. You and your brothers left clues all over the place."

"No, we didn't," Cat exclaimed.

"'Fraid so," Michael replied.

"How?"

"The lilies told me, for one thing."

"They can't talk."

"You'd be surprised."

Cat stared at him, unsure. Michael grinned at her, pleased to see her stymied. She usually left him feeling the same way.

Amy rounded the other side of the foyer.

Michael smiled in relief. A friend at last. "Hi, Amy. How are you doing tonight?"

Her answer consisted of an unhappy frown.

"What's wrong?" he asked.

"She's mad 'cause she can't go," Cat announced smugly.

"Shut up, Cat!"

"You're such a baby."

"No, I'm not!" Amy burst into tears.

Appalled, Michael went over to her and bent on his knees. "Amy, honey. Don't cry."

"Why can't I go?" she wailed, throwing her arms around his neck and weeping copiously.

"Because it's for adults," Janice said, coming into the foyer.

Michael looked up. Janice was beautiful as always— only she wore slacks and a simple white blouse. Michael wondered how to tell her The Striped Bass, an elegant four-star restaurant in Philadelphia, had a slightly less casual dress code. Michael the kitten, already doubled in size from his first day, butted his head against her legs for attention.

"Amy, I had this discussion with you before," Janice continued. "All day, as a matter of fact. Now that's enough crying. You're not going, so stop fussing about it."

Amy sniffed, then gave her mother a dirty look.

Janice finally glanced at Michael. "Uh-oh. I better go change."

"No," he said, disentangling himself from Amy and rising. He knew what he had to do. He whistled loudly. The kids froze. *Good old whistle,* he thought. "Kids! Pizza at Vito's for everyone."

"Yeah!" Amy cheered, turning instantly radiant. Heather and the triplets perked up.

"Oh, no," Janice said, shaking her head. "They've already eaten dinner."

"We could eat again. It's pizza," Heather said.

Michael smiled. "That's settled."

Janice shook her head. "If you give into a child's demands, she'll run all over you."

"Maybe," Michael agreed. "But Heather's ticked because you've had two dates. Amy's a mess because she can't go. Cat's made Lou a god, and the boys won't even speak to me. I know when I'm licked. If we take the kids, Heather and Amy will be happy for opposite reasons. Cat will have to admit Lou didn't take her and I did. She'll owe me. Chris and C.J. might actually speak to me. And David, if we can pry him from his video game, can come along for the ride. There're big-time pluses in this for me." He turned to the kids. "I don't want to hear a peep from any of you when I take your mother to dinner tomorrow night. *Just* your mother, understand?"

They all nodded.

"Good. Now go wash your hands and faces," he said, clapping twice to make them vanish.

They all scattered.

"Damn!" Michael exclaimed, staring at his palms. "It actually worked."

Janice kissed his cheek. "You're something. You know that?"

"Hell, woman, you can do better than that. I'm on a roll!"

He kissed her thoroughly, savoring the faint aftertaste of the morning's passion. She wrapped her arms around his shoulders and pressed herself against him, taking his breath when she did.

"Did I hear Vito's? Whoa! Mom!"

David was staring openmouthed at them when Michael broke away from Janice. *Oh boy,* he thought. Now things were in the fire.

"Yes, you heard right," Michael said. "We're all going to Vito's for pizza. And yes, I was kissing your mother. If you've got a problem with that, we'll talk later."

David had a funny expression on his face—half concerned, half speculative—but he shrugged. "Okay."

The rest of the kids came skittering back into the foyer, all chattering with excitement.

Michael whistled sharply. The kids quieted, only fidgeting slightly. He supposed total quiet was an impossibility.

"Okay," he said. "Everyone be on your best behavior, please. No sniping among yourselves and no sticking food in any body opening except the mouth."

The kids all giggled.

He added an incentive, feeling like he needed one. "If you guys are good at Vito's, we'll go miniature golfing afterward."

The kids cheered, making it worth losing The Striped Bass's reservation. The restaurant would probably never let him back in, he thought, not after the strings he'd pulled to get the damn reservation in the first place. Michael sighed, reminding himself to call from his car phone to cancel.

"You're brave," Janice said, as the kids filed out the door. "Dumb, but brave."

"Probably." Michael grinned at her. He stripped off his suit jacket and rolled up his shirtsleeves. "You make a real interesting first date."

"You ain't seen the half of it," Janice promised. "Lead on, fool."

"Thanks for the confidence builder."

"That's what I'm here for."

They had to take her minivan, since the kids wouldn't all fit in his BMW. Michael sighed ruefully. So much for a perfect evening.

The children really were good at dinner, either happy to be out for a treat or else taking his promise of miniature golf seriously. The pizza bill was a lot less than their other date would have been, but Michael recognized that it cost too much for Janice to manage regularly. The triplets thawed slightly, at least enough to say thanks without Janice's prompting.

The golf course was a different matter, however. The four younger ones raced from video machine to video machine, trying each one as if it would work magically without money. Then they checked the coin returns as if each machine would magically give them cash. David stopped to watch one kid play, his gaze as intense as the player's.

"I think we've lost him," Michael said.

"It's the others you ought to be worried about," Janice said, smiling smugly. "They're going to tear the place up if they're not stopped soon."

"Some date, huh?" he said.

"It's been fascinating so far. I can't wait to see what you do next."

Michael snagged Cat as she sped by them. Chris, C.J. and Amy halted as if on command. It was Caesar who had said cut off the head and the rest of the body would falter, Michael believed. Nice to know he had hit on it by accident.

"The good behavior still holds for here, too," he said. "Now, who's ready to play golf?"

A chorus of "Me!" went up.

"David! Heather!" Janice called.

To Michael's surprise, David sauntered over to them. Heather stayed put next to a good-looking blond boy about her age who was playing a video game.

"You go ahead," she said. "I'll watch Jason, okay?"

Janice looked at Michael. "You're up, slugger."

"I didn't even know she wasn't with us," Michael muttered, wondering what to do.

"Teenage girls are *never* with their families if they can help it."

"You sure, Heather?" Michael asked her.

Heather nodded, her eyes shining with anticipation. The boy, Jason, smiled at him. Michael frowned, but said, "Okay. We'll be right outside on the course."

"Nowhere else but here," Janice added. "Understood?"

Heather nodded again.

Janice grinned at her daughter. "Have fun."

Michael got the kids settled with putters. David tried out several before choosing one he liked. His stance was very good.

Michael said, "Do you play?"

David smiled dreamily. "Sometimes I go with a friend when his dad takes him golfing. I get to play then. It's great."

"You actually do something besides the video games?" Michael grinned. "My God, it's a miracle."

David just laughed.

Janice poked Michael in the ribs with her putter. "Better get the others moving, Pied Piper. In case you didn't notice, you've given them lethal weapons, a fact they're just discovering."

The triplets were whacking at each other's clubs as if they were swords. Michael leapt between them and was immediately smacked on the shinbone.

"Sorry," Cat said, looking half repentant and half pleased.

Michael bit back a curse. "Everyone out on the course."

He herded them outside, limping behind.

The kids were a riot. Michael and David helped them all with their swings, but the children forgot the instant the lessons were over. Amy danced around gleefully the entire time and couldn't hit a ball to save her soul. Chris and C.J. challenged each other over every shot, and each missed the ball half the time. Cat actually hit a hole in one. Only her ball went into the hole across the way, not the one it was supposed to.

Michael counted it, saying, "Way to go, Cat girl. A hole in one is a hole in one."

Cat beamed with joy.

David played under scratch for every hole, quietly showing yet another talent. Michael made a golf date with the boy, having a feeling he'd found a good partner. Probably David would beat him.

Heather and Jason came out eventually and joined in the fun. Michael felt as though he'd made another victory there, especially after remembering Janice's comment that teenage girls avoided their families. He gave her and Jason money to get their own putters and start their own game, like a minidate. Heather looked ready to kiss him for catching her up to her mom.

And Janice...Janice was stunning and just as much fun as the kids. She hammed it up on every swing and teased all of them, especially him when he missed. Michael felt as if he was the top recipient of her raspberry award. Her gaze sparkled with good humor and affection. Her face glowed. She laughed the most at herself, when she hit her ball straight over the boundary fence and out into the street. Michael knew he had ultimately made the right choice and given her a perfect evening.

A memory from long past slowly surfaced—one of another miniature-golf course and kids challenging each other and laughing at mishaps and antics. His cousin Raymond had always been the most competitive, but it hadn't mattered to Michael, Peter or Jared. Magic had been the driving force in those golf games. A special magic for him, who had had the least-stable family life.

As he played and teased, a part of him watched and realized that tea parties and ghost spying and miniature-golf outings were giving him back his long-lost childhood magic. The armor he had worn for so many years was now well dented and cracked. It would never fit again.

Janice leaned into him at the end of the game. "Thanks. You were right to bring the kids. They don't get out like this very much, and they enjoyed it."

"My pleasure," he said, putting his arm around her shoulders. "My pleasure."

Chapter Eleven

Love should scare the wits out of you. Isn't that reason enough not to fall into it?

—Michael Holiday
Man Can Definitely Live by Bread Alone

"I think we crossed our wires again."

As Janice made the pronouncement and let Michael in the house, she looked at his casual trousers and designer Ban-Lon shirt. Her heels and black chiffon would never match in a million years.

"You look ravishing," he said, his face crestfallen. "And I've goofed big-time. After last night, I just assumed we'd do a casual dinner and a movie."

She chuckled. "And I thought you'd want fancy again."

He looked around the empty foyer, then said in a low voice, "We could get naked and solve the whole problem."

"Oh, no. You owe me a date, pal."

He grinned. "What was last night?"

"A date with my kids. I'll go change."

"No, I will."

"Don't be silly. You're here. I'll change."

"No, me." Michael laughed. "Our first date fight."

"Mark the calendars."

"I know a place in the city where how we're both dressed will work very well," he said. "No one has to change. Besides, I like the way you look."

She grinned, flattered and pleased. "Then let's go while the kids are still behaving. Kids, I'm going!"

"Bye!" Voices piped up from all over the house.

"I wondered where they were," Michael said, as they left. "I thought maybe you had locked them in the cellar."

"Tempting, but I don't have one. Only an attic crawl space and a garage. Besides, I told them they had made a promise to behave tonight, and they would pay dearly if they didn't."

"Good thinking."

"Someone's got to outwit them."

"So I'm learning."

He really had been brave and sweet to take all the kids to dinner and golf last night. And he had made brownie points with the kids, who were still talking about how much fun they'd had. He had made brownie points with her, too. Major brownie points.

Michael took her to a little restaurant on South Street—not very trendy, but one of those places that endures all the changes over the years. Some patrons were dressed up, as Janice was, and some were casual like Michael. The two of them fit right in, just as he'd promised. The owners knew him and greeted him warmly.

"This is wonderful," Janice admitted, when they were seated at a corner table.

"Wait until you taste the food," he said. He reached across and took her hand. "I have to thank you for giving me back something I'd lost a long time ago."

"What was that?" she asked curiously.

"Magic."

Taken aback, Janice straightened. Of all the answers she'd thought he might give, this wasn't one of them. "Magic?"

He nodded. "Childhood magic. The kids did, actually. I didn't have many outings like last night when I was their age. My time with my cousins always seemed magical to me. My grandmother catered to me a little bit. I guess because of my parents' bitter fighting, she thought I needed some extra attention. She was right. After her affair, she was never the same. Those summers that had saved me were gone. Last night..." He grinned ruefully. "I guess it was a date with your kids. I hope you don't mind."

Janice smiled. "Not at all."

She could warn him that the kids wouldn't always be like they had been last night. She decided not to, not having it in her to burst his bubble with reality. Besides, he'd seen them at some of their worst moments. He had to know what they were capable of.

"What do you want from this relationship, Michael?" she asked.

"I...I want it to continue," he replied, squeezing her hand. "I'm willing to try."

His hesitation and his answer weren't what she was looking for, yet she wouldn't have been able to give a different answer if the question had been asked of her.

She smiled. "I want to try, too."

"Good." He looked around. "I don't know about you, but I'm ready to order."

A waiter appeared, as if he had been waiting for Michael's wish to be spoken.

"Wow," Janice said. "This place *is* good."

Michael grinned. "Told you." When they were alone again, he said, "Tell me about your family and your marriage. I want to know everything about you."

She smiled wryly. "There's not much to tell."

"So tell me anyway."

"My parents live in Florida, and my brother is in Massachusetts, which means my parents now sound like they were born in the South and my brother sounds like a Kennedy."

Michael chuckled.

"You know about my marriage," she said. "Six kids create a tremendous amount of pressure. Either a marriage survives that or it doesn't."

"Would yours have if your husband hadn't died?"

"I don't know," she said, then admitted her own feelings. "I doubt it. But I'm glad, in a way, that I really will never know the answer. I must have been inadequate somehow for Tom to turn to someone else, pressure or not."

"That's crap, Janice," Michael said, taking her hand again. "Men do stupid things that have nothing to do with the women in their lives. Believe me, I'm an expert on the subject."

"That's what worries me," she said seriously.

"I should rephrase that. I'm a *former* expert." He paused. "Maybe I didn't do stupid things then. Maybe I just didn't have enough incentive to do anything else. I can't believe your husband didn't want Amy. She's a wonderful child, so loving. I wish she was mine."

Janice couldn't mistake his sincerity, and a lump of unshed tears rose in her throat. She worried still about his staying power in a relationship, but whatever happened between them, she wouldn't disrupt his relationship with Amy again.

"Michael. Hello."

Janice glanced up to find a woman standing at their table. If she was a day over thirty, then Amy was forty-seven, Janice thought, her stomach churning with sudden bad feelings. The woman had flawless skin, flawless nails, flawless red hair, flawless size-six clothes and an air of self-confidence Michael Jordan would be hard-pressed to match. Knowing what was coming, Janice wanted to shrink under the table.

Michael let go of Janice's hand like it was a hot coal. He rose to his feet. "Marianne. Hello. It's nice to see you again."

"Marianne" leaned toward Michael, giving him a bird's-eye view of cleavage in the gaping slip dress she wore. She kissed his cheek. "It's more than nice to see you again, Michael. Where have you been hiding yourself?"

"I moved to Jersey," he replied.

Marianne gave a flawless peal of laughter. "You? You're kidding!"

"No. Actually, it's very nice where I am. I like it." Michael blinked, looked at Janice, then seemed to visibly shake himself. "Marianne, this is Janice Parker. Janice, this is Marianne Wright."

"Hello," Janice said, hearing her voice crack, to her disgust. She grimaced and extended her hand. "It's nice to meet you."

"Hello." Marianne touched her palm so lightly Janice wondered if the woman thought she had cooties. Marianne turned back to Michael. "Work has been a mess lately with the mayor's reelection gearing up, so I'm sure I've missed your calls." She opened her purse and handed him a card. "Call my private number at the office. I'm always there now."

Marianne whisked away, her dress clinging to every curve.

"That was smooth," Janice said in admiration as Michael resumed his seat. "Is this how the nineties dating thing works? You just hand people a card and say, 'call me?' I've got to get some cards and get with it."

He gave her a sour look. "Very funny. Marianne's no date, believe me. She's looking for a national forum for her boss." He crumpled the card and tossed it into the ashtray. "She thinks I'm going to turn into Philadelphia's version of Mike Royko and write about hometown things...like the mayor, who's got eventual White House aspirations."

"He might be pretty decent," Janice said, trying to shake her insecurities away. "He's really cleaned up Philadelphia and he's started some great projects."

"He has, but I prefer to write columns like the one I wrote late last night, about kids and pizza and miniature-golf games. That was much more fun. I wish I was at a game right now." Michael sighed. "Let me explain about Marianne—"

"No." Janice held up her hand. "Unlike you, I have no wish to know about your prior private life. It's not my business."

"And it's not what you're thinking, either."

"Then good." She glanced over at Marianne, who was seated with a group of friends, all young and sophisticated. Boy, Janice thought. She would give her eyeteeth to be in the midst of a miniature-golf game, too.

She wondered if Marianne was as elegant and sophisticated in bed. Unfortunately, she probably was. Janice felt like the farmer's daughter out at the haystack—quick and dirty.

Their meal arrived, forestalling any further talk about his past love life. Janice truly didn't want to know—or rather, she knew all she needed to know from his columns. He could peg them as exaggerations, but they started with grains of truth. She wondered what the one about her kids and the golf game would say. Probably nothing good. Her face heated as she remembered how silly she'd acted last night. *That better not be in there,* she thought.

Somehow, her spine straightened. To hell with his columns. She had been having fun with her kids—and him. If he chose to mock that, then she needed to know. She was herself—a mother, a widow. She gave all she was to her lovemaking, and she wouldn't want to change anything about herself. She wondered if Michael had ever told Marianne he thought he loved her. Somehow, she doubted it.

The rest of the dinner went better from her perspective, although they only made small talk about gardening, movies and plays they liked and other things they had in common. Yet the mood was spoiled for her.

When they got in his car after dinner, Michael said, "This wasn't what I planned for tonight, Janice."

"It was fine," she said. "The restaurant was excellent. I never had better clams casino."

"Where did Lou take you to dinner?" he asked.

She chuckled, the question surprising her. "The Red Mill Inn on the highway."

"That place with the old-fashioned waterwheel?"

"Yes. It's requisite dining in Marshfield."

"I suppose the food was good, and he didn't have any old, female acquaintances coming up to the table, annoying you both."

"The food's okay there, a step up from a diner, but no, Lou had no old, female acquaintances." She chuckled. "By the way, I like how you said that."

"Well, that's all she is. Just somebody I knew here in the city, okay?"

She laughed outright this time. "You're defensive."

"I feel like my life's on trial every second." He made a face. "I suppose I deserve it."

"Oh, you do."

"Okay, be Doubting Thomas."

"Thomasina."

"Thomasina. But I'm not going anywhere, okay?"

She smiled at him. "Okay."

He leaned across the console and kissed her. His mouth felt innocent, vulnerable and unsure. She kissed him back fervently, unable to control her automatic response to him. Trusting him was scary, yet she couldn't help herself. Not even "old acquaintances" could pull her back now. She knew it.

In her heart, she knew it.

MICHAEL TUCKED THE BOX containing his new pair of loafers under his arm and walked through the mall. He glanced at the window displays of the various stores, wondering if he might find something to give Janice that would smooth over the bump left by their first official date.

His mother often said his life-style would eventually haunt him. How depressing to discover she was right. It depressed him more to know the little meeting with Marianne had put the aloofness right back into Janice. He would just have to hang in there all over again with her and wait for the thaw. Now if only he could get a little help...

A group of teenagers came toward him, vampirish with their white-white skin and dyed-black hair. The girls wore heavy makeup that outlined their lips and eyes. The boys wore a myriad of hoop earrings in ears, nose and even eyebrows. Michael was wondering if his generation had ever looked so rebellious when he realized he knew one of the girls.

"Heather?" he asked, positive he was imagining things.

The girl paused. Sure enough, it was Heather. Her hair was slicked back as if with bear grease and her mouth was dead black. She wore a nose ring. A nose ring! Her expression held sheepishness and fearfulness at being caught in her getup. Michael didn't have to guess at that.

"Hi, Mr. Holiday," she said casually.

"Does your mother know you look like that?" he demanded, not giving a damn if he was overstepping his bounds. The girl looked hideous.

"Hey! She can do what she wants," one of the boys said.

"That's too bad," Michael said. He noted that Jason wasn't among them. These youths were far scarier. "Well, I'll be sure to tell your mom I saw you, Heather, and how...interesting you look today."

She hung her head, clearly showing she knew she was in trouble. "Okay."

"Unless..." Michael began. Heather perked up. "Unless you and I talk about this now over a soda."

Heather looked at her friends. She was silent for a few seconds. "Okay."

"Heather!" one of the girls wailed. "Don't listen to him."

"He'll tell my mother if I don't," Heather muttered defensively.

"Who cares?" a boy snapped.

"Let's go," Michael said, wanting to get her away from these kids.

Heather hesitated, looked at the others, then walked away.

He led her to the mall's food court. Heather hit him up for french fries as well as a soda. They found a small table.

Michael looked hard at her, not believing this was the

same beautiful girl of the shining dark hair and the all-American features. "Heather, there's expressing oneself and then there's chaos. You've hit chaos big-time."

"You're not my father," she said defiantly. "You can't tell me what to do."

"No, I'm not your father," he agreed calmly, while wondering how to reach this girl. "I'm your friend. You can take or leave what I have to say. The choice is yours."

Heather shrugged.

"Your mom trusts you, Heather. This would upset her a lot."

Heather shrugged again, seemingly uncaring.

Michael wondered if he had ever been that young...and that scared. For Heather was scared. He could see it in her tense shoulders and trembling hands. The girl truly didn't want her mother to know. Janice had placed a lot of trust in her, and Heather had broken that trust. Right now, only he kept her mother from knowing she had.

Unfortunately, the kids she'd been with looked like they were exercising more than individuality. She was with a bad crowd. Somehow, she had to be separated from them. He realized he had boxed himself in by implying he wouldn't tell Janice. Now what?

He looked at the nose ring. First things first. "Doesn't that hurt?"

"It's only a clip." She removed it to show him.

Michael breathed a sigh of relief. At least she hadn't pierced it. "What do you do when you have to blow your nose?"

Heather giggled a little. "You just take it out, Mr. Holiday."

"Call me Michael."

She smiled shyly. "Michael." Relaxing a little, she pulled several loops he hadn't noticed from the upper edges of her ears. "These are fake, too. And this one." She reached under her shirt and brought out yet another ring. "It's a belly ring, for your belly button."

Flummoxed, Michael said, "You kids boggle the mind. I hope to hell you don't have a ring anywhere else."

"No. Just those. They're cool." She sipped her soda.

Cool. Michael shuddered. "Thank God they're not the real things, or you really would be cool...from all the holes poked in your body."

Heather grinned. "I'm not that dumb. Besides, if I really did have everything pierced, my mom would poke a bigger hole in my body when she killed me." Heather frowned, worried. "She won't kill me, will she?"

"I would kill you if you were my daughter and I saw you like this," Michael said bluntly. "You'd be lucky if you were only grounded for the rest of high school. Aren't you glad I'm only your friend?"

In his own youth, he had responded better to adults other than his parents. Maybe Heather might. "The first time I saw you, I thought you were one of the most beautiful young women I'd ever seen. And I've seen lots of beautiful young women."

She glanced up sharply. "You have?"

He nodded. "You made me wish I was that kid Jason's age again, because girls weren't nearly so pretty when I was. Does he like this look?"

"Well, no," she admitted in a low voice. "I—I saw him yesterday here at the mall. He just acted like he didn't know me. He's the most popular boy in the ninth grade."

"That must have hurt," Michael said gently.

Tears welled up in Heather's eyes. "He seemed to like me that night at golf, didn't he?"

"Yes, he clearly liked the *real* Heather very much. This isn't you, Heather. Or at least not the beautiful Heather

I've seen. What's the attraction with that group? Is it because they look so different?''

"No. Not really." She lifted her shoulders. "They're Jen's friends mostly. She likes one of the guys. I...I don't know—''

"You really don't like looking like this, do you?" he asked, perceiving she'd been caught up in peer pressure from her friend.

She shook her head. "It's okay, I suppose. But I feel weird sometimes.''

Michael closed his lips against saying she looked weird. Instead he said, "You should do something because it makes you feel good. If it doesn't, never do it. Sometimes it's tough to say no to friends. Sometimes friends should understand that you need to be yourself. Okay. Here's the deal. I won't tell your mother...but only if you promise not to come back to the mall without her.''

"But I'd never go then, except for clothes shopping!" Heather exclaimed.

"That's the deal.''

Michael waited for her reply, silently rooting for her to make the right choice. The best choice for her.

Finally, reluctantly, she said, "Deal.''

Michael grinned at her, pleased that parental fear still occasionally won out with kids today. "And I know, because you are a mature young woman, that you'll keep our deal. Mature people honor their commitments.''

Heather nodded, looking glum. Michael smothered a smile, remembering he'd felt the same way when he'd realized he had to be "mature.''

"Okay," he said. "Let's go find that motorcycle gang you were with and tell them I'm taking you home now.''

"I've got to take this stuff off first," Heather said. "Jen

and I do it in the bathroom before our moms pick us up. It brushes out of my hair."

"Lead the way." Michael was pleased that she was ridding herself of the Lily Munster look *before* telling her friends rather than afterward.

Her friends, however, were less than delighted by her new, or rather former, appearance. Her friend Jen protested vigorously. Heather looked ready to cry, but, to Michael's awe, stuck to her promise to him. The girl had character— and probably a crush on Jason.

As they walked out of the mall, she said, "Well, there goes my summer. I have nothing to do now except hang out at home."

Michael realized she'd fall into something else that might be as unsavory as the kids they'd left at the mall.

"You can work for me," he offered, as an idea hit him smack in the face. "I need help with my gardening and remodeling. I had your mother over once to be a second pair of hands." Boy, had Janice had a pair of hands, too, that night, but that was better left unsaid. "A hundred dollars a week."

"All right!"

"Half goes into a college fund."

"Oh, boo."

Michael laughed. Heather looked relieved and happy. Probably the lesson had hit home with Jason's reaction yesterday, and his own had only seconded it.

When they got to the house, they discovered Janice playing a video game with David. Amy, who had been watching her mother, ran over and wrapped her arms around Michael's legs. Michael grinned and hugged her back.

Janice pressed the pause button. She looked curiously

from him to Heather. "Hi. I thought I was supposed to pick you up in an hour."

Heather glanced at Michael. Her face clearly showed her panic over how to answer.

"I met up with Heather there, and since she was ready to come home, I brought her. I hope you don't mind."

"I suppose I don't, although Heather's supposed to call me if she's ready early."

"I saved you a trip." Since Michael was with the friendly Parker kids, he leaned over and kissed Janice lightly on the mouth. He wanted to kiss her more and more. She was an addiction, and he couldn't get enough. Now, unfortunately, was not the time or place. "I thought I finally bombed David out of here with the lure of golf. Now you're in here."

"Hey, I'm a player upon occasion." She grinned. "I'm quite good with certain games."

"She's playing Yashi, the dinosaur," Amy said. "It's fun."

"Okay." Michael sat in an easy chair that had seen better days, but it enfolded him like a big mama embracing her baby. "By the way, Heather's going to do some work for me this summer, in the afternoons. I need a helper with my remodeling, and she's available. Works out great for me."

"And me," Heather added, sitting next to her mother. "Michael's paying me a hundred bucks a week—"

"Wow!" David said in an awed voice.

"But half has to go into a college fund," Heather continued.

Janice skewered Michael with a look. He didn't need to analyze it to know she didn't like the job for Heather. The moment they were alone, she'd kill him. He wondered how to explain the need without explaining the reason.

"You don't have to do that, Michael."

"From my point of view, I did. Or will you come over whenever I call for help?" he asked.

"You know I can't."

"Then let me have an excellent helper. Heather will be right behind your house, where you can stroll over anytime you like. I need the help, and Heather *needs* the job." He stressed the word, to get Janice beyond the "we're not charity" objection. "Now show me how to work this Yashi thing. Better still, you play and I'll make dinner again."

"Oh, no!" Janice exclaimed, thrusting the controller into his hands. "You play and I'll cook."

Michael smiled. "What an invite."

"Yeah, well..." She left the room.

Michael wondered again how to tell her what he couldn't, then decided to cross that bridge when he came to it.

Instead, he played the game. He found the thing refreshing and frustrating, funny and addicting, with his mistakes providing half the entertainment. Amy leaned on his thigh after he moved to the ottoman directly in front of the screen. Heather seemed content to sit on the floor next to him. David hung over his shoulder, giving directions and yelping in horror and amusement whenever Michael went the wrong way. He went the wrong way a lot, to everyone's merriment.

Dinner was a better success than the first time he'd eaten over. At least no string beans were stuck up anyone's noses during dinner, although the triplets looked at him as if he still had two heads.

After Amy went to bed—very reluctantly—Michael and Janice sat out on her back patio. Mosquitoes were held at bay by citronella candles and a bug zapper farther out in the yard.

"Okay," she said. "I've been patient. *Very* patient. What's going on with my daughter?"

"I would tell you in an instant, but because of a promise I made to Heather, I'll ask you to be patient forever," he said. "At least from me. I can't break the trust she's put in me. But I will say that she's in fine health, emotionally and physically. She stole nothing and wasn't arrested. Nothing *happened,* okay? She just got off a road she'd started to wander down, smart girl, and now she won't be going to the mall anymore without you. That's her half of the bargain, and that part I didn't promise not to tell you."

Janice chewed on the news for a long moment. "Okay. Obviously you discovered something happening at the mall that would displease me. And you handled it yourself."

"Yes." He eyed her warily. "I know I shouldn't have. It wasn't my place to. But she seemed to need a push in the right direction, and I was there at the opportune moment. I have not made you happy."

"You've made me bewildered." She sighed. "All right. I understand about trust, and I will honor your bargain with Heather. But she can't have the job at your house."

"She has to," Michael said. "I realized that she needed something constructive to do, and I was doing something constructive that needed help. I planned to ask David when we went golfing tomorrow morning, but Heather needs it more than he does. Otherwise, she might start sneaking back to the mall, despite our agreement. It…it's unhealthy there for girls her age. They could fall in with the wrong crowd very easily."

He had told her more than he should have, he thought.

But Janice needed the push to be convinced. Damn, these Parker women had a thing for stubbornness.

"Ah..." she said, raising her eyebrows. Clearly, she grasped the gist of the problem. At last. She leaned over and kissed his cheek. "Then she keeps the job. Thank you, Michael, for caring about my children."

"My pleasure." He took her hand and kissed it. "They're a part of you, and they're important to me." He kissed her palm, letting his tongue caress her soft skin. "I wish I could kiss more of you."

She shuddered. "I wish you could, too."

He had never experienced this kind of restraint, and it galled him. He would cope, he told himself.

He drew her closer in the padded love seat and kissed her hair. It smelled like frangipani and roses. Exotic and innocent. Unique for him. He kissed her temple. He tasted the incredible softness just under her ear. His tongue traced the delicate cords of her neck.

"You make me crazy," Janice whispered, running her fingers across his shoulders.

"I hope so."

He kissed her mouth, a tiny bird's kiss at the corner. She turned her lips to capture his, but he evaded her, content to torment her into wanting him as much as he always wanted her.

Her hands rose, pressing into either side of his face. Her mouth swooped in and caught him in a frenzied kiss. Their tongues dueled and thrust. Their teeth nipped gently. Their lips melded over and over in a promise of more-primitive delights. Michael gasped for breath when the kiss finally ended.

"Damn, woman. Where did you learn to kiss like that?"

"The seventh grade." Janice grinned. "I had a crush

on Billy Walker and I used to practice kissing my pillow every night in case he ever kissed me. He never did.''

"More fool him.''

"I always thought so.'' She shivered. "Oh, God, Michael. I don't know where we're going with this, but I won't make it in one piece.''

He knew where they were going with all this. He saw it rushing up at him faster than lightning.

For once, he wasn't afraid.

Chapter Twelve

Your past love life is your business. Never let a woman tell you otherwise.

—Michael Holiday
Man Can Definitely Live by Bread Alone

Janice and Amy walked Heather over to Michael's house for her first day on the job.

"I do know the way, Mother," Heather said, looking aggrieved in a way only teenagers can.

"Well, I know that," Janice replied, smiling gently. Amy was off in her own world, not listening as she skipped along while holding Janice's hand. "But you're a young girl going into a single man's home every day. I want others to know that I know what you're doing and I approve, so there won't be any gossip about your reputation."

Heather gaped at her. "I didn't think of that."

"I did. That's why I'm the mom."

Her oldest daughter looked heavenward, but she grinned.

Janice laughed and put her free arm around Heather as they walked together. She wondered what had happened at the mall, although she gathered that something had been averted by Michael. She wished she knew, but right now it was better to respect both him and Heather. If it were dire, she was positive she would have been told by both.

Trust. She was giving a lot of it to Michael Holiday.

He opened the front door after Heather rang the bell. He looked sensible and sexy as hell in a T-shirt and seersucker shorts. He had done things for her children that she never would have expected or even considered him to be capable of doing.

"Wow! Three beautiful women on my doorstep. How lucky can a man get?"

"Very lucky in your case," Janice said. "But I'm not staying. Amy and I just strolled around to say hello."

"Hello," Amy chirped.

"Come in for a few minutes and see what I'm having Heather do." He stretched to open the screen door. "And have something to drink. I have coffee, and juice for Amy and Heather."

"Okay," Amy said, moving through the doorway like a shot.

"David said he nearly beat you this morning," Janice commented, as she entered after Heather. David and Michael had played nine holes at the local club.

"I was rusty," Michael replied.

Janice laughed and patted his ribs affectionately. He was lean and hard. She wanted to touch him all over, yet she knew she couldn't. Restraint after opening the floodgates was a bitch.

Michael grimaced and led the way to the kitchen. "Okay, so the kid is good. Very good. I honestly thought all he knew was video games and marching band."

"I told you he wasn't a glassy-eyed, glued-to-the-TV kid."

"Are you one of those I-told-you-so people?" Michael asked.

"With bells on," Janice said.

"She's terrible," Heather added, making a face.

"I figure it's a privilege I've earned when you guys don't listen to me."

"We'll have to cure her of that," Michael said to Heather.

"All right!"

A pile of mail sat on the kitchen table. While Michael got their juice and coffee, Janice couldn't help glancing at a partly unrolled full-color poster.

"That's a promo piece my publisher's doing for *Man Can Definitely Live by Bread Alone*," he said, after he brought over the drinks. "I got it in today's mail. They're planning a half-million-dollar advertising campaign for TV, radio and the print media. Everything, really. I couldn't ask for better. Go ahead. Take a look."

She unrolled the poster all the way. In it Michael stood against a backdrop of shooting stars. He wore a tuxedo, à la James Bond, and had a gorgeous model dressed in spandex dripping off each arm. The legend read: "Come and feast on Michael Holiday's blockbuster, *Man Can Definitely Live by Bread Alone*. Mana never tasted so good!"

"That's *all that!*" Heather said, looking over Janice's shoulder and giving her approval in teenage jargon.

"Boy, they're pretty, Michael," Amy said.

"But not as pretty as your mom," Michael answered. To Janice, he said, "This was taken back in March, long before I knew you."

Janice swallowed her jealousy and insecurities. "It's a great campaign to sell the book."

Michael sighed noticeably in relief. "Thank God you understand."

She was trying to, she thought. But Michael's life-style philosophy, forgotten as he had wrapped himself around her heart, now rushed up to bite her in the behind. She felt more like the monster had bitten off half her butt while she'd been sitting down. Objectively, she could see how the poster's theme would be a draw—especially for its target audience of men. It looked fun and funny, very tongue-in-cheek. Janice wished she could feel objective. Instead she wanted to rip up the poster, fling it in his face and give him a lecture on its macho-pig attitude toward women. And then she wanted to take him apart inch by inch on a more personal level.

She forced herself to smile. "You should sell a ton of books."

He grinned. "One hopes. Let me show you what I want Heather to do."

He showed them the wallpaper and paint he'd selected to finish the kitchen walls, now that the cabinets were in place. It was all very domestic and totally at odds with the poster image. Janice tried to listen to him, but her mind and gaze kept straying to the damnable advertisement. She wished it would vanish with the blink of her eye, yet she refused to reach out and move it, or herself, out of range.

She looked at Michael, who was grinning and chatting happily with Amy and Heather. How could she expect a man like him, who had lived the confirmed-bachelor's life, to truly want something permanent with the mother of six growing children? She couldn't. Not really. Somehow she had become a temptation, forbidden territory, alluring as an ultimate conquest. Yet he had already conquered—he must know that. So the axe would fall at any time.

She gazed at the floor, all her insecurities closing in on her. But awareness of Michael pulled her gaze toward him. His shorts bared his legs, which were well muscled and

tanned. Short, curling hair lightly dusted his corded forearms. His smile was infectious as he talked with her daughters, and his eyes held a warmth that couldn't be faked.

Janice pushed aside her anxieties with a firm, mental
Stop it. Michael had said it best himself: he would have
run long ago if he was going to.

She still felt a thread of doubt when they started on their
date later that evening. Pushing qualms away was one
thing. *Keeping* them away was another.

"How was Heather's first day on the job?" she asked,
when they were finally alone in his car and on their way
to a restaurant.

"Didn't she tell you?" he asked, grinning wryly at her.

"Just that it went okay." Janice chuckled. "The prin-
cess was tired."

"She was a good helper." Michael laughed. "Can I be
a chauvinist?"

"What? You're not one already? My mistake. Okay, go
ahead."

"Heather was fine, really a help...but the wallpaper
paste was 'icky,' although she was game about handling
it. She broke two nails, and I'm not talking about the ones
you pound into wood. Her hair needed brushing every fifteen minutes. She timed it, Janice! It was the most amazing
thing."

Janice started laughing.

"And we had to renew our lip gloss every half hour,"
Michael continued, clearly immersing himself in the day.
"We talked boys, mostly Jason. Mixed in was some guy
from TV I never heard of named Andrew Keegan. Oh, and
Brad Pitt was debated, as well as whether Keanu Reeves
was really cute or was that just in *Speed*."

Tears of mirth leaked out of Janice's eyes as she envisioned Michael trapped with Heather for hours, her daughter loosened up conversationally and in full swing.

"I passed on a final answer about Keanu, having the need to uphold my macho image. By the way, I do feel on a first-name basis with the boy."

"Welcome to the world of teenage girls." Still laughing, Janice wiped her eyes.

"Is that what it was? I thought God was getting back at me for a past sin."

"What the heck do you think teenage girls are?"

He chuckled. "Okay, so what do I talk about tomorrow? And the rest of the summer?"

"Michael, I still haven't figured out the answer to those questions, although I am well versed now about cute boys. One of my best moments came when Jason, who's the school's cutest boy, or so I'm told, was my guide during last spring's Career Day. That he and I actually talked made me a hit with Heather and her friends. Oh! I believe the expression is that I was 'all that.'"

"I'm jealous." He reached over and took her hand, raising it to his lips and kissing her fingers. Janice shivered deliciously at the warmth of his skin. "So you're telling me that I have to talk to this guy, too, to be 'all that'?"

"Your reputation as a macho man will be in shreds. Truthfully, there's no hope for you."

"That's what I concluded in the column I wrote right after Heather left."

Janice stiffened. "You wrote a column about Heather? Can I see it?"

He squeezed her hand. "Relax. It was about teenage girls in general, although Heather inspired it. The thing took about twenty minutes, and the writing flowed. I wish that happened all the time."

Janice had wondered before whether her children would

give him column fodder, but to know they had twice now bothered her. "How bad is it? I'd really like to see it."

"The trust you place in me is inspiring."

"My second fear."

He grinned. "Writers hate for anyone to read their words until they're in print and not a damn thing can be done about it. Don't worry, honey. She would never recognize herself. *You* won't recognize it's her. I think I'm discovering a whole new world."

That ought to make her feel better, Janice decided. Somehow, it didn't. She wanted to question him more about his motives, about his relationship with beauties like those in the poster. She felt so damned pedestrian compared to the women he'd dated before.

How much of the poster was publicity campaign?

How much of it was really him?

Her biggest, deepest fear had always been that he *was* the man in the poster.

"I keep talking about my kids," she said, knowing she was a broken record on the subject. This car ride to dinner was a prime example. Maybe if she took herself in hand, she wouldn't feel so insecure around him. "They demand so much of my time that I'm not up on anything else anymore."

"I like talking about your kids. I told you, it's opening up a whole new world for me."

"Boy, you need help."

"Probably. Speaking of your kids, how are the triples? They haven't been traipsing through my lily bed lately. Can I take that as a sign that they are beginning to speak well of me?"

She sighed. So much for changing the subject. "They haven't said anything, which could be good or could mean they're plotting your demise."

"Why do I think I'm in trouble?"

"You might be... What's the last book you read?"

He glanced at her and smiled. "Are we being adult now?"

"Yes."

"Oh, boo. Okay, even though I wanted to plot triple counterstrategy... Last book...the latest Patricia Cornwall mystery. Maybe that will help with the triples. What about you?"

"Ah..." She thought back. "Oh, joy. I can't remember, it was so long ago. I believe I have been unmasked."

"*You* brought up the subject."

"Yeah...well. Oh, I remember." She groaned and covered her face, then said, "*Surviving your Kids and Other Natural Disasters.*"

Michael laughed. "We're back to kids again."

"And I'm totally boring you again. Sorry."

"Don't be. I like it."

They pulled into the restaurant parking lot. As Michael parked the car, Janice wondered just how long it would be before Michael stopped liking their stalled conversations.

Not long, she thought.

Yet he did seem to enjoy her company, talking about her kids and all. Maybe she was allowing what had happened with her husband to overshadow the current situation. Michael's actions were a whole lot better than Michael's image, thus far. Tom had been the opposite.

She decided she needed to relax. Just relax.

"COME OVER FOR COFFEE."

"I shouldn't."

Michael smiled. Janice's voice over the telephone receiver sounded reluctant yet wistful. "Sweetheart, we've barely had time to ourselves. A couple of dates, and I take you home directly afterward and kiss you at the door. Your father would be relieved at my manners, but I'm not. Please come over after you put Amy and the triples to bed. Surely Heather and David won't mind.''

"Heather and David think you're a god."

He grinned. "Well, then. Come over and let's be alone for a while. Please."

"Who said Peter Pan was dead?" she asked. "You're like a boy who's never grown up."

"Not me."

She sighed. "I shouldn't, but I will."

"That's what I like, enthusiasm. It strokes the libido to new heights."

"If you're not careful, I'll start writing columns on the shortcomings of men." Suddenly, she gasped. "Michael, dammit! My leg is not a climbing tree. I swear I'm having you declawed tomorrow."

"Promises, promises," he drawled. "But it's nice to know my namesake is well and rowdy and in the house."

"I may put both of you out on your ears."

"Just hurry over."

She didn't arrive until well after nine. Michael kissed her soundly, loving the feel of having her in his arms, to himself. She clung to him and kissed him back, her response all that he wanted.

When he raised his head, she said, "Coffee never tasted so good."

"Next to you," he murmured, into her hair. "I'm so glad you came."

"Me, too. I never thought Amy would go to bed. She really fought it tonight."

He chuckled. "And here I thought she was my best girl."

"Hey, be grateful the triplets went down at eight like

lambs. They're no-sleep marathoners when they get started.''

"The gods are with me." The length of her body pressing fully against him gave him ideas that had nothing to do with kids and gods. "You feel so good, Janice. I could stand here forever like this."

Her arms tightened about him. "So could I. I think I have skin hunger. I just need to be touched."

He rubbed his palms along her back, marveling at the feminine strength and fragility. "I need to touch you."

She kissed his jaw. "The things you do to me. I've lost all common sense, I think."

"Common sense is overrated. Besides, you've had way too much of it. You need to be Janice again."

"You make me feel like Janice again."

"Good." He needed to hear her say that. He needed her. Now. All the time.

As if she sensed it, she whispered, "I don't need coffee, Michael. I need you."

He kissed her once more, pouring all of his passion into it, wanting her to feel and taste his desire for her. Their tongues dueled and teased and promised.

Michael took her upstairs to his bedroom. He had seen her for the first time from this room, and fate had changed his life forever. He removed her clothes, revealing the always surprisingly strong body she nurtured. Thin, silvery lines, barely visible, stretched along her belly. Several redder ones spoke of her last child's birth. When she would have covered the lines, as she always tried to do, he brushed her hands aside and kissed them. The marks were a part of what made her who she was and he loved them. He loved her.

No "thinking" he did. No hedging. No avoidance.

He let his body say the words intimately...with every

kiss, every caress, every thrust. With his protection. When she cried out her pleasure, he heard her words of love. When he spilled himself into her, he said them in return. Love surrounded them both, and they gave themselves up to the soft, velvet darkness.

Together.

"SO WHAT DO YOU THINK of Congress's debate on government reform?"

Michael gazed at Janice's earnest face. "Where the heck did that come from? Especially now?"

Government reform wasn't on his postlovemaking discussion agenda. It wasn't on anybody's.

"I read it in the paper today. So what do you think?"

"I think you've gone nuts, honey." He kissed her. "Who cares about government reform?"

"Michael, I'm trying to be up on current events. What about the Russian elections?"

"All I know is someone won," he said, raising his head. "Can we talk about something more relevant? Like whether there's enough juice left in my fridge for later."

She sighed. "I told you. I'm broadening my horizons, to be less unimaginative."

"Oh, I get it." He chuckled and shook his head. "I told you, I like talking about the kids. And the juice."

She rolled her gaze heavenward.

"I know what we should talk about," he said, pulling her closer to him, needing to feel her naked body against his. "We've been avoiding it altogether for a while now. Let's talk about love."

She stilled.

Hurt shot through him like a knife to the gut. "You said you love me. Or was it just the sex talking?"

"I do," she said. "I love you, and I want to believe it will last. But I'm afraid."

"I'm afraid, too," he admitted. "My mother and my grandmother taught me some hard lessons. I felt betrayed by women I trusted the most to love me. I've seen your loyalty to your kids. Your *steadfastness*. It's an old word, but it fits. I want the love more than I want to follow my doubts. I find myself trusting without thought, and I find myself feeding off your doubts in a positive way."

"I know." She kissed his cheek in almost sisterly fashion. "I thought I had the most steadfast man, but I turned out to be a baby machine. Three planned children turned by chance into six. I was so busy with the kids, I didn't notice him slipping away. I was hurt by his initial unhappiness over Amy, and I think I punished him for that. He couldn't handle what life threw at him and he betrayed my trust.

"Now a man who professes, even encourages, running from commitment has somehow gotten my heart. I want to believe he's changed. I'm trusting he's trusting me. But it's hard not to be scared."

He held her tightly for the longest time. Finally, he chuckled wryly. "We're a couple of 'fraidy cats—maybe with good reason because of our pasts. Now we have to trust the future."

"Are you sure I'm what you want for the future?" she asked. "A woman with six children, three who give you grief? A woman whose main conversation is who didn't eat their peas and what will happen if one misbehaves again? A woman who has about thirty seconds a day to give to a man? A woman who's probably going to be too tired for sex three-hundred-sixty-four days of the year?"

"Okay, so you're no Cindy Crawford. I'll tell you what I see. I see a woman who's raising six kids alone and making it against all the odds. I see a woman who has infinite love to give and who gives it freely, even to a kitten, despite the demands on her time. I see a woman who puts others first yet finds time for herself. I see a beautiful woman who nurtures love and makes it grow, and I want her for myself.''

"Oh, Michael," she whispered, kissing him.

She touched him everywhere, igniting his need once more and to new heights. The telephone rang, interrupting them before he could reciprocate in kind.

Michael cursed and rolled over. His heart pounded, half from their lovemaking and half from being startled by the sudden noise of the telephone. He grabbed up the receiver. "Hello!"

Silence hung for a moment on the other end. "Is my mom still there?"

"Yes." *It's Heather,* he mouthed to Janice. He turned before she could reach for the phone. "Is anything wrong at the house there?"

"No. It's just that it's late, and David and I thought she'd be back by now."

"I kept her out after curfew, I know."

Heather giggled. So did Janice.

"I'm glad everything's okay at home. I'll send your mom back in a few minutes, all right?"

"Okay. And David wants to know if you guys are still golfing together tomorrow morning."

Michael groaned. The kid was another Tiger Woods, a teenage golf prodigy. "Yes. And tell him I'm not spotting him two strokes per hole again. He's killing me with that."

When he hung up, Janice said, "I think my daughter's worse than my mother ever was about the opposite sex."

"She's a watchdog," he agreed, then caressed Janice's derriere. "With good reason."

Janice sighed. "Much as I'd like to put gray hairs on Heather's head, I have to go. I knew I'd stayed too long. See what I mean about thirty seconds?"

"I'll take them," he told her.

And he would. He knew their future was fraught with land mines, but he couldn't walk away. He loved her.

She would have to leave him first.

Janice's phone. She ended it then to confirm the time of
the flight home. They hadn't enough money to stay too long.
Suzanne's managerial instincts surfaced.
"We have to be efficient."
"Gary made arrangements this morning to return the
land Rover. I told Eric we'd leave it at the airport for
him. Would you do that for me, Suzie?"

Chapter Thirteen

Mistaking love and sex is a big mistake.
— Michael Holiday
Man Can Definitely Live by Bread Alone

"Can I go and watch you and David?"

Janice raised her eyebrows at Cat's request. Michael and
David were about to leave for their golf match.

"Is this a psyche—out play?" Michael asked David.

David chuckled. "I don't need it."

"I wish you wouldn't say that with such confidence,"
Michael complained. "It's unnerving."

David smiled happily. "I know."

"Honest. I want to watch," Cat said. "I promise I'll be
good. I really liked playing that night when you took us."

Cat sounded deadly earnest. Janice didn't know what to
think—or how to advise Michael.

Michael hesitated for a long moment. "You and your
brothers would have to be really good. No running anywhere at all, inside or out. No spitting. No sneaking into
the steam room or the flower beds."

"I don't do any of that stuff," Cat said indignantly, then
paused. "I *won't* do any of that stuff, okay?"

"What about your brothers?" Michael asked dubiously.

Chris and C.J. looked at each other, then back to him. "We don't want to go."

Janice realized the inseparables were separating, growing up.

"So now can I go?" Cat asked again.

"We're happy to have you with us," Michael said. "Tell you what. We'll rent you some kid's clubs, and you can practice while we play."

Cat's eyes turned round as saucers. "Really?"

"Really."

"Sure you know what you're doing?" Janice asked in a low voice when Michael kissed her goodbye.

"No. I'm hoping David will protect me. Be prepared. You may have to come to the rescue."

She grinned. "I don't know. I think you're winning her over."

Cat made a face.

"Maybe."

She sent the three intrepid golfers off to the links with only a slight qualm for Michael. He looked so damn good in that print polo shirt and khaki trousers, the ultimate golfing uniform. Their relationship had deepened over the last few weeks since they had talked about love. Janice finally had hope that the house of cards she expected to collapse at any moment had stronger foundations.

Amy put up a protest when she came out of her room and discovered Cat had gone with the guys. To Janice's surprise, Heather offered to take her sister to the park for the morning, her workday not beginning until Michael returned. Janice had heard that Heather's friend Jen had been caught shoplifting at the mall. Having two and two to put together finally, Janice was grateful to Michael for interfering with Heather...and to Heather for listening to him.

Chris and C.J. decided to go with the girls, and Janice suddenly found herself alone in the house.

The place was silent. Janice strained her ears, but an unopened tomb couldn't have been quieter. Life would be like this for her one day. She wasn't sure she'd like it.

But in the meantime, she intended to enjoy it.

She decided to read the morning paper, despite the work she ought to be doing. The hardware-store monthly reports could wait. So could setting up Lou's contracting-business account. She'd been pleased to get the job from him and hoped the man could work something out with his ex-wife.

Michael the kitten clambered up on her lap after she settled at the kitchen table with the paper and a cup of steaming tea. Janice sighed as the feline, now more adolescent than baby, curled up on her lap and began to purr.

Then she laughed wryly. "Okay, so one kid is still here."

She stroked the cat, which purred even louder, content with the attention. He had survived his first weeks of massive attention from six children without a nervous breakdown. In fact, he was getting a little fat and lazy. She had a feeling the kids were sneaking him extra treats by the handful.

She read through the world report and business sections without a single outside interruption. A miracle. Unfortunately, she couldn't help wondering how Michael was doing with Cat. Janice would have loved to be a bird for a moment and fly over to see how he was surviving.

"I'm so bad," she murmured to the cat, who never flinched.

Her good mood shattered, however, when she unfolded the newspaper's features section. Glaring up at her was the damnable picture she'd seen on Michael's book poster. An in-depth story from one of the international wire services about the book took up two-thirds of the large page. Instinct told Janice—screamed at her—not to read the article.

She did, anyway.

The story emphasized his confirmed bachelorhood. It stressed his dating history, which included a well-known actress/model and a wealthy socialite. He was quoted as saying the book was fun to write and philosophically incorrect, and that he didn't much care that it was. He was living the life he wanted to live—that *all* men could live if they truly want to. Several quotes from the book were printed as teasers for the reading public. Among them:

Be honest with a woman. She'll hate you for it now, but you'll thank yourself for it later.
Never evade your taxes. Always evade a deepening relationship.
Women never want to keep the relationship simple. Make sure you do.
Always protect yourself in a relationship. If you do, you'll pass any paternity suits with flying colors.

Janice remembered that, since the first time she and Michael had been together, he had always done the protecting. She had thought it was a courtly gesture, especially with her past pregnancy record. Now she wondered if he expected entrapment. If he did, what a shining statement about her integrity that was. But the pièce de résistance teaser was:

Love is an overrated emotion. Flirt with it, but never quite succumb.

Janice set down the paper and clenched her jaw. She tried to tell herself that this was only hype—the old Michael, the columnist Michael, not the Michael she loved. Doubts shouted at her. Why would he be golfing with two of her kids and hiring another as his helper? Or was he flirting with love? Not quite serious? Yet if he wanted a shallow relationship, why would he say he loved her?

She lifted the cat from her lap and stood. Restless, she began to pace. It didn't help. Knowing she needed to work off her panic, she set Michael the cat on the chair and went to find her exercise mat. She carried it from her room to the backyard, not caring that the sun was blazing hot and the humidity rivaled a steam bath. She found peace whenever she was outside, alone. Maybe she would be able to set aside the dread growing within her.

Thirty minutes later, she was drenched from head to foot and drained of all energy. Her limbs felt like gelatin. Yet her brain still raced. Although knowing she needed to replenish her liquids, she continued to sit on the mat and just stare at her garden. The plants were green and healthy, the beds free of weeds and the blooms nurtured to fullness.

She had thought Michael's love had held such promise as her garden showed. She had backed away once before from him—hadn't even wanted to get involved with him in the first place. Now she had given her heart, despite all reservations to the contrary. He'd asked her to trust him. She had. All his actions were opposite from this article. The mixed message couldn't be missed.

She should have paid more attention to the fence, she thought. The flowers stopped there, allowed to go only so far. That's what the fence symbolized. Hadn't Michael made it stronger? Hadn't he needed to shut the world out?

She knew the sun beat down on her a long, long time before she heard the swish of feet across the grass.

"You exercised and I missed it. That's my most favorite thing you do. Could you grab your ankles and do that stretch—"

She turned and looked at Michael. His grin faded. "Janice! You're red and pale at the same time. How long have you been out in this soup?"

"I don't know." She looked around, as if just awakening. The movement left her feeling light-headed. Her stomach churned. "Awhile. Almost since you left."

"That was hours ago. Too long. Dammit, woman, you know better." He helped her to her feet, his touch strong and warm. "Let's get you inside and get some fluids into you."

"How was the golf game?" she asked as they walked into the house. Michael carried the mat. "How was Cat?"

"Cat was great, an angel." He smiled wryly. "I wish I could say it was me, but she really wants to learn the game. You better not have given yourself heat exhaustion."

"I haven't." But she might be close to it, Janice thought. Heat exhaustion seemed a fitting punishment for her stupidity. She'd allowed the heat of passion and love to overrule her normally cool head.

In the house, Michael sat her in a kitchen chair. The air-conditioning swept over her skin in a chilly caress. He fixed her a tall glass of orange juice from the refrigerator. Janice drank it, the cold, almost-sour liquid soothing her parched throat. It tasted like satin, she thought, as her body cooled and righted itself. Her head cleared.

"No more Swami of Marshfield imitations," Michael said sternly, staring at her with concern. "From now on, please contemplate your navel here in the house. Or better still, let me do it. I *love* contemplating any part of your body. Hey!" He picked up the features section of the newspaper, which she'd left on the table. Obviously, it had caught his attention. "It's my article. I heard this was coming out soon. They interviewed me for this a few weeks ago."

"Mom, where's Chris and C.J.?" Cat asked, coming into the kitchen just as Michael began to read the article.

"At the park with Heather and Amy. They'll be back shortly." She sipped more juice. Her body felt calm now, waiting for the inevitable. She filled in the time with her daughter. "Mr. Holiday said you guys had fun."

"Yeah, especially when David beat him," Cat said, glancing at Michael and grinning.

"Go ahead. Rub it in, girl," Michael said, not looking up from the paper. "And I used to think I was a scratch golfer."

Cat laughed. "You scratched that tree when you threw your six iron at it."

Michael grinned and tousled her hair. Cat took the gesture of affection with good grace. Janice's heart wrenched in two. How could he say all those things in the article, demeaning love and lasting relationships?

He set down the paper. "From a marketing standpoint, it's great, especially with a ten-city publicity tour coming up...but I'm glad I wasn't here when you read it. I know now why you're upset. I thought you were, under the heatstroke."

"I'm not," she said.

He blinked. Cat turned the paper around to face her and began to read. Janice took it from her daughter.

"Mom!"

"Cat, honey, why don't you go to the park and get the crew? Michael's home, so Heather needs to get back to work."

Cat frowned. Finally she said, "Okay."

After she left, Michael began an explanation of the article. "Most of that was done months ago, before we met. The reporter only asked supplemental questions when she called me. She had the bulk of it from my publisher's publicity department. Of course, she took the most controversial parts of the book, because she's working from a feminist angle. It's a great one for a story, so I can't blame her for using it. I'm a journalist. I understand it. But I'm not happy to be portrayed this way. It's just hype for the book.''

"No," she said.

"Yes, it is—"

"No, Michael. All these things in here reflect how you really feel about a loving relationship with a woman. And that's cynical. Love doesn't exist for you."

"But I love you, Janice. I know it exists with you."

She shook her head. "It doesn't matter. I can't handle this. I can't love with insecurity. I don't know that I'll ever feel secure with you. I'll be waiting forever for you to revert to this." She tapped the newspaper.

"I know my reputation wasn't the best. But I've changed. I told you all that before."

"Maybe you have changed," she conceded. "But with this book, you'll be thrown right back into single life again. You'll go back to your old self. I understand your wariness about women and commitment. It's okay." A sob escaped her throat and she gulped. "It's okay to be what you are, Michael. I love you, but I can't take the risk, not with my children involved."

"I love the kids!" he snapped. "Don't use them to cover your own insecurities. I knew I had to jump through hoops to prove myself to you. I accepted that. I don't blame you for needing to be sure. But how sure can I make you? What the hell else do I have to do? What more do you want from me?"

"Nothing," she whispered.

"I'm not going anywhere, Janice," he said. "Nothing's chased me away yet, and there's been plenty that could. *Plenty.*"

"Please, Michael. Understand."

"Sure," he said. "I'm just trying real hard not to feel betrayed again by someone I loved and trusted."

"I'm not betraying you," she replied, stricken that he would see her words that way.

"You're using something against me that I can't help. That's a little too convenient for my taste. Am I paying for your husband?"

"No." She shook her head again. She wasn't betraying him or making him pay for past hurts. She knew that. Soon, though, he would be grateful to her for breaking up with him. It would save him a lot of trouble in the end. "Maybe we're both confusing sex with love."

He glared at her. She cringed from the terrible expression on his face, as if she had stabbed him in the heart.

"I have to get out of here," he said, "before I say or do something really stupid. Like you just did."

He stormed out, slamming the front door behind him hard enough to rattle all the picture frames in the house.

Janice sat at the kitchen table, feeling like a leaden weight crushed her chest. Her eyes burned. Her throat ached with tears. She'd hurt before, but somehow not like this. Love had shown its promise in what most would have assumed were weeds. And she had pulled it out because it was planted in the wrong place.

Cat came into the kitchen. Obviously the child had seen that fireworks might start and had hung around. "Wow! What was that?"

Janice looked at her nine-year-old. The child was already tough as nails. "I hurt him, Cat. I love him and I hurt him and I'm so sorry that it was the right thing to do. For him."

She laid her head down and cried.

MICHAEL HAD A PLAN.

He needed one, he thought, after the way Janice had dumped him.

The old Michael would have skipped away happily,

grateful to avoid being the heavy in a breakup. The new Michael, however, wasn't giving up so easily. Hurt by what she'd said, he knew his past had come home to haunt him. He knew he'd have to prove himself with her, but she just wasn't seeing that he had.

Above all, however, Janice was scared.

Ironic, he thought. He had spent years running from commitment only to be outrun by someone who epitomized the word with her children. She wanted to protect them from him. Well, he would show her they didn't need protection.

His first step involved Heather.

"Oh, it's so pretty," she said later that morning, while standing back after they'd put the last new baseboards into place in the kitchen.

Michael looked around in satisfaction at the new maple cabinets, the almond state-of-the-art appliances and the contrasting wallpaper. *Home and Gardens* couldn't have done better.

He patted Heather on the shoulder. "Great work. *Great* work."

Heather giggled. "I didn't think we'd make it when the wallpaper kept rolling down on our heads that day."

"A slight setback." He glanced at her. "How's your mom?"

Heather frowned. "Okay. I guess."

That sounded promising. "You don't seem sure. Is she ill? Is anything wrong?"

"No, she's not sick. Just kinda funny. Mopey, like Amy gets sometimes. And me." Heather grinned, looking for one breathtaking moment like Janice's double. Someday she would break hearts—if she wasn't already.

Michael began with a broad hint. "I haven't been to tea with Amy for a while now. I really miss it. Think we could

take a break for the rest of the afternoon, before we start
the next project?''

"Will I get paid?" Heather asked, going right to the
most important thing for her.

Michael chuckled. Heather had more of her sister Cat
in her than he'd realized. "Sure. Now, I haven't talked
with Amy about the tea—"

"I'll tell her," Heather volunteered, right on cue.

As soon as she said the words, Michael realized that
what he was doing was wrong. He was wrong. "I'm sorry.
I've done something I shouldn't. I love Amy, but that's
not why I want to have tea with her. Your mother broke
up with me, and I'm trying to get back in through you
kids. It's not right or fair to use any of you."

"You really like my mom?" Heather asked.

"I love your mom."

Her eyes grew wide. "*Dag*. It's kind of disgusting in a
way, but neat."

"Gee, thanks," Michael muttered.

Heather blushed. "I just meant...you're both so old."

Michael laughed. "Oh, I'm feeling much better with
that."

Heather clamped her hand over her mouth. She lowered
her palm after a moment. "Don't worry, Michael. I'll help
you. It'll be so cool. Why don't you come over with me
now? Amy never turns away a tea party. And if she can't
have one, I'll make up some reason for you to be there.
I'll get you in. You'll see."

"But I'll be using Amy then."

Heather waved a hand in dismissal. "She loves you.
She'd want to help. In fact, she'd bug Mom to death to
see you. David'll help, too. He'll give you video-game
lessons. Since you don't have the software, you'll have to
come to our house. For *hours*."

"Thanks," he said, grateful that she accepted him and

thought her siblings would, too. Well, most of them. The triples were noticeably absent from the strategizing. But he'd work on that.

Amy came through like a champ. She ran for her Pooh Bear and tea things, setting up the party on the patio in record time.

While she did, Michael stared at Janice, drinking in the sight of her. Her profile had never looked more beautiful, her neck more kissable, her shoulders more caressable.

She never looked up from her computer, however.

"How are you?" he asked finally.

"Fine," she said, gazing at her monitor.

"You notice I'm not going away."

She said nothing.

He walked up behind her. Her perfume drifted across his senses. Her hair reminded him of chocolate silk bound in a shining hank. His fingers wanted to touch it. He reached out and took her heavy ponytail in his palm. The individual strands clung to his hand as he stroked it.

"Don't run away from me," he said.

She said nothing.

"I'm ready!" Amy called, popping in the doorway.

Michael sighed and let go of Janice's hair.

"We'll talk later," he promised.

Janice hit a few keys, then shut down her computer.

"I have to go food shopping," she announced, and left the room.

Michael gaped, having had the rug pulled out from under him.

Amy's charm never wavered during the ensuing tea. Even Pooh Bear's personality grew. But the magic wasn't quite there for Michael. His mind was on the woman at the food store.

He refused to be daunted by his first defeat.

David came through for him next.

"Hey, come in for another video-game lesson," he invited, after a golf outing. The kid grinned knowingly. "Mom's home."

Michael smiled. "I owe you."

"Nah. I'm winning at golf. That's enough."

"You Parkers love to rub it in, don't you?"

"Yep."

Again, Michael invaded Janice's sanctuary. Again, Janice found an excuse to escape. Michael played video games for over an hour, but her trip to the milk store was clearly turning into a marathon. He got her message. She wouldn't restrict him from spending time with her children, but she wouldn't change her mind, either.

Michael finally set the controller down. "Forget it, David. Nice try, but she obviously wants nothing to do with me anymore. Eventually, I've got to get that message into my brain. In fact, I think I've already gotten it."

"Hey! Don't give up," David said.

"Sometimes you have to pay for past mistakes, no matter how many times you say you're sorry and you're putting it right." Michael sighed. "Maybe this is my payment. I love someone who's afraid to love me."

"She cried."

Michael turned to find Cat standing in the doorway of the television room.

"She cried?" Michael echoed.

Cat nodded. She came into the room. The child normally had a hard-edged wariness to her. Now she looked unsure and vulnerable. "Mom cried and said she hurt you and she was sorry." Cat paused. "And that she loved you."

Michael nearly fell off the ottoman. Not that the confession surprised him—every instinct told him Janice did love him—but who had relayed the confession did. Cat.

"See?" David said with satisfaction. He added sensibly, "You can't give up now, Michael."

"Damn right I can't." Michael wanted to hug Cat, but sensed she wasn't ready to get that close. He held out his hand for her to shake. "Thank you, Cat. You have no idea how much I needed to hear the words."

She took his hand gingerly, and as they shook, Michael felt like he was forging a little bond with her. After he let go, she asked, "So will you take me golfing again?"

Her ulterior motive for helping him was a self-centered one. He'd take it. "How about now?" He would do anything to get through to this child. "I might actually beat David this time."

"Yeah. He might," David said. "We'll leave a note for Mom so she knows where we are. It'll tick her off that we're having fun with Michael."

Cat grinned. "Sounds good to me."

Out of the mouths of babes.

Unfortunately, over the next few days Janice managed to evade all the "babes'" efforts on his behalf to get them together.

Undaunted, the kids finally sent out the sure thing.

Michael was in the midst of deadheading the spent blooms of a black-eyed Susan when he noticed a monarch butterfly being stalked in his backyard by a suspiciously familiar looking feline.

Michael the cat was "lost" again.

"Michael? Michael!"

The soft, yet urgent call came from one pair of kissable lips. Michael the human stepped behind a bush and waited. Sure enough, Janice tiptoed into view, her need to find the cat overriding any reluctance she might have in entering the yard. *God love trespassers,* he thought. He himself did.

She looked gorgeous to his eyes, her body as slender and mesmerizing as ever. Even her frown didn't mar her serene features. She always surprised him. She always tantalized him. He ached for her as he had every night.

The cat meowed when he saw her and ran over, the butterfly having flown out of its reach.

"Can't you find another place to run away to?" she said in a low voice, while scooping the animal up in her arms.

"No, he can't," Michael said, stepping out into the open.

Janice shrieked and whirled around, clutching the cat to her breast. It squirmed, clawing at her hands, and she dropped the creature. "Dammit, Michael!"

"Which one?" he asked.

"Both of you. You scared me."

"Good. Maybe you'll come to your senses about us."

She slumped. "Michael, please. Let it go. It's best for us."

If she had held her ground with coldness, he might have felt justified in badgering her to defeat. But her emotional surrender entered his heart like a knife.

He came over to her and took her in his arms. She cried against his chest, wetting his shirt.

"What can I do to prove to you that I'm here to stay?" he asked against her hair.

"Nothing," she said, between tears. She sniffed, then looked up at him. "You've got a book to publicize, a book that holds all the philosophy you've believed all your life about relationships. You've protected yourself emotionally. I understand. God, I wish I didn't, but I do. You're flirting with love right now, even if you don't see it yourself. I just can't be here when you come to your senses."

He kissed her. She tried to resist, but he demanded the response she was capable of giving. Her mouth softened and twisted in unison with his. Her tongue mated with such exquisiteness that he thought he would die of it. He would wither from its lack.

When the kiss finally ended, Janice picked up the cat.

"What can I do?" he asked, feeling helpless.

"Nothing," she whispered. "I can't take the chance."

She left him in the garden. Never had he felt more betrayed. And yet, he had ultimately been betrayed by himself.

A breeze ruffled the blooms of the little impatiens, the moonbeam coreopsis, the tall coneflowers. It drifted across his face, refreshing his senses.

Bringing him a promise.

JANICE LISTLESSLY PUSHED the sponge along the counter. Crumbs from breakfast toast dropped to the floor. She looked at them, then shrugged. She didn't care. She didn't care about anything.

No, that was wrong, she thought. She cared about her children. She wasn't hiding behind them, despite Michael's accusation. How could she not see that he would leave her? All his own words pointed to that. He just hadn't woken up to it yet. He would. That was a surety. How could he not, after all the things he wrote about women and love? Seeds might sprout, even grow a little, but eventually love would die within him. He had been too hurt in his long-ago past. She couldn't fight that.

"Hey, Mom!" David called from the television room. "Michael's on TV!"

Janice straightened, every fiber of her body urging her to run and see him. She willed herself to stay put. "That's nice."

"Don't you want to see him?"

"No," she lied.

"But Mommy! It's Michael!" Amy wailed.

"He looks sick!" Heather called out.

Sick reverberated through her like a golf ball flying through the air on its way to a hole in one. She raced into the television room. All the kids gathered around the TV, watching the screen.

Michael sat with the host of a popular show, on a cozy armchair-interview set that millions of people around the world knew well. Michael was in the process of answering one of Matt's initial questions. He didn't smile. His eyes looked ringed, and his face was pale. Was he sick? The thought crawled through her, making her feel ill that she wasn't with him, to care for him.

"They probably didn't put makeup on him," Janice said, hoping she was right.

"Makeup!" the triplets exclaimed in disdainful unison.

"They have to put makeup on, dingdongs," Heather said, snorting in disgust at their ignorance. "Otherwise they look sick on TV."

"Jean-Claude Van Damme doesn't wear makeup," Cat said. "And I'm not a dingdong."

Heather and David laughed. "Yes, he does. Everyone does, right, Mom?"

"Right, and now I'm wondering why you called me in here if you already knew that." Janice glared at her daughter.

"Oh, ah…" Heather fumbled.

"He's talking about us!" David said, turning up the sound.

"…They live behind me. Six kids," Michael said, a smile lighting his face.

Janice could feel heat suffuse hers. Whether her cheeks burned from anger or panic, she didn't know. But she couldn't leave now. She *had* to watch, to hear what he would say about her and her family.

The host laughed. "Six children! How does a confirmed bachelor like you move into a house that has six children living across the backyard? Isn't that the antithesis of what your life should be?"

"Actually, it isn't." Michael leaned forward in the chair. "It was the best thing that ever happened to me.

Man Can Definitely Live by Bread Alone is a compilation of stupid opinions by an ignorant man, written over the course of an idiotic decade. I truly didn't understand what love was then. I avoided it. I thought it would hurt me. Then I moved in behind a woman with six kids. I never knew before the joy of playing with a four-year-old, of watching the blossoming of a beautiful young woman, of seeing the promise of a fine young man. I've even learned there are ways to survive adolescence. At least I hope I survive the triplets. But I like them, too. They've given me back the childhood magic I'd thought I'd lost years ago. All of it was unexpected to me. But above all, I love their mother.''

Janice's heart leapt, then pounded so hard that the world dimmed for a moment, until all she was aware of was Michael's voice.

"She's a wonderful, gracious, beautiful, giving woman...." Michael paused, then added, "I love her, only I've scared her away with this book and what it portrays of me. If I had it to do all over again, I would toss the manuscript in the trash. It's worthless and useless, a fraud now, frankly—"

A yelp erupted offstage, followed by a crash. Both Michael and the host turned to look.

"That's probably my publisher's publicist fainting dead away with shock," Michael said, shrugging his shoulders. "I'm sorry about that."

"But this woman with the children..." the host urged, clearly knowing he had a tiger by the tail.

"I don't know what to do to show her I've changed," Michael replied. "That the man who wrote this book was dumb and dumber, and now he understands. I've tried. God knows, I've tried, but I don't know what to do to convince her I'm not the man in this book. I just want to love her. And the kids. For the rest of my life."

"Oh, God," Janice moaned, shocked and shaken by his so-very-public confession. "Oh, God."

Her knees buckled and she collapsed onto the arm of the big, stuffed plaid chair. Michael was still talking. Somehow her brain registered and yet didn't register what he said. *He loved her.* She had done a terrible thing to him, and yet he still loved her.

The kids stared at her, mute. Accusing.

The telephone rang.

Heather, being a teenager, responded like one of Pavlov's dogs and raced for the phone. They could hear her voice from the other room.

"Hello? Yes! Yes, that's us, Mr. Harper... Well, they were kind of dating...."

"Mommy," Amy said, getting Janice's attention. She sliced to the heart of the matter. "Michael loves us."

Janice found her voice. "Yes. Yes, he does. I was scared that he didn't at first, and that he might stop loving us, but I think that's not true. I think if he can tell the world he loves us, then we should believe him. I was wrong not to have more faith." An idea occurred to her. "I have something to do."

She stood and walked out of the room.

"Where you going, Mom?" Chris asked, the first of the kids to catch up with her. The others followed behind him.

"I've got to show Michael I love him." She stopped and looked at all the kids. "Heather, hang up the telephone." When she had all their attention, she said, "Kids, I love Michael and he loves me. I want to bring him into the family, if he'll have us, but you six have to want it, too. Do you?"

Amy flung her arms around Janice's legs, shrieking, "Oh, yes! He would be my daddy, then."

Heather grinned. "This is so neat."

David said, "Hey, I'll get free golf all the time if he lives with us. I won't say no. Besides, I like him."

"He's okay," Chris and C.J. replied, a big concession for them.

"I suppose he's all right," Cat conceded, in an even-bigger concession for her.

Janice breathed a sigh of relief and smiled at her children. "Okay, guys, let's go take down a fence and refuse to take no for an answer."

MICHAEL PULLED UP in the driveway and sighed. *Home sweet home,* he thought, deciding publicity tours were overrated—especially when they were abruptly cancelled by a furious publisher. He expected the breach-of-contract lawsuit subpoena would be served any day now.

He got out of the car and slammed the door. Three look-alike kids descended on him from out of nowhere.

"He's home!" they yelled, running around him and yanking on his arms. It was the first time they had touched him without a show of reluctance. "We didn't know when you were coming home! Hurry, hurry!"

The triples reminded him sharply of his first encounter with them. Only this time they seemed a whole lot friendlier. He didn't automatically count that as a plus.

"Where am I going?" he asked, although he allowed himself to be dragged along by Cat, Chris and C.J.

"In the backyard," they said in unison. "Wait 'til you see what Mom did."

Concern rose up inside him. "Is she all right?"

They giggled. "Come on!"

He rounded the back corner of his house and stopped in his tracks. He gaped. His fence was down. The normal view of high, flat-topped slats had vanished. He could see straight through to Janice's garden. Even her back patio was visible in the background. Her plants and shrubs looked as if they mingled with his own already. In fact, they all had an oddly beautiful symmetry and contrast, as if they belonged together. As if they always had.

His heart pounded with hope and caution.

"Mom!" the triples shouted. *"Mom!"*

"What the heck happened to my fence?" Michael asked, finally moving again.

The kids laughed maniacally.

He found that a narrow path had been carved through the two gardens, not quite straight but not overly crooked, either. The back door to Janice's house opened and Amy came flying out into the yard. She raced across the grass and plowed right into him, almost knocking him down.

"Hurrah!" She held his legs in an iron grip. Raising her head, she said fiercely, "Just say yes."

"To what?" Michael asked, lifting her and kissing her on the cheek.

"I'm not allowed to say," Amy told him. She shook a finger in his face. "Say yes. Okay?"

"Okay."

Amy screamed. "He said yes!"

"Amy!"

Janice's reprimanding tone was not lost on the little girl. She put her arm around Michael's neck and said, "I only told him to say yes and he did. I didn't say nothin' more. Honest, Mommy."

Michael shook hands with David and patted Heather's shoulder. Both teenagers practically glowed with anticipation. Michael refused to get his hopes up.

He finally turned to Janice, who smiled almost shyly, it seemed to him. He wanted to kiss her. He wondered if she knew about his disastrous interview on national television. He wondered what she was thinking.

"What happened to my fence?" he asked. "And what am I saying yes to? A new one?"

"No." Janice cleared her throat loudly. "I have been a fool. I was the one scared of love. I didn't trust you, no matter how much you showed me I should. I was the ignorant one, Michael, not you. I don't blame you if you never want to see me again—"

"Mom!" The kids sounded like a Greek chorus with its latest-and-greatest doom hit.

"—But in case you don't...will you marry us?"

Michael grinned past the lump in his throat and the relief in his heart. "Janice. Damn, but you make me crazy."

"I hope so."

"Come here."

She did, wading her way through her children. He kissed her.

"That means yes," Heather announced, clapping her hands.

"I told you!" Amy shouted smugly, practically in Michael's ear.

The kids hugged them, nearly knocking them over.

He didn't care. He kissed Janice with all the love he could muster. Suddenly, he understood about his fence. No more barriers would keep them apart.

She had made the ultimate commitment in life: to nurture love.

And so had he.

Epilogue

Men. Women have to love them. No one else will.
> —Janice Parker-Holiday
> Men Need Bread Every Day

They held the wedding in the back garden in late August.

Michael said "I do" among the candytufts and hollyhocks, the tall feather grasses and the speedwell, the daisies and, of course, the moonflowers. Gardens were for lovers, lifelong lovers. Where else would he be married?

After he happily sealed his fate, he kissed his bride. Janice had never looked more beautiful, with her dark hair brushing her shoulders and her doe eyes sparkling with happiness. Her simple, cream silk gown skimmed her slender figure. He knew he would remember her this way for the rest of his life. He tasted the promise on her lips. He would honor that promise. He would always honor her.

The kids, who served as special bridesmaids and groomsmen, all hooted their approval, while the guests clapped.

Michael finally released Janice and grinned at everyone. People stood and cheered, obviously enjoying his surrender to love. He'd surrender anytime when it came to Janice.

"I love you," he whispered, as they walked up the aisle, husband and wife.

"I love you, too," she whispered back, squeezing his hand tightly.

The kids trailed behind.

Cousins Jared and Raymond Holiday looked at each other in chagrin as the wedding party passed by their seats. Even without the same last name, their features would have marked them as relatives of the groom.

"First Peter, now Michael," Jared said, shaking his head over the capture of Peter Holiday by Mary Ellen Magnussen earlier this year and then Michael's marriage. "Look at them." As he nodded in their direction the couple kissed tenderly. "He's caught."

"I never thought either of our cousins would fall from bachelor grace," Raymond agreed. "Michael especially. He always seemed to have things so together about love and women. I hope he did a prenup at least."

"No," Jared said. "I asked him about it, but he refused. He said he was sharing everything with Janice."

"He's crazy!" Raymond exclaimed. "His book is actually climbing the bestseller charts."

Jared chuckled. "That was a stroke of genius on his part, even if he didn't know it. People buy it to get a great laugh. I understand another publisher is talking to Janice about a book on how to live with men."

"Maybe Janice ought to get a prenuptial agreement from Michael." Raymond shuddered. "All this is not for me, man. I'll stick with flirting over the radio airwaves, thank you very much. But no woman in my life. Like I said before, love's overrated."

"*Way* overrated." Jared pursed his lips. "I've seen too much about the disasters of love at first sight in my practice. No thanks. If I ever marry, and I doubt it, it will be to someone whom I've thoroughly researched and I know will be a good mate for life. If love happens, that's fine. If not, I've got a lasting marriage.''

''Hell, I don't even want that....''

Life would be totally different, Michael thought as they set up the kids in the receiving line. They were excited and fidgety, but no whistles were needed to bring them into line. He and Janice weren't sure what to do with the houses yet and had decided not to worry about it all. They could keep one as a sanctuary, he supposed. They'd probably need it.

He had had no desire for children of his own, probably a holdover from his own youth and feeling of abandonment. That was okay, because he had six now. He wasn't looking for more, truthfully. To Janice's relief, he thought in amusement, glancing over at his bride.

''Are you sure you don't want a honeymoon?'' she asked.

''When do we have time?'' he countered. ''School starts next week, and David's got band practice two days a week, with golf on the other days, since he made the school team. Heather's joined field hockey, so she's got practice, too, and the triples have three soccer games in the next nine days alone. Let's not forget the biggest event of all—Amy starts kindergarten. We can't be away for that. It's a huge step. Isn't it, Amy girl?''

''Yep!'' Amy said proudly.

''I'll make it up to you,'' Janice promised.

Michael kissed her. ''I'll hold you to it.''

A woman stood next to some tall pampas grass in the back part of the joined gardens. She wore a white, flowing gown and a wreath of flowers in her graying hair. Her eyes held the wisdom and patience of the ages. Serenity graced her beautiful, mature, yet young face. She wasn't worried that anyone would see her eavesdropping on the moment.

People never saw Mother Nature herself, only the grandeur she brought forth.

She had taken this second job and nurtured the married couple to this moment. She had cradled the newborn love the two had begun, chased it back in the proper direction as it hared off and let it go finally when it matured. Like the garden she stood in, love needed endless diligence to reach its fullest bloom. Now it had for Michael and Janice. They would spend the rest of their lives together.

Mother Nature glanced at Peter Holiday and his new wife. Cupid, that little devil, had done well. The two other Holiday men... *Not too long now for them*, she thought. The seeds had been germinated, although their growth would go to others to nurture in their own ways.

Satisfied with her work, she turned away from the wedding. As Mother Nature walked through the garden, she touched the moonflowers.

Suddenly, in the middle of the afternoon, their buds opened in full bloom.

HARLEQUIN

Temptation.

and

HARLEQUIN

I N T R I G U E®

Double Dare ya!

Identical twin authors Patricia Ryan and Pamela Burford bring you a dynamic duo of books that just happen to feature identical twins.

Meet Emma, the shy one, and her diva double, Zara. Be prepared for twice the pleasure and twice the excitement as they give two unsuspecting men trouble times two!

In April, the scorching **Harlequin Temptation** novel #631 **Twice the Spice** by Patricia Ryan

In May, the suspenseful **Harlequin Intrigue** novel #420 **Twice Burned** by Pamela Burford

Pick up both—if you dare....

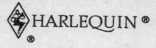

HARLEQUIN®

HARLEQUIN ULTIMATE GUIDES™

HAVE A LOVE AFFAIR WITH YOUR KITCHEN... ALL OVER AGAIN!

Get great tips from great chefs! Find out how to:
- get the best produce
- create the most enticing meals
- cut preparation time
- set a table guaranteed to make 'em go WOW!
- turn culinary disasters into triumphant cuisine

Want to be the star of every meal? Then you'll have to find out

What Great Chefs Know That You Don't

Available in June, at your favorite Harlequin/Silhouette retail outlet.

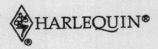

HARLEQUIN®

On the plus side, you've raised a
wonderful, strong-willed daughter.
On the minus side, she's using that
determination to find

A Match For
MOM

Three very different stories of mothers,
daughters and heroes...from three of your
all-time favorite authors:

GUILTY
by Anne Mather

A MAN FOR MOM
by Linda Randall Wisdom

THE FIX-IT MAN
by Vicki Lewis Thompson

Available this May wherever
Harlequin and Silhouette books are sold.

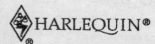
HARLEQUIN®
®

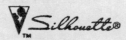
Silhouette®
™

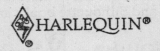